DERAILED

DERAILED

MARY KELIIKOA

W☮RLDWIDE

TORONTO • NEW YORK • LONDON
AMSTERDAM • PARIS • SYDNEY • HAMBURG
STOCKHOLM • ATHENS • TOKYO • MILAN
MADRID • WARSAW • BUDAPEST • AUCKLAND

For Robb, my forever, who never let me give up on my dreams.

For Marcille Shepherd and Marilyn Norris, my mom and sister. So blessed to be able to say you are my family and my best friends.

W⊕RLDWIDE™

ISBN-13: 978-1-335-42463-1

Derailed

First published in 2020 by Camel Press, an imprint of Epicenter Press, Inc. This edition published in 2021.

Copyright © 2020 by Mary Keliikoa

Recycling programs for this product may not exist in your area.

This edition published by arrangement with Harlequin Books S.A.

For questions and comments about the quality of this book, please contact us at CustomerService@Harlequin.com.

Harlequin Enterprises ULC
22 Adelaide St. West, 40th Floor
Toronto, Ontario M5H 4E3, Canada
www.ReaderService.com

Printed in U.S.A.

ACKNOWLEDGMENTS

This book has been long in coming and therefore there have been many who have been part of its journey. I offer sincere gratitude to each of them and apologize now if I miss a few, which I'm sure I will.

To my first writing group, Becky Lien and Richard Mann, who encouraged the first draft. Their enthusiasm and support during those early years helped me fall in love with the craft of writing in the first place and made it fun.

Thank you, Brenda Drake, for the tireless hours that you put in, and to the Pitch Wars family for a contest that truly works to lift aspiring writers.

To Kellye Garrett and Sarah Henning, my mentors and my friends, for guiding me through the Pitch Wars journey and fielding my questions and offering support since!

To Author Accelerator, who teamed me with my friend and coach, Kate Pickford. Thank you, Kate, for seeing that final piece that was missing. I wouldn't have gotten here without you. Thank you for being tough on me and helping me believe I could do it.

To my wonderful agent, Michelle Richter, and Team Fuse. So grateful every day that you are in my corner.

To my editor, Jennifer McCord, and everyone at Camel Press for pushing me to make my book better and helping me make it shine.

To my beta readers, Jessica Jett and Bonnie Matheny. I feel like a rock star every time you read my writing. I hope I can continue to live up to the expectation. And to Dianne Freeman, who is the best critique partner and friend a writer could ask for. Thank you for knowing it would happen even when I wasn't sure.

To all of those who shared my Pitch Wars journey and my writing friends, thank you for cheering me on! And to Sisters in Crime and Mystery Writers of America for creating a place for mystery writers to learn, network and grow together. So glad to be part of both of your amazing groups.

Thank you to the Portland Police Department and Detective James Lawrence for answering all of my crazy and borderline "Is she about to commit a crime?" questions. Your feedback and ideas helped me bring those areas to life and you have my gratitude. If I've made any errors on the procedural side, it's all on me for not asking the right questions.

For all of those who have helped *Derailed* become what it is, I can't say that I'd even have been writing again, or entered it into the contest, without my husband Robb's encouragement. For being my sounding board, for believing that I would be published, for holding me when I cried and for cheering me on in between, you are my rock. It's all the sweeter knowing I can share this with you. *Aloha au ia 'oe.*

ONE

PORTLAND, OREGON HAS as many parts as the human anatomy. Like the body, some are more attractive than others. My father's P.I. business that I'd inherited was in what many considered the armpit, the northeast, where pickpockets and drug dealers dotted the narrow streets and spray paint tags of bubble-lettered gang signatures striped the concrete. In other words, home. I'm Kelly Pruett and I couldn't imagine living anywhere else.

I'd just finished invoicing a client for a skip trace and flicked off the light in the front office my dad and I used to share when a series of taps came from the locked front door. It was three o'clock on a gloomy Friday afternoon. A panhandler looking for a handout or a bathroom was my best guess. Sitting at the desk, I couldn't tell.

Floyd, my basset hound and the only real man in my life, lifted his droopy eyes to meet mine before flopping his head back down on his bed. No help there.

Another rap, louder this time.

Someone wanted my attention. I retrieved the canister of pepper spray from my purse and opened the door to a woman, her umbrella sheltering her from the late October drizzle. Her angle made it hard to see her face, only the soft curls in her hair and the briefcase hanging from her hand. I slipped the pepper spray into the pocket of my Nike warmup jacket.

"Is Roger Pruett in?" she asked, water droplets splatting the ground.

She hadn't heard the news and I hadn't brought myself to update R&K Investigation's website. I swallowed the lump before it could form and clutch my throat. "No, sorry," I said. "My dad died earlier this year. I'm his daughter, Kelly."

"I'm so sorry." She peered from under the umbrella, her expression pinched. She searched my face for a different answer.

I'd give anything to have one. "What do you need?"

"To hire a P.I. to investigate my daughter's death. Can you help me?" Her voice cracked.

My stomach fluttered. Process serving, court document searches, and the occasional tedious stakeout had made up the bulk of my fifteen hundred hours of P.I. experience requirement. Not that I wasn't capable of more. Dad had enjoyed handling cases himself with the plan to train me later. In the year since his death, no one had come knocking, and going through the motions of what I knew how to do well had been hard enough. Now this lady was here for my father's help. I couldn't turn her away. I raked my fingers through the top of my shoulder length hair and opened the door. "Come in."

"Bless you." She slid her umbrella closed and brushed past me.

After securing the lock, I led her through the small reception area and into my office. A bathroom and another office that substituted for a storage closet were down the long hallway heading to the rear exit. Floyd decided to take interest and lumbered over. With his butt in the air, he stretched at her feet before nearly snuffling my soon-to-be client's shoe up his nose. She nodded at him before vicious Floyd found his way back to his corner, tail swaying behind him. Guess he approved.

The woman looked in her mid-sixties. She had coiffed hair the color of burnt almonds, high cheekbones, and a prominent nose. She reminded me of my middle school librarian who could get you to shut up with one glance. "Would you like coffee, Ms…?"

"No thank you. It's Hanson." She settled in the red vinyl chair across from my dad's beaten and scarred desk. "Georgette Hanson."

My skin tingled when she said her name.

"My condolences on your father," she said.

"Thank you." Her words were simple, and expected, but her eyes held pain. Having lost her daughter, she clearly could relate.

"How did it happen?" she asked.

I swallowed again. With as many people as I'd had to tell, it should be getting easier. It wasn't. "Stroke. Were you a former client of my father's?"

She waved her hand. "Something like that." She lifted the briefcase to her lap and popped the latch. Her eyes softened. "He was a fine man. You look just like him."

My confident, broad-shouldered, Welshman father had been quite fit and handsome in his youth. Most of my adult life he'd carried an extra fifty pounds, but that never undermined his strong chin, wise blue eyes, and thick chestnut hair. I'd been blessed with my dad's eyes and hair and had my mom's round chin. But since

I'd ballooned a couple of sizes while pregnant with Mitz, I knew which version she thought I resembled. "What were you hoping he could do for you with regards to your daughter?"

"Find out why she's dead." Georgette shoved a paper dated a few weeks ago onto the desk and snapped the case lid closed.

A picture of a young woman with a warm smile, a button nose, and long wavy brunette hair sat below the fold on the front page under the headline: WOMAN STRUCK BY MAX TRAIN DIES.

I winced at the thought of her violent end. "I'm sorry. Such a pretty girl."

"She was perfect." Georgette pulled off her gloves, her eyes brimming. "The train destroyed that. Do you know what a train does to a hundred-pound woman?" Her voice trembled.

To avoid envisioning the impact, I replaced it with the smiling face of Mitz, my eight-year-old daughter. Which made it worse. If anything ever happened to her... How Georgette wasn't a puddle on the Formica eluded me. I took a minute to read the story. According to the article, Brooke Hanson fell from the sidewalk into the path of an oncoming MAX train downtown at Ninth and Morrison Street. The police reported alcohol was a contributing factor. "They detained the sole witness who found her, Jay Nightingale. Why?" I set the paper down.

Georgette brushed her hair away from her forehead flashing nails chewed to the quick. "At first, the police thought he had something to do with her fall. He told them he'd seen my Brooke stumble down the sidewalk and teeter on the edge of the curb. Supposedly, he called out the train was coming and she didn't hear him. He made no effort to get her away from those tracks. When the autopsy showed she'd been drinking, they wrote her death off as an accident, released Mr. Nightingale, and closed the case."

Their decision couldn't have been that cut and dry. "How much had she been drinking?"

"You sound like the police." Georgette lifted her chin and met my gaze. There are many stages to grief. One of them anger, another denial. Georgette straddled both, something I knew plenty about. "Not sure...exactly. You'll have to check the report."

I scanned her face for the truth. "You don't know or you're afraid to tell me?"

She massaged the palm of her hand with her thumb. "The bartender at the Limbo said she'd had a few before he'd cut her off and asked her to leave. None of that matters because Nightingale's lying. He had something to do with her fall. He may have even pushed her. At the very least, he knows more than he's telling."

My eyebrows raised. The police weren't perfect, but they had solid procedures in death investigations. They would have explored that angle. "What are you basing that on?"

"My gut."

A mother's intuition while undeniable, alone didn't prove foul play. "Did the MAX operator see Mr. Nightingale next to her at any point?"

"He didn't even see *her* because the area wasn't well lit."

"Do you have his name?"

"Chris Foley."

I jotted the information down. "What do the train's cameras show?"

"There weren't any. And no passenger statements because the train was done for the night. But Brooke shouldn't have even been in the vicinity of that train."

"Where is the Limbo located?"

"Ten blocks from where she was hit."

A half mile, give or take. "Could she have been heading to catch the MAX to go home?"

"Brooke detested mass transit. The people who ride during the day scared her. She wouldn't go there at night. Besides, she lived south of town. The train wouldn't have taken her there." She sighed. "I'm telling you, she wouldn't be that far from the bar unless someone…" She closed her eyes.

Georgette talked in circles attempting to make sense of it all, but I had first-hand knowledge of drunk people doing things out of character. Given what she'd described, I could understand why the police had closed the matter. Even so, her devastation gripped my heart. And something had brought her out on this rainy Friday. "What are you holding back, Ms. Hanson? Why do you feel so strongly Mr. Nightingale was involved that you'd come to my dad for help?"

She stared at her hands as if they held the answers. "Brooke had changed in the last year. Become more distant. Not visiting. Missing our weekly calls." The corner of her mouth turned upward in a sad smile. "We used to go for pie once a month. She loved pie. Apple pie. Cherry pie." Her smile melted. "One day she was too busy and couldn't get away. When she did, she didn't look well. Stressed."

"Did she say what was bothering her?"

"No. She shut me out, which she'd never done before. Now to have been killed by a train downtown when that Nightingale fellow was close enough to stop it from happening? He's involved. I can feel it." She straightened. "Until I know what happened that night, I won't rest." Georgette reached into her purse and produced an envelope grasped in her right hand. "Here's three thousand for you to find the truth. Please say you'll help me."

Despite steady work from a few law firms around town, and an adequate divorce settlement, being a single mom often meant more month than money. Georgette was offering twice what I made in a good month of process serving and that would go a long way in taking care of my little girl. Not needing to ever rely on my ex would have been incentive alone, but there was more to it than that.

I'd recognized Georgette's name the moment she'd said it. At the reading of my dad's will, his lawyer had handed me a handwritten letter. It was a request from my dad that if a Georgette Hanson ever came to his door asking for help, I should assist and not ask questions why. It had meant nothing at the time. I'd figured it was due to his unending dedication to his clients.

Because Georgette had a connection to my dad in some capacity, that sealed my decision to at least try and help her. While I'd been directed not to ask questions, even he would have needed the obvious one answered before he took her money.

"You said she'd changed. Is there any chance she might have… I mean, was she depressed? Could she have stepped…"

Georgette cut me off. "Stop." Her eyes grew wide

with denial and the damn broke. Tears poured over her cheeks; her shoulders shook, buckling from the weight of her anguish. The anger and determination she'd used as a mask crumbled, and each passing second exposed another layer of her gut-wrenching grief.

I shifted at witnessing her raw emotion, bracing myself against my own around my father, and my thoughts on Mitz. Tears stung my eyes, unsure how to comfort my client when I struggled to do that for myself.

She muffled a wail with the back of her hand and finally drew in deep breaths until the sobs subsided.

I grabbed a box of Kleenex behind me. She already had a handful of tissue ready from her purse. I'd back off the notion of suicide—for the moment. The woman didn't need any more distress than she'd already endured.

She sniffed hard a couple of times and sopped up her face with the tissue. "I'm sorry."

"Don't be." I swiped under my eyes with my fingers, gaining control over my thoughts. "I'm not sure I'll uncover anything new, but I will look for you."

"Thank you." She composed herself and stuffed the tissue back in her purse for the next inevitable breakdown.

I handed Georgette one of my dad's old contracts, explaining my hourly rate, and a couple of authorization forms that might come in handy if requesting any case files was necessary.

She signed her name without bothering to read the fine print. She stood, the vinyl chair screeching against the hardwood floor startling Floyd. Her expression softened. "How old are you?"

"Thirty-two."

"Brooke was a couple of years older, but pretty, like you and with the same flowing brown hair and kind eyes." She sniffed. "I came to Roger because he could get to the heart of things. If you're like him, you'll find out what happened to my baby."

I'd never be as good as my dad, but I did possess his mule-like stubbornness to get to the bottom of things. My ex could attest to that. "I'll do what I can."

She nodded. "Brooke was a good girl. She loved animals, ran every morning, and worked for the law firm Anderson, Hiefield & Price. She was the head accountant there." Her face beamed with pride before her chin trembled again, but she held it together.

"It might help if I get a better sense of who she was." I slid the legal pad to her. "If I could get her address, I'd like to start there."

Georgette jotted the information down and pushed it back to me. She dug into her purse and produced the key. "I haven't brought myself to go there yet."

I gave her a sympathetic smile. "Are there family or friends I should start with?"

"Besides my husband, Chester, there's just her sister, Hannah, who lives in Seattle. They weren't close." Georgette cleared her throat. "She never spoke to me about friends or boyfriends. Honestly, with her work schedule, she didn't have time for any."

With my own social life lacking, I related. "Do you have her cell? I'd like to check who she had on speed dial."

She shook her head. "It wasn't among her belongings."

What thirty-something didn't have their phone

glued to them? Unless the impact of the train threw it. Another image I pushed away. I rounded my desk and walked her out of my office.

"Please keep in touch on how the investigation is going," she said.

I assured her I would. She squeezed my arm to thank me as she left. With a twist of the deadbolt, I rested my shoulder against the door and closed my eyes. Mitz would get hugged a little closer tonight.

At my desk, Floyd trotted over and sat at my feet. He rested his chin on my lap while I added a few more notes. His sixth sense of when I needed him never faltered. I tucked the notes, along with a couple of divorce petitions into my bag to serve in between outings with Mitz.

It was early enough to get to Brooke's place, about twenty minutes away, and to the grocery store so Mitz and I weren't eating PB&Js for dinner. The faster I got started and found answers, the sooner Georgette could begin healing. If I was lucky, Brooke's phone would be sitting on her nightstand waiting to be found.

Before getting up, I pulled the letter from my dad out of the top drawer and unfolded the paper. I traced the ruts in the desk we shared with my finger as I read his words. Georgette's name was there in black and white. I had wanted to ask her more about how she knew my dad, but he'd been explicit in his request. He was a good man, albeit a tough man that I didn't question. Nor had I ever felt the need to. It hadn't been easy for him after my mom died, and we became the Two Musketeers. We may have run out of time for him to teach me everything he knew about being a P.I., but I'd learn as I went. I had no other choice. Helping Georgette was the last thing I could do for him. And I would.

"Ready to boogie, Floyd?" I flicked off the lights and Floyd padded behind me down the narrow hall to the back door.

We jogged to my yellow 1980 Triumph Spitfire, a gift from my dad when I graduated. "You know the routine, buddy." Floyd stretched himself halfway into the car, and with a grunt, I lifted in his other half. He tripped over the manual gearshift and settled into the passenger seat as I slunk behind the wheel. The engine started right up, for a change.

Brooke was a couple of years older than me—far too young to die. Was Nightingale involved in her death? Did he know more than he was telling? Or was he just a helpless bystander who could only watch Brooke fall because she was drunk off her ass? I had a feeling I'd be returning the bulk of Georgette's money after putting in some legwork. With a case the Portland police had already closed and an eyewitness who'd already been cleared, what other possibility was there?

TWO

My phone navigation led me straight to Brooke's apartment at Meadow Verde, located far south of Portland in Burlingame. The buildings I passed needed serious renovation, but given the lack of graffiti, there didn't appear to be much gang activity in this part of the city.

Georgette had been right about the MAX not traveling this direction. Rundown bus stops lined the thoroughfare; no train tracks in sight. I spied a 7-Eleven and zipped in for a coffee refill in my travel mug before continuing. Black coffee, the older the better, had kept my eyelids open on more than a few stakeouts. Now I wouldn't know how to function without it.

Meadow Verde consisted of two-level rectangular blocks with outside entrances leading to each unit. By the aged avocado green and darker shade trim, they had a solid 1970s vibe. Each of the six buildings measured at least half a football field. The two tenants upstairs shared a stairway with rusted wrought-iron railings. Brooke's place was on the left, upper floor of the first block.

Coffee in hand, I climbed out of my car with Floyd at my heels. The drizzle had stopped for the moment. I let Floyd sniff around the bushes while I refueled and scanned the parking lot for any tenants I could ask about Brooke. There was no one. Aside from a few cars parked in their stalls, the dreary complex looked abandoned.

Floyd settled back in the car and I ascended the stairs to Brooke's unit. The door's paint was cracked and faded. A dead houseplant in a chipped pot sat in the middle of Brooke's and her neighbor's lifeless entries. I unlocked the apartment and stepped inside, a combination of decades old cigarette smoke and mustiness hitting my nose first. A dim overhead light in the foyer revealed worn, dark parquet floors. Straight ahead was the living room. I veered right into the kitchen.

The countertops and appliances were the same avocado green as the exterior, and the linoleum was an unattractive mix of pea green and yellow paisley swirls on a cream-colored base. The fridge was empty, and a half-full jar of peanut butter sat next to a box of Ritz crackers in the cupboard. A girl after my own heart.

A nook with a small dining table jutted off the kitchen and opened into the living space covered in gold shag carpet. A futon, a beanbag chair, and a thirteen-inch box TV balanced on a stack of yellowing newspapers were all that inhabited the room. This apartment didn't jibe with my impressions of Brooke. Or Georgette's assertion that her daughter had been the head accountant of a downtown law firm who'd pulled down decent money. I'd pictured Brooke living in a clean, neatly decorated home, with modern appliances; a woman with beauty and class. This environment reflected neither.

Intrigued, I checked out the bedroom. The same gold shag continued with indentations where furniture had been at some point over the last thirty years. Now, not even a mattress or a nightstand.

Inside the closet, a sweatshirt, a couple of cocktail dresses, and a few pairs of jeans hung. Slippers and high heels were scattered on the floor. Nothing said office attire. An Army-type duffel bag propped in the corner contained lacy underwear, bras, and T-shirts. A thin comforter and a pillow were rolled together. No way Brooke had slept with that sorry excuse for bedding.

In the bathroom, a bottle of generic shampoo sat on the rim of a tub so dingy with soap scum I couldn't identify its original color. Two thick, blue terry-towels were flung over the shower rod. I scanned the empty bedroom again on my way back to the kitchen. With no personal effects or real electronics, including Brooke's phone, I could only conclude that Brooke Hanson hadn't lived here in quite some time. I wasn't convinced she'd even visited. What would be the point? Nothing here said "home." Yet this was where Georgette believed her daughter lived and the key worked to let me in. Brooke could have been in the process of moving out and with her being distant, failed to update her mom. I had an idea where I could check that theory. An arrow labeled "Manager" had been pointed to a few buildings down when I'd driven in.

I secured the apartment and knocked on the manager's door a few minutes later. A man in his mid-thirties answered, his straw blond hair dented from a hat. He had a boyish face with a ruddy complexion, and a gap the size of the Columbia River Gorge between his two front teeth. He wore five-pocket jeans, the hem resting on brown boots, and a plaid western shirt. He'd look more at home in a barn pitching hay.

I introduced myself. "I'm looking for some information on one of your tenants, Brooke Hanson. Got a minute?"

His eyebrows knitted together. "Kinda busy right now."

"It won't take long."

He inhaled through his nose. "I can tell you she's deceased, if that's any help,"

His resistance made me rethink identifying myself as a P.I. up front in the future. "That's why I've been hired by the family. I'm looking for more than that."

He hesitated and gave me the once over from head to toe. "My dinner's on the stove, but if you wanna wait…"

"I can do that."

He opened the door wide, turned and strode down the hall. "By the way, I'm Luke," he said. I followed to the living room where he left me before disappearing into his kitchen. Smoke from a frying pan filled the pass-through between the kitchen and living area. The smell of a rib-eye made my mouth water.

"Nice to meet you," I said, inspecting his living space while he finished up. The two-bedroom apartment had a different layout than Brooke's place. Furniture, stacks of books, and boxes—one with a leather saddle balanced over the top—took up nearly every inch. Like at my house, I could write my name on his dust covered shelves. He had a few pictures of a horse, couple of ribbons on the wall, and a collection of shiny belt buckles on display.

"You want a beer?" he hollered.

Tempting, but I hadn't eaten since breakfast. "I'll take a pop if you have one."

He returned a moment later with a Bud Light and Pepsi and waved me over to the dingy gray-striped sofa while he plopped down across from me in a matching armchair.

"Watcha need to know?" he asked, lifting the tab on his beer and sipping the foam off the top.

"I came from Brooke's apartment and it's pretty empty. Had she been moving out?"

"Don't know much about that. Never been in there. Wouldn't the family know?" he asked. He put down the can and swooped up a pack of Camel's from the coffee table. The man had a problem with being idle, reminding me of my fidgeting eight-year-old daughter. He tapped out a cigarette. "You mind?" He extended the pack to me at the same time.

"No, thanks." If it had been a box of chocolates, it would've been a different story. I took a drink of the pop. "I'd have thought they would. There's been a lot going on, they may've forgotten."

He took a drag and nodded.

"When did Brooke move in?" I asked.

"Been at least a year or more. I'd arrived before that from Texas and needed a cheap place to stay. Got to be friends with the existing manager and when the job came open, I took it. Gives me more time with Chance."

"Chance?"

"My horse. I rope, game, that sort of thing. This job here gives me free rent and money in my pocket. I work out at the barn, close it up at night, and clean some stalls. Get free board there, too."

Luke did something he loved and worked his life around it. Had to admire that. "You're not here a lot then?"

"During the week sure, but I'm at events on the weekends." He inhaled another drag on his cigarette and coughed.

I held my breath while he exhaled. "Did you see her around often?"

"Not much. When she was here, she was quiet."

"Any friends drop over?"

"Couldn't say."

"How about a boyfriend?"

He stretched his neck from side to side and flicked the tip off his cigarette into a clay ashtray on the coffee table. "None that I ever saw. If she did, she could have been staying at his place, I suppose. Come to think of it, hadn't really seen her much in the last few months."

Luke wasn't as helpful as I'd hoped he'd be. "Did she ever mention anyone's names to you—like Jay Nightingale?"

"Nope."

"She get along with the neighbors?"

"No complaints."

I shifted on the sofa. "Anything else you can tell me about her?"

"Can't think of nothing. Other than she never looked like she belonged here. Like a rose in a land-fill. Not saying this is a landfill."

Luke and I agreed on that point. "Is it possible the apartment could have been used for something else? Like drugs?"

He straightened. "Geez, I'd have heard about that from a neighbor by now if it was. As for Brooke, what few times we talked was polite chitchat. She was out of my league, for sure."

I took a slow drink of my pop and ran my fingers

along the seam of the sofa arm at his comment. "Did you like her?"

He cleared his throat. "Course. I like everyone who lives here."

"Oh," I said, setting the can down. "The way you said *out of your league* sounded like there was more to that."

"Nah. I meant she was fancy. Everything I'm not. Anything else?" He stood.

I couldn't blame him for wanting to get back to his steak, but I didn't move. "Did she pay her rent on time?"

"Always, and usually ahead."

"That unusual?"

"Not for Brooke. She didn't like having to worry about it."

Brooke had to be staying someplace else. The answer of where wouldn't come from Luke. I finally stood and thanked him for his time.

He walked me to the door. "Sure a shame her dying and all."

Yes, it was.

I headed back to my car. If Brooke had a boyfriend serious enough to stay with, she'd done a good job of hiding him from her mother. Or had she? The inconsistent phone calls might have been a clue that someone else was taking up her time.

At my car, I inserted the key into the lock and glanced up at Brooke's bleak apartment. A light that had been off when I'd left now illuminated the kitchen window. Someone had come home.

THREE

My pulse raced as I climbed the stairs two at a time wondering who was in Brooke's place. After two un-answered knocks, I unlocked the door and stepped in-side. But no one met me in the entry and the kitchen was clear. I peeked into the living room—empty as well. The wiring could be faulty, which wouldn't be shocking given the overall state of the complex. More likely, I'd been distracted with my confusion of Brooke and this unit when I left the first time.

Annoyed at myself, I went back in the kitchen, slapped off the light, and had my hand on the door to leave when the rush of running water stopped me.

I retraced my steps to the living room. The sound of the shower on full blast and a woman's voice floated out from the master bathroom where I'd failed to look. She was singing. I crept into the bedroom. A cocktail dress and heels were piled in the middle of the gold shag. I could wait for the mysterious bather right here and give her a heart attack when she came or go outside and knock on the front door again in a few minutes. Except if I went out, she might not answer.

The element of surprise could work to my advan-tage. In process serving, if the defendant didn't ex-pect me, they didn't have time to hide or leave before I arrived. In this case, terrifying a woman could make her put up her guard, get me thrown out, or even shot.

The water shut off. No more time to debate. I darted out of the room and waited a few beats before shouting, "Brooke, is that you?"

A long pause. "Ah, no. It's Trina. Who's there?"

Trina? "I'm a friend of Brooke's. I hadn't heard from her and was checking to see if she was okay." I didn't intend to lie, but I'd started the ball rolling.

"I'll be right out."

A minute later, Trina appeared, one of the plush blue towels wrapped around her body, the other turban-style around dark brown hair. Mascara smudged beneath her green eyes. She held the towel tight with one hand and wiped under her eyes with the other. A couple of inches taller than me, she was pretty, in a fresh scrubbed kind of way. Based on the minimal blemishes on her face, I pegged her in her early twenties.

"How'd you get in?" Her sculpted brows drew together.

For having found a stranger in her apartment, she was quite chill. Brooke's friends dropping by could be normal. "The door was unlocked." Her forehead creased. Before she gave it more thought I said, "Have you seen Brooke?"

She met my eye. "How do you know her?"

"We worked together years ago and made plans for coffee today. She never showed."

"You haven't heard then. She's dead," Trina said, her face blank.

I put my hand over my heart. "She's what?"

"Two weeks ago. Hit by a train."

I expected tears, a grimace—any sign of loss as she delivered the news. There were none. "Serious?"

"I didn't buy it at first either. Apparently, she'd been drinking and fell. Stupid, really."

"Were you two roommates?"

Trina scratched the tip of her nose. "Brooke didn't live here. I mean, she used to. When she moved out, she let me stay to get back on my feet. Surprised she didn't tell you she'd moved."

"It may have slipped her mind since we talked business." Luke didn't know either, or the fact she'd been subletting the place.

"You say you were good friends?" she asked.

"She helped me when I needed it. How about you?"

She shrugged. "We knew each other."

Enough for Brooke to offer up her place; not enough to elicit a tear about her death. Interesting relationship. "I'm in a dilemma. When I saw her last, I'd given her my taxes to figure out because she was a whiz at those things and the IRS is on my butt. That's why we were meeting. I'm assuming she has my paperwork at her place. If it's not here, where's home?"

Trina bundled the towel closer around her. "She never said."

Strange, even if their arrangement was landlord and tenant. "Do you know anyone else she spent time with who would?"

"No. We didn't generally hang."

"Was she staying with a boyfriend?"

Trina chuckled. "You two weren't that close, were you?"

My face flushed. Afraid she'd caught onto my lie, I didn't respond.

"Brooke didn't live with anyone, let alone a man."

"I had no idea she was doing well enough to have

two places." Even so, why fork out money for two houses? Especially when the second was this one. "I'll try where she worked. If I don't get my documents back, I'll be screwed. Any place else you can suggest?"

"Can't help you. I need to get going."

"Sure," I said. "Have you thought about where you'll go now that Brooke's gone?"

Trina yanked the towel off her head, her wet hair clinging to her bare shoulders. "I'll figure it out. I always do."

"Were you out?" I asked, wondering why Trina had been wearing a cocktail dress on a cold Friday afternoon.

She laughed. "Just got home from work. But I'm getting ready for a rad party that will go all night."

"I remember those days." Not really. At her age, my all-nighter consisted of rocking a screaming baby to sleep.

Trina rolled her eyes, like she read my mind. "Let yourself out." She walked into the bedroom and shut the door.

While I'd only confirmed my suspicion that Brooke didn't live here, that was sufficient. Georgette said things had changed with Brooke. Her not living where she told her mother could have been one of those things.

I headed out. Before the door closed behind me the sound of baying struck my ears. Floyd.

Sprinting down the stairs, I squinted into the setting sun. The silhouette of Luke about a hundred yards from my car with Floyd at his side made my heart catch in my chest. "Hey," I hollered, running his direction. "What are you doing?"

Luke turned around and sauntered my way with no sense of urgency. "This here your pup?" he asked, drawing closer. "Found him wandering."

I screeched to a halt in front of him unsure how that was possible. Even if I'd unlocked my car before going upstairs, Floyd had never tried to get out before. If he had, he'd never succeeded. "How'd you find him?" I knelt next to my furry friend inspecting him and ruffling his ears. He gazed at me with those big eyes. I willed him to tell me what happened. He licked my face instead.

"I was taking out my garbage and found him nose to the ground. He seems fine. No worse for the wear."

Being a hound, Floyd was born to pick up a scent and follow it. That didn't explain how he'd gotten out of the car. And what were the odds Luke would be going by at that moment? "Lucky for me and Floyd." I stood, scanning Luke's face.

"Happy to help."

My gut said it wasn't that simple. When I'd come down the stairs, Luke was walking away from the apartments. He could have been letting Floyd sniff before turning him back. Except Floyd howled, which didn't happen unless he was upset. I'd be making sure my doors were locked in the future. I held my hand out for Floyd's lead. "Thanks again."

"No problem. What were you doing back in Brooke's place?" He lifted his head towards her apartment while handing me the leash.

"Forgot to turn off a light. That's all." If Luke didn't know about Trina and Brooke's arrangement, I wouldn't educate him. Seeing him with Floyd had me too freaked out.

Impolite or not, I turned without another word and took off with Floyd in a trot back to my car. At my Spitfire, I wrangled him in fast and sped away. The more distance from Meadow Verde, and the more my boy settled into the passenger seat unphased by the event, the more I calmed. My thoughts returned to my visit.

Georgette's assertion that something sinister happened to Brooke didn't have any teeth to it yet. My father's request for me to assist could be short lived. The apartment had revealed no connection to Nightingale—let alone feeling connected to Brooke who hadn't lived there recently. There might be a boyfriend, but none anyone had seen. And no phone to search for names and numbers.

What now? What would Dad do? That might become my motto in this case and I knew. He'd start back at the beginning, which meant the police file. Hopefully my contact, Officer Kyle Jaeger, was on duty. With the phone on my lap, I punched speaker, and hit SEND.

FOUR

WHILE THE PHONE RANG, I envisioned Kyle with his six-foot frame and wavy blond hair. We'd met at the court-house a few years ago when Dad had sent me down to check on some warrants on a missing person. I'd run into Kyle, literally, on the stairs, sending his cof-fee skyward before it drenched him. Over a million apologies and another steaming mug, we'd become friends. Or more like friendly acquaintances as I saw him around the courthouse on a regular basis. While his true domain was at the Justice Center, sometimes he'd help me personally when I needed information for process servicing. Since the divorce, my interest in him had drifted into the more than friends category. However, up to this point, coffee hadn't advanced to lunch.

When Kyle answered, his voice resonated like a bass guitar. "Hey, Officer, it's Kelly Pruett."

"Ms. Pruett, how are you?"

A little more formal than I'd have liked. "I'm good and hoping for an assist. I'm working a case involving Brooke Hanson, the woman who died a few weeks ago when she was hit by the MAX train."

"Hanson, of course. I was among the first respond-ers."

Even better. "You're exactly who I need to talk to then. Could I swing by and see you and the file?"

"I'll be here for another hour to chat. I'll need an authorization for the file. Who you working for?"

"The family."

He sighed.

There was something to that sigh. I'd ask more details when I saw him in person. "I've got the necessary form. Give me your email and I'll send it over."

He did and we disconnected. Traffic crawled as I approached the Morrison Bridge. I took the 405 and exited onto Everett Street which put me in the Pearl District with all its trendy shops and eateries. Ninth and Morrison, where Brooke's accident occurred, was two blocks over after I crossed into southwest via Burnside.

Dad had often talked about checking the scene before he started a case. It gave him a feel for what happened, making it real. While Georgette's grief had made it real for me, it might give me a better sense of the incident and pose some additional questions that Kyle could answer when I saw him. With an hour window, I had time to swing by.

Many office workers had already raced out of town for the weekend giving me my pick of street parking. I pulled to the curb across from the MAX tracks and sent Kyle what he'd need to allow me file access.

With Floyd counting lamb chops in his sleep, I climbed out and trotted over to the corner. It was after six, and darkness shrouded the tree-lined street. The wind ruffled the leaves of ivy covering an old brick building which filled half the block. The scent of rain was in the air and I imagined that night: rain starting or ending; the swaying tree branches making the dim light from the overhead lamps dance across the sidewalk and the tracks. The vibration of the tracks as the MAX approached; a scream followed by a heavy noise as Brooke fell under the train. The squeal of metal on metal that had pierced the air as a hundred tons tried to stop. I shuddered, stepping to the curb and looking down at the rails laid in cobblestone. There was such a narrow space between the sidewalk and the MAX, and nothing protected a pedestrian from walking into its path.

The idea of Brooke standing in this spot, her life cut drastically short, sent an unexpected wave of sadness through me. Life could change on a dime, leaving behind things undone. Regrets of words that should have been spoken. I closed my eyes missing my dad and wondering why he'd left me this task to help Georgette when he hadn't trained me to fill his shoes. He was the seasoned detective. The muscle in my jaw twitched. He should be the one here handling this.

The wave passed through me before I opened my eyes. No amount of wishing would change the fact he wasn't here. He must have thought I could handle a case on my own or he wouldn't have left me the letter. I had to believe that and I couldn't disappoint him and not try. I refocused on Brooke.

In the dark and shadows, she would have been difficult, if not impossible, to see. A step or fall off the sidewalk while the train passed would be a quick death. Or a shove, as Georgette believed. Could the witness Nightingale have saved her?

The MAX drew near. The faint whir blended with other city noises, making it almost stealth-like in its approach. Brooke had been drinking to the point a bartender cut her off. Even if Nightingale was yelling, with that level of inebriation, Brooke might not have understood the danger.

The train loomed, its headlamps brightening the road ahead. As the MAX passed, sidelights flashed into the trees, the rays lost in the foliage. Cameras were mounted on the train. Georgette had said the train that hit Brooke didn't have them. She could have been wrong. I waved to the operator, curious if he saw me. No hand raised up in response. With the lack of lighting, the trees were an effective camouflage.

With the Tri-Met website on my cell, I found the Public Information Officer's number on the Contact Us page and dialed. If Georgette had been mistaken about the cameras, this case would be over sooner than later. It wouldn't address the dingy apartment, but it could offer a definitive answer on what happened to Brooke that night.

A woman, sounding like she'd sprinted to the phone, answered on the fourth ring. Kids screamed in the background.

"I'm sorry, wrong number," I said.

"You calling Tri-Met?"

"Yeah."

"Then you're good. I'm Angie Carmichael. I worked from home today."

"I appreciate your answering. I'm Kelly Pruett of R&K Investigation. I'm working with Brooke Hanson's family."

"They hired an investigator?" she asked.

"They want to understand what happened the night their daughter died. I'm hoping you can confirm whether there's any video footage available from the train involved."

"Unfortunately, there's not. As we reported to the police during their inquiry, Homeland Security funding came through late last year for cameras. The train involved in the incident hadn't been retrofitted yet."

No such luck on a speedy resolution. "Can *you* tell me what the MAX operator saw at the scene?"

"I can't even discuss whether it's a man or a woman."

That part I already knew. "Back to work yet?"

She didn't answer.

"How about why it was determined to be an accident so quickly?"

"The police made that decision. From what I understand, the witness said he'd seen the victim running down the street. She approached the tracks, stumbled and fell. Our operator didn't see her though since the trees are pretty thick in that area."

"That's true. I'm at the site now."

"And if you've read any of the papers, you know alcohol was involved."

"Right." I wasn't learning anything new.

Children shrieked in the background again.

"I need to let you go," she said. "There anything else?"

No. I thanked her and clicked END before slipping the phone into my back pocket. So far, the lone eyewitness was Jay Nightingale. Despite what Georgette thought had happened, he might prove my best chance of getting the facts. And the train operator might have more to share about the incident. As might Officer Jaeger.

ON SECOND AVENUE, I swerved into a matchbox-sized spot across from the Justice Center. I'd spent longer than I thought at the scene, and had to hurry before Jeff dropped off Mitz.

As I jumped out of my car, Kyle walked out of the building.

"Kyle," I yelled, jogging across the street and admiring his sculpted body in his blue jeans and red jacket. His bangs swept to the side, he had a strong jawline and tan skin. I imagined him strolling up from the beach, blond hair tousled, a surfboard tucked under his muscular arm. I didn't have a lot of personal details about Kyle, except that he was thirty-six and single. And yummy. "Did I misunderstand?"

"Not at all. I thought I'd be here longer, then realized I had a class tonight. Sorry to be running out on you." He glanced at his watch. "I can give you a few minutes." He flashed a smile that lit up his eyes and revealed deep dimples.

My breath caught at his sexiness. "Appreciate it. I wanted to hear more about your take on what happened the night Brooke Hanson died. Specifically, I heard the department deemed her death an accident?"

His smile disappeared. "Yeah. We worked alongside the transit detail and of course the coroner's office who made the final determination. After that, the matter wrapped pretty quick."

"Didn't you detain the witness, Jay Nightingale?"

"Not for that. We took his statement at the scene. When he first saw Ms. Hanson, he assumed she was drunk, which the tox report confirmed. Her blood alcohol came in at double the legal limit. He'd said he'd tried to save her from falling into the train's path by getting her attention, but she didn't hear him. We were about to release him when we ran his name through our system and found he had a bench warrant. We had to process him at that point and held him until he could bond out."

At double the limit, how'd Brooke even walk? Three drinks and I'd be down for the count. "Was suicide considered?" Georgette not entertaining the idea didn't make it implausible.

"The evidence and interviews we conducted didn't support that. The family didn't indicate any depression or recent breakups with a partner either."

"Mr. Nightingale was never viewed as a suspect?"

"Not by us. The victim's mother is another story. She's tried to put a different spin on it." His voice sounded tight.

That must be the reason for his earlier sigh. "You clearly disagree with her take."

"She's called my sergeant every day wanting us to reopen the case."

I shifted from one foot to another. "She lost her daughter and wants answers. You can't blame her."

His face softened. "You're right. Anyone would be devastated. But she also wants someone to blame, and there isn't anyone."

"She has a theory Nightingale was involved. That he may have pushed Brooke into that train. I swung by the accident scene before getting here. If he'd been standing on the corner like he claims, and Brooke stood in the middle of the block, he could have reached her in time, if he'd tried. Perhaps he was already standing next to her and pushed instead."

He shook his head. "You've definitely been talking to Ms. Hanson and I'll tell you what the department told her. While it sounds noble to rush to the aid of a stranger, most people don't. Especially if the stranger's drunk, and Mr. Nightingale had been drinking himself. And people often don't realize there's a problem until it's too late. His not being able to save her doesn't make him guilty of any wrongdoing." Kyle glanced at his watch. "Officially I can tell you there were no signs of struggle; nothing to indicate she was dragged to the area where she fell. No other witnesses or evidence to say she'd been pushed. Every indication is Brooke Hanson left the bar alone and died alone."

My mouth twitched from side to side. "Hmmm, alone—except for Nightingale." I'd caught something else he'd said. "What do you mean officially?"

His eyebrow arched. "Did I say that?"

"You did."

He ran his hand through his hair and checked his watch. "I don't get to have opinions at my rank. I defer to my sergeant, field supervisor and the coroner."

"But…"

He shrugged. "I need to get going."

I didn't want to make Kyle late after he was nice enough to stand on a street corner and discuss the accident and I needed to go myself. But it sounded like his viewpoint differed from the official report which warranted another conversation. "Any chance I could come back to look at the file?"

He gave me a faint smile. "I'll be working Saturday night into late Sunday morning. Give me a call before you come down. I'll give you a call if there's a chance I won't be here."

"Perfect."

He glanced at his watch again and flashed a broader

smile. "I'll see you later." He began to jog away when I realized he might not have my phone number.

I called out. "I'll leave my cell on your work voice-mail."

He waved, an indication he heard me, as he disappeared around the corner.

Between Kyle and what I'd found earlier, I was feeling a bit pleased with myself. I'd followed my first lead and might be onto something. Dad would have been proud. I glanced at my phone. Crap. I had five minutes to get home.

FIVE

THE LIGHTS OF my Belmont house lit up the night from two blocks away even though rain had begun to fall again. I'd tried to let my ex, Jeff, know I'd be sliding in on the dot, but he hadn't answered. On the way, I'd also left Kyle my info. Giving him my number had been a dream for a while, except I'd always pictured more romantic circumstances.

Jeff's car was nowhere to be seen when I pulled past the *Deaf Child at Play* sign we'd posted years ago at the street and into my drive, which meant he'd been early, dropped Mitz and ran. It also meant he'd let his mother, Arlene, into my house. She'd lived next door since my family moved here when I was five. I stared up at the three-story 1930s Cape Cod I'd grown up in and inherited from my dad and prepared myself.

Floyd and I entered through the unlocked door next to the single car garage and he and I both shook off the wet from our walk in. If the garage wasn't filled with boxes from my move here last year, I could pull in like a normal person and not even have to be outside. Someday I'd get to it. Maybe. I let Floyd lead the way upstairs.

In the kitchen, I found my former mother-in-law at the stove. The steam billowed up from a saucepan. With dinner so far underway, Jeff had dropped our daughter much earlier than our agreed time. This was a first to have Arlene cooking in my kitchen when I got home. I wasn't sure how I felt about it.

At sixty-eight, Arlene was trim and classy in brown tweed slacks and a cream silk blouse. The pixie cut of her highlighted graying blonde hair suited her narrow face. She had a white apron with red cherries tied around her waist. She'd brought it from home as there were no aprons in my kitchen. Dad was the fast food king and when I dared to cook, I wore old sweats for more coverage.

"Hey," I said, dropping my bag on the counter. "The door was unlocked downstairs. I'd appreciate it if—"

Arlene cut me off. "About time you got here. Busy day at the office?"

I sighed at the queen of deflection. "I'm right on time." Barely, but it counted. "And yes, a new client stopped in before I left and I ran downtown. I called Jeff to tell him I'd be close, but he didn't answer." Too busy letting his mother in, no doubt. "About the door being unlocked…."

"Don't be such a worrier. We got here twenty minutes ago. I didn't think you'd mind him letting me in to start dinner. Didn't want Mitz starving to death."

"No, we wouldn't want that." I ignored my reflex to snipe back. Arlene meant well, and our relationship had always been a push pull. But how I felt about her being in my kitchen was becoming clear. I was going to need to set some boundaries. Later.

"Tell me about your *new client*. What fun deliveries do they have you doing this time? Another subpoena?" she asked.

Arlene never hid her distaste for my father's profession. Or that I had been his shadow. When other girls were wearing dresses and playing with dolls, I was playing shoot 'em up with Jeff and pretending to solve cases.

"No subpoenas this time." I stood a little straighter. "An actual case."

"Since when do you do that?"

"Since one came to my door looking for my dad and hired me instead." I didn't include the information on my dad's letter about helping Georgette. It didn't feel relevant.

"Do tell?"

A paper napkin rested on the counter. I grabbed it up in both hands for distraction. "So far, it's looking like an accidental death, which I'd love to get to the bottom of sooner than later. Any chance you could come back after I get Mitz in bed?" Despite our *struggling to understand each other* kind of relationship, Arlene did help me out when she could and a Friday night would be the perfect time to hit the Limbo.

"Can't. My book club is meeting." She frowned. "Your case already sounds time consuming. You think you should be investigating when you spend so little time with Mitz as it is?"

I wrung the paper. "Jeff and I spend the same amount of time with Mitz. Like him, I have bills to pay, a child to clothe, and a house to keep up." Why did women always have to justify working when men could simply say they had things to do? Arlene may never have had to work, but she knew I had been for years. After my mom died, I practically lived in Dad's office doing filing when school let out and full-time after graduation. My only break had been from the time Mitz was born until she started classes. Not that

Arlene ever approved of any of that. Why did I always feel so guilty? "No worries. I'll start Monday." The Limbo might have to wait after all.

"Good. You have things planned for Mitz this weekend then?"

"Plenty." Not really. Mitz and I had more fun winging it. "I can take it from here. Thanks for getting Mitz settled in."

Arlene waved her manicured hand. "It's nothing. I'm just making some quinoa, and chicken is in the oven." She poured in a cup of the fine grain, put a lid on the pan, and reduced the stove to simmer. "I've already whipped up a salad. Don't you want me to finish?" With a faint smile, she raised her eyes at me.

I waited, expecting her to point out that the recited menu had not come from my cupboards. She said nothing. She didn't have to. Despite my best efforts, with the death of my father and my marriage in the same year, what few domestic skills I did possess had slid downhill. I made a note to put in an order with the grocery store and have it delivered tomorrow.

"That would be great," I said. "I'm going to find Mitz." As I walked out of the kitchen, I dropped the napkin in the garbage and thought of Jack—Arlene's husband. He'd died years ago, before Jeff and I got serious and she never remarried. If he'd been around, she might have been different. Instead, I became her project. When I wouldn't let her mother me after my mom's death, she focused on Jeff's and my relationship and tried to direct my life in other ways. I needed to go to college, not work for my dad. Learn to cook, not become an expert on take-out. Zig left, not zag right. Divorcing Jeff had made no difference because that had been another mistake. In her eyes, I never made the right choices.

In the living room, I rehashed my conversation with Georgette while dropping the blinds and climbing the stairs. She'd mentioned Brooke becoming more distant in the last year. She'd also used the word *perfect*. Distant and perfect didn't sync. Family dynamics could have played a role in the shift. I only needed to look in the kitchen to confirm mother and daughter relationships, in any form, could be challenging. Did that distance indicate there'd been a problem in Brooke's life that contributed to her dying? It certainly told me why Georgette might not know why her daughter had moved out. Or to where.

At the top of the stairs, I turned off the light and passed by my dad's bedroom. The door was closed and locked. I placed my hand on it to say hi, the way I did every time when passing. Like Georgette who hadn't gone to Brooke's apartment, I had yet to go into that room. In fact, other than making sure Mitz had a place to be, I'd changed nothing about my dad's home since moving in. I wasn't sure I ever could. Between that, and not feeling motivated, the boxes downstairs may never get unpacked.

A pair of red Converse sat in the hallway and a Pokémon backpack leaned against the bedroom doorframe. Inside, Mitz sat on the bed, her back to me. Her red curly hair fell around her face as she cuddled Floyd, who'd scaled the toy box to join her. Not wanting to scare them, I entered the bedroom, swinging wide so Mitz would see me.

The minute I came into view, she let go of Floyd and leapt my direction. I opened my arms just in time to catch my girl. She wrapped her long legs around my waist and her arms around my neck and squeezed. I held her tight, emotions from earlier flooding back. After a long moment, I let go and she slid down.

"Hello Ladybug," I mouthed and signed.

She smiled, giving me the sign for I love you, a lot like a hang ten, but with the index finger standing up along with the thumb and pinky.

I returned the sign and hugged her again. Mitz had been Deaf since birth, a result of Waardenburg syndrome that came from my family's side. At first, I'd felt horrible; like my faulty genes had ruined my daughter's life. I had learned a lot in the last eight years—including Deafness wasn't a curse. Mitz had learned to sign in her first years, and with speech therapy to say some words. We were all motivated to adapt.

She pulled away and signed. "What's wrong?"

"Nothing, silly. I missed you." My arrangement with Jeff had Mitz with me every Friday through Monday. At the time of our divorce, Mitz was in school. It was less disruptive for her that she spend the weekdays with him since he lived close to the Washington School for the Deaf and worked from home as a software manual writer. Smart phones and video chat helped us communicate in between, but our four days wasn't enough.

We cuddled on the bed and Floyd wiggled between us. I caressed his silky ears while Mitz showed me her graded schoolwork from the last week and a math paper and art project due Monday.

The video phone rang and the lamp in Mitz's room flashed in sync.

Arlene had picked up downstairs. "It's Jeff," she yelled from the bottom of the stairs.

"I'll put Mitz on," I hollered back. It was my turn to be old school with the video phone. I liked the ability to have a landline and not be dependent on cell service and social media channels. Signing was also easier to read with the bigger screen.

"He wants to talk to you." Sweetness dripped from her voice.

I smiled and signed, "It's Daddy. He wants to talk to me." Mitz smiled a bit too broad, and Floyd gazed up at me. I answered, keeping the video portion off and turned my back so Mitz wouldn't see the grimace on my face. "What, Jeff?"

"Hey Kel. How are you?"

"I'd be better if you'd had your mother keep Mitz with her until I got here. I get this arrangement is new to all of us, but I don't need an inquisition the minute I get home."

"Sorry. She doesn't listen to me any more than she listens to you, and I had to run."

"Yet, you're calling me now. Must have been urgent." He didn't respond. Arlene insisted on helping, and neither of us were good at telling her no. "Whatever. What do you want?"

"To say hi and find out how you are. How you really are."

After cheating on me more than a year ago, now he wanted to check on my emotional status. It was a bit too late for that. "I'm marvelous. Thanks for asking."

"No, I mean…would you like to go out?" he blurted.

I turned to see Mitz squinting at me. Was she trying to decipher my side of the conversation? I smiled and turned away. "I don't think that's a good idea. And I can't believe you'd ask with Mitz here tonight." Saying no to Jeff was easy—crushing my daughter was a whole different story.

"I've said I'm sorry. You know I love you. Mitz loves you. You're still pissed and I understand that."

"You act like we're separated and I'll get over this. We're divorced, Jeff. I didn't make the decision lightly." It had been anything but easy. Even now twinges of pain and guilt jabbed me.

"It's never too late to right a wrong. If you gave me a chance—hey, I bet our initials are still carved in that oak in the backyard, right?"

"We were twelve. If that's your measure of whether I still have feelings for you, I'll take a chainsaw to that tree in the morning."

"You're impossible."

"I'm not the one who had the affair."

"One night of drunken sex is not an affair," Jeff said.

True. But the cheating had capped off what I realized later was an already failing marriage. "Rationalize it any way you'd like. I need to go."

"One dinner date, that's all I'm asking. It won't kill you, and it'll make Mitz ecstatic," Jeff said.

"And give her false hope."

"It's talking, Kel."

His offer did give me an idea. If Arlene would stay tomorrow night, I could get to the Limbo sooner than later. If Jeff and I were going out, she'd say yes since she wanted us back together. And if I were up front about my motives with him, it might work out. I could get closure for Georgette and finish the job my father had asked me to do, both of which ranked higher than Jeff's feelings. "Okay. Fine. Tomorrow night. I have some business to conduct though while we're out."

"Sounds good."

"This isn't a romantic interlude, right?"

"Nope. I'll pick you up at seven."

I reached out to Mitz and ran my hand through her curls while appraising her freckles. She had Jeff's and Arlene's brown eyes. My rounded nose. My father's strong chin. "Make it nine. Mitz will be in bed by then."

"Cool. Can I talk to her now?"

I flipped the video switch on the phone and signed, "Daddy wants to talk to you. Come downstairs when you're done."

At the top of the stairs, I sat down and pulled out my cell. With a few minutes before dinner, I'd update Georgette.

She answered. "You're calling sooner than expected. What have you found?"

"It's more what I didn't find," I said. "Brooke hasn't lived at the address you gave me for a while, and there's a young woman subletting there."

"Who?"

"Her name's Trina and she's more acquaintance than friend. The place is old and run down. There's no furniture, and no personal belongings. I wouldn't say Brooke lived in squalor, but it's pretty shabby."

"That can't be right. Brooke had money."

"You'd said she was an accountant."

"No, I mean, last year she paid off our house. I can't see her living in a place like that if she could afford to help us. It makes no sense."

I agreed. "Trina thinks Brooke lived somewhere else but didn't know where. Do you have any clue where I should begin?"

"I don't. Brooke said she lived there and I believed her, even though I'd never visited. If I offered to come her way, she was always too busy and never home. When we did get together, she insisted we go somewhere to meet."

"For pie?"

Silence. "For pie," she finally whispered.

"You're sure there was no boyfriend?" I asked.

Georgette confirmed again that Brooke had never spoken of one.

I promised to keep her updated and clicked off.

"Dinner," Arlene called from the kitchen.

"Be right down."

I went to get Mitz. Brooke hadn't wanted her mother to see Meadow Verde because she hadn't lived there. Yet she had enough money to pay off her parents' house. People didn't do that unless they had money to burn. If that was the case, why keep the ruse alive? If it was for her mom's benefit, I didn't see the purpose of that. But a low-rent apartment wasn't a one-way ticket to the train tracks. What had led Brooke so far off course?

SIX

THE NEXT MORNING, I jolted awake, the MAX train bearing down on me, its horn blaring. The horn quickly became a chirp, and the flashing light on my cell indicated an incoming text. Mitz and I had fallen asleep on the couch after dinner, making Arlene happy by asking her to stay with Mitz while Jeff and I went out later tonight, and watching Guardians of the Galaxy. I'd suggested The Princess Bride but had been outvoted by Mitz who wanted adventure over a love story, and Floyd who liked barking at the raccoon. Adventure worked for me.

I nearly fell on the floor as I detangled myself from my daughter and reached for the phone on the nearby end table. Kyle had sent a text that said his schedule had changed some, but he'd be on tomorrow morning.

I shot him a *thank you* and got an *any time* in response. I rested the phone near my heart. Who was I kidding? My story could use some love in it and talking to him last night in front of the police station had rekindled my smoldering crush. I just didn't know how Kyle felt. At least he had my number and could get a hold of me if he wanted to—more than he'd had a day ago.

Mitz stirred, her arm flopping off the sofa's edge. I left her to sleep and from the front sundeck, let Floyd out for his morning ritual to make sure the shrubs hadn't moved during the night. In the kitchen, I poured some coffee and I settled at the dinette table.

With Mitz out for a couple more hours, I had time to get the contact information for Jay Nightingale and Chris Foley. From my phone, I went into one of my trusted databases that I used for process serving. Within a short time, both last known addresses and phone numbers came through. At seven thirty, it was too early to call. I moved on to Brooke Hanson. The only information that popped up for her was the Meadow Verde apartment address. Curious to learn more about her, I opened Facebook.

My dad never approved of these methods and preferred researching the old-fashioned way which meant beating the streets. I loved the speed of technology. The details found by the push of a few buttons made process serving more efficient. Most people had no problem spewing everything about their lives on Snapchat, Instagram, and Twitter: from the gut-wrenching breakup with Mr. Abs of Steel, to seventy-three artsy shots of a bowl of handcrafted granola. Without realizing it, they often pointed me right where they intended to be down to the hour.

The search completed and a professional athlete and an image consultant popped up—neither the Brooke I wanted. The other possibilities numbered at two hundred and twenty. Narrowing the search to Portland, it dropped to seven. Six pictures didn't match. The seventh didn't have a picture and stated *Details Not Shared Publicly.*

The other social media channels showed the same result—a big nothing. Whatever Brooke enjoyed in life, she didn't share it with the world—we had that in common. If nothing else, she'd been a smart girl.

A Google search linked to the local newspaper, The Oregonian, and her obituary. A couple of the on-line people-finders reported her as 34 and living in Portland. No other information. Because most of those sites derived data from social media, that could explain the lack of info, and left me no closer to finding where Brooke had lived at the time of her death.

Next, I moved on to Jay Nightingale. Other than the information found in my database, no new information was on Google, and about fifty nationwide scrolled up on Facebook. None in Portland. Since many people listed hometown instead of current city on their profile, this didn't mean anything. And he might go by a different name. Without more solid info, there'd be no way to narrow it down.

I got up and dumped my coffee in the sink and returned to the dinette. The clock read nine. While Mitz was still out, most people should be up by now, including the MAX operator, Chris Foley. I punched in his number and hit SEND. Five rings later, voicemail picked up and I left my name and number.

Mr. Foley had been the easy call to make. My stomach knotted as I brought up Jay Nightingale's number. My client believed he'd been involved in Brooke's death and being a newbie to investigating, I didn't want to screw it up. It would have been nice to have my dad to talk to, but he didn't back down from much. A phone call wouldn't have phased him. I had to believe he'd say go for it. I hit Nightingale's number and waited.

"Hello." A man answered on the first ring, his voice flat.

My mouth felt liked I'd chewed on a sock. "Mr. Nightingale?"

"Who's asking?"

"Kelly Pruett. I'm a private investigator helping Brooke Hanson's family."

"Why you calling me?"

"They're looking for closure. Since you witnessed what happened the night their daughter died, I'm hoping we could set up a time to talk in person."

He cleared his throat. "Last time I did that, I ended up in the county hotel for a few nights."

"Frustrating after trying to help, I'm sure." I tried to sound understanding. "But you're the last person to see Brooke alive and I'd love to get your version of events."

"I can't."

"I'm sure witnessing her death was traumatizing."

"You don't know the half of it." He raised his voice.

I winced at his tone before remembering agitated was good. Dad always said *excited people run at the mouth*. "Exactly. That's why we need to talk." I had to think of something to get him to meet me. "It can be cathartic to talk things out. Meeting could help you, too."

He laughed, in the way you do when you know the person is full of it. "I doubt that."

"Why not try? I'm a good listener. You'd be helping Brooke's family find peace. At the very least, give me a few minutes so I can go back and tell her parents we spoke."

He paused. Finally, he said, "I told the police everything I know."

"I'm sure, but it could take weeks for me to see

the report. You could help them sooner than later." A white lie couldn't hurt.

"What kind of things do you want to know?"

I chewed on my lip. "Like, did you ever see Brooke before that night?"

"Never."

"What state was she in when you first saw her?"

He didn't answer.

I pressed. "You called out to her, right?"

He hesitated. "Yeah."

"My questions will be that easy."

"Well, that's about the gist of it, lady. No point in meeting."

I was losing him. "Imagine it was your daughter running down a dark street and dying so tragically. You'd want answers about what happened to her. Please, Mr. Nightingale. The family's a complete wreck." Sympathy and guilt usually swayed me. I crossed my fingers.

The pleading tone in my voice worked because after another long beat he said, "Fine."

"Thank you."

"Where're we meeting?"

"How about ten o'clock at the Limbo on Tenth. I'll buy you a drink."

He blew out a breath. "The Limbo?"

"Yes. Do you know where it's at?"

"No, but I'll figure it out."

"Brooke's family will appreciate this."

He cleared his throat again. "It was a screwy night. Not what I signed up for, that's for sure."

"For everyone involved."

"Not for everyone," he said, bitterness in his tone.

My heart double timed. "What do you mean?"

"What time again?"

"Ten." Afraid he'd change his mind, I said, "And whatever we discuss, I'll keep as much as I can confidential. You have my promise. How will I recognize you?"

"I'll have on a brown flat cap and leather jacket." Before I could say more, he disconnected.

The phone cupped in my hand, I rocked back and forth on the chair looking forward to our meeting at ten o'clock. I hoped I could push him enough to find out who had him so pissed off.

AT EIGHT O'CLOCK SHARP, I pulled back the comforter for Mitz and sat on the edge of her bed while Floyd stretched across the foot. We'd spent the rest of the morning finishing her homework, putting away groceries, and the remainder at the zoo.

She hung on my neck with one arm, her brown doe eyes drooping but pleading. "Can I stay up 'til Daddy gets here?" she signed with her free hand.

"Not this time. You'll see him later." Sometimes I let her eat too much candy. Or stay up too late. But I'd always protect Mitz. Tonight, that meant not confusing her about Jeff and I going out. She let go, her bottom lip protruding, and crawled under the covers. Her pout didn't last long. "Have fun with Daddy."

I bopped her nose with my index finger and gave her a peck. "Absolutely. Daddy and I are friends."

"Good friends?" she signed.

"Good friends, who have one very important person in common."

She smiled.

"Now sleep, Ladybug."

By the time Jeff arrived at nine, she and Floyd were
conked. Arlene had shown fifteen minutes earlier and
had found her way to the living room while I finished
up in the bathroom until the doorbell rang.

"Don't you look pretty," he said when I answered.

I'd picked a navy T-shirt dress that brought out my
blue eyes and fell above my knees. Two-inch heels put
me a hair under Jeff's five ten frame. My brown wavy
hair rested on my shoulders, framing my oval face,
and I wore teardrop diamond earrings and a pendant
my mother had left me. I'd gained weight with Mitz,
mostly in my butt, and rarely put on a dress. Not that
it was necessary in my line of work where my jeans
and warm up jacket were a second skin. Despite that, I
did feel good, even if my sole motivation was to blend
in at the Limbo in hopes of discovering as much info
as I could. "Thanks."

Jeff brushed my arm as he entered. Strands of his
oatmeal brown hair were tucked behind his ears. His
trimmed mustache and beard accentuated his rounded
jaw. He looked good without effort. I tugged at the
skirt of my dress, making sure the fabric laid smooth,
and hating myself for feeling insecure. No matter how
much I denied it, his affair or one night-stand as he
called it, had taken a bit of my self-confidence.

In the living room, Arlene peered up from her knitting over half-moon bifocals. "You two all set?"

I twisted the blinds closed on the window near her.
"Think so."

"Tell us more about the case you took on." She laid
the garter stitched scarf on her lap.

I closed the remaining shades and checked the lock on the French door to the sunroom.

"Like I mentioned before, I'm looking into a death that could be as accidental as the police say it was." Along with the shabby apartment and Kyle's unofficial take on the incident, Nightingale had me believing there could be missing pieces to the story, but I hadn't jumped to Georgette's conclusion that he, or anyone, had killed Brooke.

"You've never done investigative work," Jeff said.

"Not the kind my dad did, but I am a licensed P.I. And I'll learn as I go and finally be doing what my dad said he enjoyed most about his work."

"It wasn't always easy for him," Arlene said. "Investigating is dangerous, which is why he kept you out of it. If I recall correctly, a few bricks found their way through his office windows a time or two."

He'd also dodged a few tire irons and replaced some slashed tires. He'd made people nervous and there were inherent dangers in his line of work. While I was finding investigating more interesting than the stakeouts he'd put me on over the years, at this point the case was only about fulfilling my dad's wishes. "Yes, and he took them in stride; I learned that much from him. And he didn't keep me out of anything. He'd planned to dig into training me right before…" I cleared my throat. "Anyway. I can hope I'm half the P.I. he was."

"That's what we're worried about—that you'll be like him and cause yourself problems," Jeff said. "You don't do anything halfway. Mothering our daughter should be your priority."

The hairs on my arms prickled. "Mitz is my priority. Always."

"Jeff's not saying you're not a good mom," Arlene interjected. "We just both want you around for our sweet girl. I'd think you'd feel the same given your mother wasn't. And the safest place is at home."

Sometimes the gap between Arlene and I was as large as the San Andreas fault. Her parents had been older. Maybe that explained her archaic ideas. "I hear your concerns, and know they come from a good place, Arlene, but I haven't told you everything. My father left me a letter indicating if this woman ever came looking for him, that I should help her. Which is what I'm doing. I also do need to pay bills and showing my daughter how important it is to pursue her passion is very important to me."

"You'll get your half on our house when the values raise enough for me to get a loan on it," Jeff said an edge of defensiveness in his voice.

"I'm not saying that. I'm saying I want my independence."

"Since when is being a P.I. a passion? What's wrong with process serving?" Arlene asked. "Not that I've ever thought that was a good idea, but as you mentioned, it does pay the bills."

"Nothing, and I'm not sure being a full-fledge P.I. is yet, but last night, I got a three-thousand-dollar retainer. Mitz is always asking about some camp she'd like to go to. And she has my dad's overbite. You know braces will be in her future."

"My insurance would cover a lot of that," Jeff scoffed.

He had me there. "You're missing the point. I need the ability to care for my own kid."

He frowned. "You're going to actively be looking for these types of jobs, aren't you?"

"I didn't seek out this one. It came to me and I feel bound by my dad's request to see it through."

"And?" he inquired.

He knew me too well. "And yes, if this one goes well, I'll evaluate how this works. That's what I should be doing. That's what my dad would be doing," I said with more confidence than I felt.

"Great. So more to come once you get to the bottom of this Hanson woman's death."

I froze. What did he say? "I never mentioned my client's name. How'd you know that?" I asked as Jeff's face turned red.

His mouth opened and closed like a fish before he spoke, "I did my own investigating."

"Have you been following me?"

Jeff threw his hands up. "What kind of freak do you think I am?"

"You tell me. You know so much about what I'm doing."

"Mitz is my daughter too. What you do affects her, and that affects me. I called around."

I bit the inside of my lip afraid I might take off a chunk. "I don't buy that."

"Okay, you two," Arlene said. "Quit bickering. Jeff knows you don't ask for help easily, and when I told him you took on your first case, he wanted to make sure you were okay."

I'd be okay if this conversation could be over. I marched across the room to grab my purse and turned to him. "Since I didn't tell you any details, I want to know who you called, Jeff."

I flipped open my purse flap and dug around for my keys, bypassing my planner. My hand stopped near my case notes that were sticking out. I'd left my purse in the kitchen when I'd gone upstairs to see Mitz last night. Those notes detailed my meeting with Georgette and the list of places I wanted to visit. It also had the word MURDER with a big question mark scribbled right across the top—no doubt what had ignited this entire conversation. My chest tightened.

"I'm waiting. How'd you know about Brooke?"

"I just did," Jeff said.

"The two of you could at least be honest with me," I said pulling out my notebook. "Why would you snoop in my things for information, Arlene?"

She brought her hand to her chest. "I didn't snoop. I moved your purse and it fell open. When I saw what you'd written, I got worried. As you should be."

"There's nothing to be worried about. My client's opinion on what happened to her daughter is not mine. Yet, anyway. And it certainly didn't give you the right to call Jeff and get him involved."

"I'm sorry you see it that way," she said.

"How else would I see it?"

She resumed her knitting. I focused on Jeff and plopped on the couch. "How'd this go down exactly? Your mom called the minute I went upstairs and told you I wanted to go to the Limbo? Is that what prompted you to ask me out?"

"No," he said, without conviction. "I'd planned on that a long time ago." He walked over and sat next to me. "Someone has to watch out for you, and for Mitz."

He could watch out for Mitz all day long and I wanted him to do that. But he'd given his rights up on me when he screwed my friend. I wanted them out of controlling my life but I had a stronger desire to prove to them and myself how capable I could be. I stood. "What now? I need to get to the Limbo tonight." I addressed Arlene as I got up. "Will you please stay with Mitz?"

"Since you've already made up your mind on this, yes. My mom will stay," Jeff announced.

"I will?" Arlene said to Jeff.

"Look, you two," I said, "I'm handling a small matter for a grieving mother at my father's request. I hoped you would both understand. Thank you for staying, Arlene. I'll be back soon." I grabbed my jacket from the closet and strung my purse over my shoulder as I headed for the door.

"Fine," she said.

"Wait. What about dinner?" Jeff said.

"Stay with your mom."

"I'm going with you."

If I got in the car and drove away, he'd follow. "Whatever." I made a mental note to change the house locks at the end of this case and to keep my purse and client files not so accessible until then.

SEVEN

THE SILENT TREATMENT had driven Jeff crazy since the time we were five years old. After the interaction with him and his mother, I was fine with employing it now. I glared out the passenger side window for the twenty-minute drive downtown. Other than sarcasm, I had nothing left to say. He sensed silence was the wisest course of action because he didn't say a word.

He pulled his Subaru into a parking lot down the street from the Limbo, and backed into a space butted up against a gray building. I jumped out and didn't wait for him while he prepaid the ticket machine. He caught up before I crossed the street.

"What's your plan here?" he asked.

"Just gathering information."

He nodded. "Is there something special I can do to help with that?"

"Not really. It might be better if you wait in the car." I hadn't finished being annoyed.

He kept stride with me.

I didn't think he'd go back and wait, and I did have until ten before Nightingale showed. "My plan is to chat with the bartender. Can you find a corner and blend in?"

"I can do that."

His being agreeable was wearing me down. "Okay, but don't talk to anyone. If you see a guy come in wearing one of those golf caddy hats and a leather jacket, would you let me know?"

"We could both sit at the bar like we're a couple?"

"Thanks but I'm working a case."

"That's cool."

I threw him a sideways glance at the lack of arguing. We reached the front door and I grabbed for the handle.

Jeff got there first. "Allow me."

Ignoring his attempt at redemption, I breezed past. Inside, a brass-railed mahogany bar ran the length of one end. Hunter green and plum-colored booths lined the walls and high-top tables littered the middle. A cover band played current hits on a makeshift stage, and a group of twenty-somethings gyrated on the parquet dancefloor. The plaque on the wall indicated a capacity of two hundred people could squeeze into the space. A quarter full now, the hot spot would be packed in another hour.

Jeff found a booth near a table filled with a group of women with short skirts, plunging neck lines and heavy makeup. At the bar, I settled on the farthest end from an Asian man and his very pale girlfriend whose light brown shock of hair surrounded her face. The bartender strutted over. In his early thirties, he had longer mousy brown hair on top, and the sides were shaved. While I wasn't a fan of the look, his muscles strained his white rayon shirt and black vest nicely.

"What'll it be?" He chomped on a piece of gum while rocking a stainless-steel shaker in his hand. A blonde waitress watched with her tray ready.

"Whatever light beer you have on tap will work." When the bartender returned, I slid over a twenty and told him to keep the change, hoping to endear myself. "Great band."

"They draw a good crowd."

I took a frothy drink. "You worked here long?"

"Couple years." He wiped down some wet spots on the bar.

"Bummer to get stuck working Saturday nights. Happen often?"

"Always. Tips make it worth it." He winked at me and blew a small bubble with his gum.

I took another drink. "Then you probably saw the lady in here a few weeks ago who fell onto the MAX tracks."

His shoulder twitched. "Seen her? I'm the one who cut her off." He looked me over. "You a cop? Because I already told the cops what I know."

His tone suggested he wasn't keen on talking to anyone official again. This could be easier than I thought. "No. I'm a friend. Kelly Pruett." I extended my hand.

"Derek." He gave me a weak handshake. My father warned me that limp-handed greetings were a sign of insecurity, but Derek had swagger with no obvious signs of what those insecurities might be.

"Did you interact with Brooke much?" I asked.

"Not really. She didn't hang here at the bar and I don't generally talk to the customers on the floor."

"Did you see her at her table?"

"She was hard not to notice."

Even from the grainy newspaper picture Georgette had brought in I could tell she was beautiful. "She usually by herself?"

"Not always. Sometimes a guy would come by."

"Her boyfriend?"

He rubbed his nose with the back of his hand. "Didn't pay attention."

"How about that night?"

He dried a tumbler with enough pressure to make it squeak with each turn of his wrist. "She was here alone."

"Could she have been waiting for someone?"

He shrugged. "Hard telling from my vantage point."

I nodded. "I understand you cut her off that night. Her family says you also kicked her out. What brought that on?"

Derek hung the glass in a rack. "Brooke was smashed, which was fine. The girl liked to drink. That night though she had an attitude to go along with it."

I took another drink. "That was new?"

"I don't want her family getting the wrong impression, but Brooke could be a real piece of work. She always thought she was out of everyone's league, kind of a high-rise girl. Drinking made it worse."

His comments didn't jibe. "If you don't talk to customers not at the bar, how do you know that about Brooke? Had you cut her off before?"

"No. If the waitresses were busy, she'd come up to the bar for her drinks like she did that night. When I refused to serve her, she became belligerent. That's when I asked her to leave."

"Isn't that a normal response from people to being cut off?"

"Of course. I kick them out too." He popped another bubble.

His pride in having that power showed. It also couldn't be easy dealing with the inebriated. "Do you think something might have happened that night to set her off? Say, could she have been here alone because she got stood up?"

He didn't answer and a waitress clad in a black miniskirt laid a ticket in front of him. "Two screwdrivers," she said.

Derek bent down to the fridge.

The waitress turned to me. "You talking about that woman who died?"

"Yes. Brooke Hanson. I'm a friend of the family."

"Sad," she said.

"Very." I glanced at my beer. "Derek says she was bombed and obnoxious that night. Was that normal?"

"She was, but I don't know anything else. I just serve the drinks." She scribbled something on her order pad, tore off the sheet, and slid it under my hand.

Our eyes met briefly before Derek stood up.

"I need a coffee nudge," she said.

"Got it." He turned his back to us and headed for a set of glass mugs.

The waitress grabbed the screwdrivers and I palmed the paper off the counter, and into my lap. It read, "Meet me in the alley at 11." I glanced at the waitress for confirmation but didn't get any as she headed for her customers.

Derek returned as I dropped the note in my purse. "You were telling me what you thought might have set her off more than usual," I said.

He scrunched his face. "I was?"

"M-hmm."

He shook his head. "Not sure. It's not like we had a conversation. She came up to the bar and was already plastered."

"I was curious about that. They found her with double the legal limit in her blood. Why didn't you cut her off long before?"

His shoulder twitched again. He didn't like his actions questioned. I could relate. "When I don't see the customer, I can't gauge how much they're drinking. But when she came up and tried to order with me, I knew she'd had too much. We exchanged some words and I escorted her to the door."

"Did you call her a cab?"

"No."

My eyebrows raised. "You left a drunk woman standing outside the bar by herself?"

"I wanted her loudmouth out. She had a phone. I figured she'd called for a friend to take her home."

Where was that phone? "Except she didn't go home."

He stretched his neck from side to side. "Wherever she went, she went. I don't know what she did after she left here."

Was his sudden defensiveness guilt for not having done more?

He took a couple of shot glasses off a shelf and filled them with sake. He walked them to the couple on the other end and set them down. They must be regulars, as I hadn't seen them order.

When he came back I said, "Did you know the guy the police arrested, Jay Nightingale?"

"Nope."

"How about the man who stopped by Brooke's table?"

"Nope."

Derek's one-word answers reflected his shift in attitude. Two more waitresses had come on duty and a small crowd had made their way to the bar placing orders, closing my window of opportunity.

I left my half-empty glass on the counter and slid off the stool. "Thanks for chatting. It means a lot to the family."

Derek's shoulders drooped. "Wish I could've been more helpful. It was a shame what happened to her. Tell them I'm sorry for their loss." His frown was sincere.

"I will."

As I made my way to the door, I searched for Nightingale, not seeing anyone wearing a hat or leather jacket. Jeff finished his drink and followed me out.

"Are we done?" he asked.

The autumn wind had picked up. "Not quite. I'm expecting someone about now."

"Who?"

"The witness to Brooke's accident." I glanced at my watch. It was after ten. "Did you see anyone matching the description I gave you?"

"No."

"He must be running late. I have to wait until eleven for another meeting anyway. You should go home to Mitz and relieve your mom. I'll catch an Uber."

"I already called and everything's fine there."

"Great, but it's not necessary for you to stay."

"What did the note from that waitress say?" he asked.

"You saw her pass it?"

He nodded. "In the mirror behind the bar."

Had anyone else seen the exchange—like Derek? That could explain his change. "She wants to talk with me out back. That's why I suggested you go."

"And leave you to meet a stranger in a dark alley by yourself?"

"I can handle it."

"You've made that clear." Jeff tilted his head back. "I'll get the car and we can wait in there until your meeting. I'll park so we can see the front door in case your guy shows up."

The night air permeated my jacket, and I would have a better vantage point to see those coming and going by, sitting out front than inside the bar. Despite my need for independence and not to feel smothered, it would be nice to know Jeff was waiting. "Thank you."

Jeff jogged to the parking lot. I leaned against the building replaying what Derek had said. He'd asked Brooke to leave, escorted her out, and left her about where I stood. Even if she had her phone, he should have called her a taxi. Wouldn't a good bartender do that? Wouldn't a decent human being? Unless he did believe she called someone herself. If I found her phone, I could check that myself. I could ask Kyle to obtain the information, but the law was pretty specific. Without a subpoena, which only happened with an active police investigation, he wouldn't be able to.

I scanned the wet street, the parked cars, and the Limbo building with its two recessed doorways. Brooke Hanson was single, young and pretty, and a party girl from what I'd gathered. None of that answered what had made her walk the ten blocks toward downtown where her path crossed with the MAX. Or if she was here on a Saturday night alone or waiting for someone. I wrapped my jacket closer around me as Jeff came into view. The waitress might be able to fill in the blanks.

EIGHT

JEFF KEPT THE engine running and heat blowing while we sat in his car close to the Limbo's entrance. With an eye out for Nightingale, I called his number. It went straight to voicemail. When I had him on the phone, I should've pressed for more specific answers on what he'd seen that night, and why he'd sounded bitter. I'd made a rookie mistake and now I'd be hunting him down.

My thoughts had shifted to the waitress when Jeff said, "Since I have you alone, can we talk?"

My safety wasn't the only thing on his mind when he offered to wait with me in the car. I suspected what it might be and folded my arms over my chest. "If you're going to defend Arlene—please don't."

"I'm not, but you were kind of hard on her."

"She invaded my privacy."

"Sounds like it was innocent, but I agree she can have an odd way of showing she cares. She just doesn't want Mitz to be motherless, like you were. You can't blame her for that."

I pressed my cheek against the window, willing Nightingale to walk up the sidewalk and save me from this conversation. He didn't. Arlene had stepped in after my mother died on a clear Thursday night in early June. My mother's car accident and instant death were moments I never allowed myself to think about.

I couldn't. I'd had to be strong for my father then, and now I was afraid to let even a glimmer of light in on the subject. Arlene had tried and I'd pushed her away. Right or wrong. But I didn't have time to feel or talk about this. "Her heart is in the right place, I suppose, but I'm alive and well. When I'm not with Mitz, I'm a phone call away. Your crack implying otherwise was just wrong."

"I agree. I'm sorry."

"Apology accepted." I sank deeper into the seat. "And I was serious about suggesting next time she have Mitz stay at her house until I get home."

He nodded. Some tension eased from my body from getting that off my chest.

"Like I said, my mother wasn't what I wanted to talk about. I wanted to discuss us."

I might be better off waiting outside; except I couldn't avoid him forever. If I could manage to hear him out, perhaps we could finally move on. I shifted my back against the door to avoid the handle. "There is no us, Jeff. Sleeping with my former friend was a betrayal."

"It was once, and Linda and I were drunk. We never saw each other again."

"She moved to California."

"No." He shook his head. "I didn't want to see her. You always focus on the bad stuff. There was plenty of good. Mitz for one."

"She's the best thing. But you seem to have forgotten the reality. You've never liked that I worked for my dad and would have been happy for me to stay at home and be a wife and mother like your mom."

"What's wrong with that?"

"For some, nothing. For me, everything. My dad raised me right along with having his profession, and I wanted both worlds for myself. After Mitz started school, we agreed it would be fine for me to go back to work with him. Obviously, it wasn't fine and the passion between us died. Our marriage was over before Linda. I came to realize that when it happened." I acknowledged. "Let's face it, our sex life had sucked for a while."

"Whoa."

"Whoa, what? It's true."

"I've *always* loved you."

I had loved him too. I always would. He'd been a part of my life; a part of me. That's why I had to put on the tourniquet so tight I felt numb. "Was love enough that night?" A familiar heaviness filled my chest and he didn't answer. "You know, when the sex dried up, I figured we were exhausted from everything it took to get Mitz on the right track after we learned she was Deaf. When you and Linda had that affair, I realized you weren't too tired for sex, you just didn't want it with me."

Those feelings of rejection were hard to talk about. I had lost my friend and my husband in that one-night stand. Then my father.... The realization squeezed my heart and a stupid tear came out of my eye.

Jeff held the steering wheel and bounced his head lightly on the rim. He had no response because I was right. Finally, he said, "I do want you to be happy. For us to be happy. I wonder if we owe Mitz another chance to find that together."

"We owe it to her to be good parents, which we both are in our own ways. What we owe her is to get along. The thing is, you have this image of what you want Jeff. I'm not that person. I never was and I can't pretend to be something I'm not."

He nodded. "I know."

"If it makes you feel better, I have forgiven you."

Jeff kept his head on the wheel and turned to look at me.

Our eyes met. "Okay, it's a work in progress." I yielded to his skepticism. "But you and I will always be friends. We have one great kid between us, and she deserves the best version of us both." It was almost eleven and it was time for me to meet the waitress. "Besides, you don't need my forgiveness."

"Yes, I do. As much as I need you in my life." He leaned across me.

I shifted away from the door and froze as his body drew close to mine. Heat radiated from him, and the faint scent of spicy deodorant soap and citrus cologne drifted into my nose. I had always loved the way he smelled.

He grabbed the handle. "You don't want to be late." He shoved the door open.

When he straightened, I slid out, closed the door and didn't look back. I ignored the ache. Despite how he'd devastated me, I would always care for him, even if I couldn't go back to what we were. Mitz would hopefully understand that someday. We were all going to have to live with disappointment, including Arlene.

DRIZZLE REFLECTED IN the amber streetlamps as I made my way down the side alley and onto the backstreet where two back doors hung open. The Limbo kitchen's door had to be the one nearest the Dumpster that smelled of grease and onion rings.

The waitress stepped down from that doorway, letting the screen slap closed behind her. She lit a cigarette as I drew closer. "Thanks for meeting me. I'm Amanda Dixon," she said.

"Kelly Pruett." I extended my hand, and she shook it with a firm grip. "I take it you knew Brooke?"

She took a long drag. "As a customer, yeah."

I shifted on my feet to keep warm. "What did you want to talk to me about?"

"Since you were here asking questions, I figured you'd want to know that Brooke knew the guy they arrested."

"Jay Nightingale?'

"The witness to her dying, right?" she said.

"Right. Did she know him from here at the bar?" I asked.

"I assume so. He showed up some Saturday nights, although he never stayed long."

"Did he and Brooke get together when he came in?"

"No."

"Talk?"

She shook her head.

"I'm not following why you think they had a connection."

"He'd come in and order a shot of scotch. While he waited, he'd hit the dance floor. Once he got his drink, he'd finish it fast, pass by Brooke's table, touch it, and leave. Few minutes later, Brooke followed." Whisking the bangs from her face, she pursed her lips on the cigarette.

"Derek said he'd never seen Nightingale before."

She took a drag. "He's always behind the counter. He doesn't know most of the people unless they come up for a drink."

That matched what he'd said earlier. "Did that exchange with Brooke and Nightingale happen the night she died?"

"Yup."

"But Derek said he'd cut her off and escorted her out."

"She was on her way out anyway." Amanda combed her fingers through her hair, fluffing the sides.

The girl liked to mess with her hair. "Because Nightingale had left moments before her?"

She nodded. "And came by her table and touched it."

I thought back to my conversation with the bartender. "Derek had said she was here alone, but sometimes a man would join her. Was that Nightingale?"

"No," she said, quickly.

"You're certain they weren't the same person?"

"Hundred percent. Nightingale is tall and part Latino. The other guy is short and stocky with black slicked back hair." She flicked an ash from her cigarette. "He also wears an onyx pinky ring with one of those big diamonds in the middle. He works that gaudy thing like it'll take his finger off if he keeps at it."

"Charming."

One side of her lip curled. "Slimy is more like it."

It was hard to imagine Brooke with someone like that. I couldn't place her at Meadow Verde either. "Did Brooke ever tell you she knew Nightingale?"

Amanda lifted her head and gazed at her cigarette.

"I never talked to Brooke, other than to get her drink orders."

Was there more than tobacco in that cigarette? "Did you talk to Nightingale about her?"

"No. Just took his orders too."

Amanda was providing nothing more than conjecture. "I need something else."

"I'm telling you what I saw. Brooke was always busy talking or texting. Guess that's why I noticed when she'd finally look up. That's when I'd see their eyes meet and he'd walk over right before he left."

"Was she on her phone that night?"

"Yeah. Always."

Amanda's observations sounded cloak and dagger. Why wouldn't Nightingale call or text Brooke to come outside? Why the secret code, if there even was one? "You're certain it was Nightingale?"

She nodded.

I didn't have a picture of him to confirm her description, but their limited interaction brought up another question. "How did you know his name?"

"He whipped out an American Express and handed it to me a while back before realizing he had enough cash. His name struck me as funny."

"You remember that?"

"I'm good with names." She gathered the collar of her shirt closed.

Georgette felt strong enough that Nightingale might be involved in Brooke's death to seek my father out. If Amanda was correct, Nightingale had known and seen Brooke prior to the incident, which he denied. He'd even said he didn't know where the Limbo was located when I asked him. What else had he lied about?

"The other man you mentioned, pinky ring, did you get the impression he was her boyfriend?"

She looked at her feet and blew out a stream of smoke. "Don't know. He eyed her like he had a thing for her, but Brooke acted indifferent towards him."

He could be a bar rat hitting on her. Bars were full of men who trolled for dates, or one-night stands. Exactly why I stayed clear of them. "Was he here the night she died?"

She looked up at the streetlight and shook her head.

I took that as a no. "Anything else you can think of that would be helpful?" I stuffed my hands in my coat pockets. The rain came down harder.

"That's it."

I started to shiver. "Why didn't you tell me this at the bar?"

"Derek had a thing for Brooke. Didn't want to bum him out more than he already is."

I'd derived the exact opposite from my conversation with him. "He made it sound like he didn't think much of her."

"Derek likes to give the impression of lots of things. He did."

"Was it mutual?"

"Couldn't tell. She was a hard read. Standoffish, if you know what I mean."

Sounded like a theme with Brooke and men. He could have made a move on her that night and she'd blown him off. That would explain why he acted curt the more we'd talked.

I gave Amanda my card and thanked her for the info. "If you think of anything, please call."

She studied my name. "I didn't think you were just a friend. That's why I wanted to talk to you."

So much for blending in. "What was your first clue?"

Amanda's eyes glimmered. "I get feelings about certain things. Kind of like Brooke and Mr. Nightingale. Call it intuition, if you want."

That intuition had suggested Nightingale had been less than honest and I'd confirmed Brooke had her phone that night. I was curious who the guy might be who had Brooke's attention. Given he wasn't here the night she died, it might not matter. With the lack of physical contact, he didn't sound like a boyfriend, and neither Amanda nor Derek knew much about him. "Did you tell the police any of what you've told me?"

"No. I snuck out the back when they came in and questioned Derek." She shifted on her feet and glanced away. "I have a stack of parking tickets I can't afford to pay and probably a warrant. Last thing I need is the cops on my back."

"Then why tell me?"

"You're not a cop." Her forehead puckered. "My sister was killed in New York a few years ago. Some asshole took her purse before he stabbed her and left her to bleed out. The cops said they tried to find her killer, but they didn't try long. When I looked myself, I came up empty. Guess I wanted to change that for Brooke's family. If the family hired you, it means they don't believe Brooke died accidentally. That's good. Perhaps the truth will come out."

My skin tingled, and not from the cold. "What's the truth?"

The back door flung open and Derek stuck his head out sending my stomach into a nosedive. Amanda startled. He gave me a *what the hell are you doing out here* look before glaring at Amanda. "We're getting slammed. Get your ass back on the floor."

She stomped out the cigarette. "Let me know what you find out." She slipped my card into her pocket and disappeared into the kitchen.

Frustrated at the question left hanging, I thought again of Nightingale and how he'd played me. If what Amanda had said was true, he'd probably never intended to show. Was he afraid to be recognized?

NINE

THE LIGHT OF morning crept through the blinds of my childhood bedroom. Yellow ruffled curtains still hung over the windows, along with the same white furniture I'd begged for when I was ten. New was the queen size bed and the comforter that I was snuggled into—about the only thing besides my clothes that I'd unpacked from the boxes in the garage.

I rolled onto my back to find my wide-eyed, fresh faced girl inspecting the mole next to my right eye.

"Morning Mama. You're being a sleepyhead," Mitz signed.

She was usually the one I had to rouse out of bed. I yawned and with a burst of energy, grabbed her and pulled her close. She squealed and laughed, while I threw the covers over our heads.

She wiggled out and Floyd, who'd followed her in, woofed at the foot of the bed and shook his head, sending a string of drool in the air. "Ewww," we said in unison and laughed.

Melting in a slow slide off the bed, she hopped to her feet. "We're making breakfast for you. Hurry," she signed before darting from the room, Floyd scuttling behind.

The smell of savory pork sausage blending with the sweet scent of Belgian waffles wafted through the house. Jeff had slept on the couch last night. After midnight when we'd returned, he said he didn't feel well, and Arlene didn't have the spare bedroom made up. I'd thrown him a pillow and gone to bed. So much for not confusing Mitz.

Dragging myself upright, I stretched. Wearing pin-stripe bottoms and a T-shirt, I rummaged through my dresser and found a sweatshirt which I tugged over my head before shoving my feet into Scooby Doo slippers—a Christmas gift from Mitz last year. A quick glance in the mirror confirmed my brown hair needed taming. I pulled it back into a ponytail and went downstairs, brushing my fingertips on my dad's door on the way. The daily ritual comforted me.

In the kitchen, my daughter sat focused on the red light on the waffle maker. When she saw me, a satisfied grin covered her freckled face.

"It smells wonderful," I said, and with my hand in the shape of a C, I moved it from the middle of my chest to my stomach, the sign for "I'm hungry."

"Daddy let me mix the waffles."

Jeff looked up from his sausage flipping duties. "And a fine job she did." He nodded at me. "Glad to see you've joined the living."

I didn't respond and Mitz continued. "My job is to make sure they're perfect."

Floyd had anchored himself dead center in the kitchen, waiting for a handout.

"Need help?" I asked. They exchanged glances and wrinkled their noses, probably remembering some of my other breakfast failures. "What? I can manage eggs." Sometimes.

"We got it," Jeff said, not willing to take the chance.

I poured myself a mug of coffee. "Chicken. Both of you."

They laughed and Mitz shooed me out. Fine. With nothing to do but wait, I grabbed the cordless and made my way to the sunporch. I had some unfinished business anyway. A couple of sips of coffee later, I punched in Jay Nightingale's number. The phone rang and rang. Ten times to be exact with no voicemail picking up.

Next, I tried the MAX operator. No answer there either, but I left a message. "This is Kelly Pruett again," I said after the beep. "I promise not to take much of your time but would appreciate a call back."

In the dining room, Mitz had set the table with my best dishes that had once belonged to my mother, and carried in a fruit salad for spooning onto the waffles. Jeff followed with hot maple syrup in a gravy boat.

"It looks great," I signed to Mitz. I met Jeff's eye and he shrugged. We'd do anything to make Mitz happy.

We sat down to breakfast and dished up, talking about Mitz's friend who had a crush on a boy. "How did you and Daddy meet?"

Jeff eyed me as he drenched his waffle in syrup.

I smiled at Mitz and signed. "You know this story silly. I've known Daddy for a very long time."

"Well, I don't like boys," she declared with emphasis as she flicked her hands in a discarding motion before digging into her waffle.

I held back a chuckle and was about to ask more about that, but she was already onto a summer camp she wanted to attend next year that had canoes. At eight, topics were often all over the place, and I was glad not to have to revisit the subject of me and Jeff. Even happier not to have to worry about her falling for boys quite yet. There'd be plenty of time for that. Though her opinion showed that no matter what age, hearing or Deaf, relationships were complicated.

A half hour later and having moved on to Mitz' upcoming field trip, my phone rang.

The MAX operator. Finally. "Mr. Foley, thank you." I excused myself from the table and walked into the living room.

"I've been under the weather." He had a wheezy cough. "Apologies for not getting to you sooner. What can I do for you?"

"I've been hired by Brooke Hanson's family to investigate her death. I was hoping we could meet."

He sneezed. "Are they planning to sue? Because I should make sure it's okay with my supervisor to talk with you."

I'd expected that. "Understandable, but I'm only looking for your observations of that night and have already talked with your public information officer."

He sneezed again. "Suppose it'd be fine then if you can make it today. Schedule has me working tomorrow if I'm up to it."

With Nightingale's no show stinging, I said, "Today it is."

"Bring a mask and come sooner than later. This stuff is nasty. To be honest, I may crawl back into bed."

With his address confirmed, I clicked off and turned around to Jeff's glare.

"It's Sunday morning," he said.

Mitz glanced up at me, as she got up from the table and carried her plate to the kitchen.

When she was out of sight, I met Jeff's gaze. "I'm aware of the day. Unfortunately it's when he's available and I can't miss the opportunity. It won't take long to zip past there with a few questions, run to the precinct and check on a file."

"With Mitz?"

"Of course. I might even be able to get us a tour of the police station."

He stretched his neck from side to side. "That's not such a great idea."

"Why? It'll be like *take your kid to work* day. You know how much I enjoyed hanging with my dad when he took me with him on his cases. Mitz is old enough to enjoy that too."

"Except I don't want my kid doing your kind of work."

His reaction shouldn't have come as a surprise, but it did. "*Your* kid?" Wow. I wrung my hands trying to dispel the hurt. "I think you mean *our* kid and it's my time with Mitz."

His face softened. "Fine, I'll give you that, but don't you think Mitz would have more fun if she came back home with me? I don't mind and I won't have to worry about what she's doing."

"Why worry at all? She'll be with me." Mitz had returned from the kitchen and stood at my side. She had a knack of knowing when to appear. I gazed down at her, then back at Jeff. Though I didn't want her to go, I was in new territory with this being a potential murder case. While I expected my interview and stop at the police station to be quick, it might make more sense for Mitz to be with Jeff. "Breakfast was wonderful, sweetie," I signed. "I have a few errands to run. You'll go with Dad and I'll pick you up this afternoon." Mitz, unphased, gave me a quick hug and sprang away with Floyd right behind her.

"This is what I was afraid of," Jeff said. "That you'd be like your Dad." His lips pressed in a hard line.

"You mean getting to the bottom of this case and doing a competent job so my client can rest easier? Yeah, you're right. Dad was like that. He wanted to solve things. I'm finding that I feel the same way." If I could solve this case, my dad would have reason to be proud of me. I would be. I hadn't realized that until this moment.

"No. That he always chose work over you."

My eye twitched. "I'm not choosing work over Mitz. You're the one that doesn't want her to come with me for a few hours this morning. I know my father and I had a different routine than what you grew up with, but unlike you, I can't do my job from home. You and I will have to agree to disagree. Let's not blow this out of proportion. I'll be by later to get her."

Jeff left to find Mitz without another word. Head back, I stared at the ceiling, Jeff had been right about my dad. I hated to admit it to myself much less to him. Dad always chose work over family. Except it hadn't bothered me. He was a superhero. Out there saving the world…or at least helping those who needed him to rest easier in his little corner of it. It had been the source of countless fights between my parents. One ending with my father storming out and not returning for a couple of days. Had my mother felt like Jeff? Or like me as I stood in the middle of the living room, the ticking wall-clock the only sound. It was something for me to think about as I found myself liking the investigative work. Knowing Jeff and Mitz were about to leave, I felt more alone than I had since my divorce.

But I had to press on if I intended to give Georgette some peace of mind. Hopefully, it wouldn't take too long. I'd ask a few more questions. That's what my dad would have wanted me to do.

CHRIS FOLEY'S MODEST sage-green ranch-style house with a white country porch was located fifteen miles away in Beaverton. Orange mums decorated terra cotta planters between the walkway and manicured lawn with clean sharp edges. Pulling the collar of my charcoal Nike jacket closed, I rang the bell and admired the display of pumpkins and dried corn stalks tied with bailing string near the front door.

Mr. Foley answered wearing flannel pajama bottoms, a long sleeve T-shirt, a terry blue robe, sleeves rolled up, and a fabric belt tied around his ample belly. Brown corduroy slippers covered his feet and his shiny scalp shone through his thinning hair. I put him at about seventy. He had rheumy eyes, like he'd not let up on sneezing since we last spoke, and he smelled of clove and cinnamon—and whiskey.

I took a step back and introduced myself. "Thank you for agreeing to see me."

"Sure." He proceeded to hack up a lung. "I'd invite you in, but I'm contagious and the wife whipped up a hot toddy. Can't talk long."

That explained the whiskey. "No worries. I have a little one at home. I'll stay out here."

He nodded. "I was surprised to hear from you. I'd filled out a bunch of reports at the scene." He sneezed, covering his face with a mottled hand. "Thought I was pretty thorough."

"You did," I said, as if I'd seen them. "I had a few more questions about the witness, Jay Nightingale."

He shifted his weight. "What do you need to know?"

"For starters, what was your impression of him at the scene?"

He frowned. "A basket case. Course, who wouldn't be after witnessing what he did."

An image of Brooke's mangled body skimmed my mind before I shoved it out. "Did you get the impression he knew the victim?"

He shook his head as if trying to jar the thoughts loose. "The contrary. When I first saw him at the corner, I thought he was going to run off. I hollered for him to hold it right there. By the way he looked at me, all wide-eyed, he'd seen it happen. If he knew her, you'd think he'd have tried to help her, not leave."

When my dad had his stroke, I'd found him on the floor of his office. I had run to him, not away. But when the paramedics had declared him dead, I'd wanted to take off by myself. If I didn't have Mitz, I would've put at least a hundred miles between me and Portland. "Could it have been a reaction to being in shock?"

"No doubt. He kept reciting the same thing over and over."

"What was that?"

"That he'd called out and she didn't hear. Always struck me as odd."

"How so?"

"The way he said it, I suppose. He sounded rehearsed."

"Did he say anything else you felt was strange?"

"I'd heard him say, 'shit,' and 'goddamn her,' a few times."

"Referring to Brooke?"

"That was my guess. He could have been angry at having witnessed the accident in the first place. Videos they make us watch for training say people react to trauma in all kinds of ways. Even suffer from that PTSD afterward—the kind our boys get when they've come back from the Middle East."

"No other witnesses, correct?"

Mr. Foley shifted his weight back to the other foot. "Far as I could tell."

That should have been a yes or no answer. "As far as you could tell?"

"I mean. Yes. Of course."

I nodded, feeling bad that I was keeping him from bed. "Did you see Brooke prior to her fall?"

"No." He shook his head.

"Did you see anyone else in the area?"

He coughed. "Would have put that in the report if I had."

He was agitated with my questions. "I'm sure you've been through this a dozen times. Almost done."

He nodded.

"Who takes control at the scene when there's an accident?" I asked.

"The operator, in this case, me, at least until the police arrived. Between them and the transit authorities, they handled everything from there." His voice faded from over-talking.

I gave him a sympathetic smile. "What did you do then?"

"They transported me home, I guess. It's all a blur. Took a few days off. I won't lie, I'm suffering from some of that PTSD myself, but I got back to work. Until this damn cold zapped me." He wrapped his arms around himself. "I need to lay down."

As I'd suspected. "Absolutely. Have you been with Tri-Met long?"

He lifted his chin. "Thirty years. I'm set to retire at the end of next month."

Dad would have hit his thirtieth anniversary next year. "Congratulations."

"It's been a good run." He gazed at his feet; his eyes glassy. "I almost made it accident-free."

"It wasn't your fault," I offered.

He nodded. "People think the train stops on a dime. It doesn't. Even if I'd seen her…"

"I know." I handed him my card. "If you think of anything else, please call."

Head down, he closed the door.

I slid back into my car, and caressed Floyd's ears. "What a way to end a career," I said as I backed out. Floyd listened so attentively, I expected him to agree. He cocked his head while I replayed Foley's remarks about Nightingale being upset at witnessing Brooke's death. "I'm curious about Nightingale's comments," I continued my one-sided conversation. "It does sound weird that he'd blame the victim, shock or no shock."

The police report might shed some light. Kyle had said that officially Brooke's case was deemed an accident, and Nightingale had been released. He'd held his personal position back. Time to see if I could get him to share that view.

TEN

BEFORE MAKING THE drive from Chris Foley's house to the Justice Center, I'd texted Jeff to tell him my progress, and he'd sent back a "no hurry." He and Mitz had opted to spend the day at OMSI and to catch an animated Planetarium feature. With Jeff's brain for writing software manuals, all things science fascinated him. It also had him seeing the world in black and white. Much like Arlene. Dad and I saw the orb in all its shades of gray.

Thankfully, Mitz had a nice balance of both and enjoyed his science, and my love of puzzles. Knowing she was having fun lessened my guilt that I had to work.

With an assurance that I'd walk my furry friend soon, Floyd and I parked in front of Chapman Square where amber gingko leaves covered the ground and bench-lined pathways. Where some cities built green spaces to bring in nature, Portland had been built around parks and trees.

Dad and I had shared many lunches here when we were downtown. When remembering those simple moments, I missed him the most. We'd talk about how much he loved investigating. He handled so much on his own, with the promise of giving me more later. Later never came. Not until Georgette needed help. Perhaps it was his way of making sure I'd get a taste of investigating, one way or another. Had he known she would show up one day? I had wanted to ask more about their connection, but he'd been explicit. I just wished we'd had more time.

On the first floor of the Justice Center, the receptionist called for Kyle and I waited in the lobby until he appeared with a file tucked under his arm. My whole body relaxed at the sight of him. I didn't have to defend my being a P.I. in his presence and that grounded me. His being sexy as hell didn't hurt either.

Kyle led me to a small conference room and closed the door. "It's good to see you again." He pulled two chairs away from the table for us and set the folder on the table. "This is all I have on the Hanson case. It's pretty straightforward."

I smiled at his gesture and plucked a notepad and pen out of my bag. "Before I look, I was hoping we could talk about Nightingale first. Earlier, you said he'd been detained."

Kyle took a seat, and I slipped into the chair next to him. "Right. He had a warrant for a failure to appear on a burglary charge that he was unaware of."

"Unaware, or hoped you wouldn't find?" I asked.

"Unless he's a good actor, I'd say unaware."

I'd have to trust Kyle on that. "His having a criminal record didn't make you suspicious of his version of what happened that night?"

"Not at all. Burglary isn't a violent crime, and a hearing's not a conviction. Remember, the coroner and the subsequent investigation supported Brooke's fall was an accident."

"You did say that was the official stance. I sensed

you had a different one." I scanned his face for a sign I'd read him correctly.

Kyle's forehead creased, revealing deeper lines around his eyes than I'd noticed before. "His testimony was consistent throughout. The way he held himself bothered me at the time." He leaned back in his chair. "Not that it mattered. My superiors didn't concur."

"What if I told you the MAX operator might agree with you?"

"How so?"

"He thought that Nightingale repeating he saw Brooke fall, and trying to help her sounded rehearsed. He also ranted things like 'goddamn her.' When I'd talked to Nightingale, he said it had been a screwy night, but not for everyone. The way he'd said it sounded bitter."

"That first part is consistent with the operator's written statement. That's an interesting comment by Nightingale though. I did feel Nightingale acted odd too, but the higher-ups didn't believe there was anything suspect about his actions, and they have more experience in that arena."

He didn't appear bothered by their dismissal. I would've been. "Did Nightingale say whether he'd ever met Brooke before?"

"Said he didn't."

I tapped the pen on the table. "He may have been telling us the same lie. I have a source that says different."

"Who's the source?"

I didn't have the same legal limitations as a lawyer. I also didn't want to get Amanda in trouble on her parking tickets. "A waitress who'd seen them in the bar at the same time, including that night."

"Were they together?"

"They'd make eye contact, and he'd pass by her table on his way out, and she'd follow."

He rocked his head side to side. "Sounds like no and a lot to read into a look."

"Nightingale had agreed to meet me last night and said he had no idea where the Limbo was located. If my source is correct, he lied."

"How reliable is the source?"

"Credible and adamant it was Nightingale." Why would she make that up? "That said, the bartender, Derek, said he'd never heard of him. Derek, by the way, according to this source, had a thing for Brooke which he didn't indicate when we spoke."

"What makes you think one is telling the truth more so than the other?"

Less than twenty-four hours ago, I hadn't met either of them. "When you put it that way, I'm not sure."

He gave me a small smile. "Truth is, they could both be right. Brooke and Nightingale may have been there at the same time and not realize it. It's speculative to say he passed by her table on purpose. Leaving at the same time could be a coincidence. It's not a leap if Derek did like Brooke. From all accounts, she was a beautiful woman. And a waitress on the floor is going to see things differently than the guy working the bar."

In one swoop, Kyle had punched holes in all my theories. "I'll give you it's not the best lit place I've been in, and she could be reading things into the situations that aren't there. Except Nightingale did lie to me about knowing the location."

One side of Kyle's mouth turned up. "Or confused. There's the Limbo on 21st, the Limbo Lounge in southeast, and Gumbo Limbo on the waterfront. Portland has well over a hundred bars in downtown alone."

"I mentioned Tenth specifically. I don't buy it."

Kyle shrugged. "Limbo Lounge is on the other side of the river on SE Tenth."

Across the river wasn't that far. If he'd been confused, he could have swung by both. I'd make sure and ask Nightingale when I got my two minutes alone with him. "Did Mr. Foley also mention he thought Nightingale was going to run off until he demanded he stop?"

Kyle frowned. "I don't recall that."

"Could be something?" I said, hopeful.

"Embellishing after the fact happens. That's why we conduct interviews right away before the brain starts adding things that weren't there. In this case, the fight or flight mode could have been in play for those few minutes after the incident. Fact is, Nightingale made the right choice which speaks louder."

Nothing I'd offered held water. I flipped through the pages looking for something Kyle couldn't crush. I checked the police report, and scanned the coroner's report, pictures of the scene, and Nightingale's testimony. The names were redacted, but it was clear who's statements belonged to whom. Nightingale's confirmed everything Kyle had said. Chris Foley's lined up too.

Next, I perused Derek Stromenger's statement where he confirmed Brooke had been drinking, became belligerent, and he'd escorted her out. Amanda said Brooke had been leaving anyway, but Derek wouldn't have known that. And would only be true if

Amanda's take on Nightingale and Brooke communicating was accurate, which Kyle had me doubting.

I kept reading. At the bottom of the page, a discrepancy popped out. Derek had told Kyle that a woman had followed Brooke out, but returned shortly after. He'd assumed she'd gone to help Brooke. He'd specifically told me Brooke was alone and he'd thought she'd texted someone to come get her. "What's this about?" I pointed to the paragraph.

Kyle scanned the text. "Exactly what it says. If you read further, he amended his statement the following day. The person who he thought followed Brooke wasn't anyone he knew and they'd come right back in. He couldn't give a description. He'd also forgotten that he'd taken a short break after Brooke left. With the bar being so busy, he realized he'd been mistaken and hadn't recalled the events correctly."

My bullshit meter flashed. "If he removed Brooke from the bar, he'd be watching to make sure she didn't return. He'd know if someone followed her out."

"Agreed, which is why I followed up and found another waitress on duty that night who concurred with his recollection. With it being a busy Saturday night, Derek could have been wrong. Again, the death was deemed accidental, and the matter was closed."

Amanda hadn't mentioned anyone following Brooke. Derek could have been mistaken. For clarification, I put another visit to the Limbo on my list.

Pulling my notebook closer, I confirmed Brooke's address was the one her mother had given me. The one where she didn't live—which reminded me… "I'm trying to find Brooke's phone. Was it found at the scene?"

"Anything that belonged to her would have been returned to the family."

I was afraid of that. With a final scan, I slapped the file closed and tucked my notepad into my bag. "Thank you again."

He smiled. "No problem. What's next for you?"

It was noon on Sunday, and Jeff and Mitz would be busy until much later. "I'm heading to get that interview Nightingale promised me."

His brow furrowed. I expected a lecture. Instead, he said, "Let me know what you find out."

His words were the opposite of what I'd been hearing the last couple of days and a reason to stay in touch. I extended my hand as I stood. "I will."

He held my hand, his grasp warm and strong. After a moment, and a shake, he let go. When he did, his hand lingered next to mine, sending heat to my face. He pulled back and I cleared my throat. He didn't make eye contact and I flung my bag over my shoulder, leaving Kyle in the conference room. Had I read more into it?

Before climbing into my car, I grabbed Floyd and we circled the park before hitting the road. Nightingale lived on SE Grand. I almost dialed him again but opted for a surprise visit instead. That way he couldn't stand me up.

ELEVEN

NIGHTINGALE LIVED IN a dilapidated four-story brick building built squarely in the city's old warehouse district. Once considered the ugly wart on the city's nose, revitalization efforts had been underway in the area, and the building now housed low-income apartments.

Before getting out of my car, I took a long drink of the coffee I'd bought at the Mini Mart and straightened the paperwork from the divorce petition I'd served on my way there. The respondent, a forty something Hispanic man, had his kids with him when he'd come to the door. The scowl on his face said he hadn't expected me. Mitz's disappointment when we told her of our plan to divorce played in my head. The things once-loving couples turned adversaries did to their kids. Whether they meant to or not. I'd never relish this part of my job. I'd prepare a proof of service later and get it to Carla at Baumgartner & Sokol.

Leaving Floyd in the car, I entered Jay Nightingale's building. The bare bones lobby was bright and airy. Exposed metal ductwork against sky-blue painted ceilings confirmed its former life as a warehouse.

I rode the elevator to the fourth floor, determined to get my interview. I drummed the palms of my hands on my thighs to dispel the apprehension of confronting the man who'd blown me off. The elevator doors opened to three brass-framed Tuscany landscapes hanging on the wall and a waist high glass table with a silk arrangement atop. Two tall, black doors mirrored each other at opposite ends. Nightingale's apartment, 401, was on the right.

As I approached, a shiny object caught my eye. Stuck in the space between the carpet and wall was an iridescent button made of Mother of Pearl. Someone was going to be disappointed when they realized they'd lost that. Mitz would love it and I swooped it up, sliding it into my jacket before ringing the bell.

While waiting, I listened for footsteps that didn't come. Nightingale couldn't avoid me this time because I wasn't leaving without answers. I pounded on the door and it creaked open. My heart thumped in my chest. Obviously Nightingale had forgotten to secure his door. With my fingertips, I pushed the door open wider and stuck my head in. The foyer, a six by six space with a divider adorned with a copper sculpture, blocked my view of the main living area. To see the full apartment, I'd have to walk around the wall.

"Hello," I called. "Is anybody home?" No one answered.

The thump in my chest turned into a full-on drum procession. A normal person would close the door and come back later. A normal person didn't have Roger Pruett's DNA. A locked door would never have deterred him, and this door was unlocked. If I left, Nightingale might continue to ignore my calls.

My stomach joined the brigade at the notion of stepping into the apartment and trespassing the minute I did. Regardless of being a P.I. or Roger Pruett's daughter, I wasn't above the law. Nightingale could be inside though, and not have heard me. Before my good sense could debate that likelihood, I strode through the entry and around the divide, stopping on the other side.

Plush white carpeting covered the vast living room. A white suede sectional surrounded a square glass coffee table with Asian architectural magazines and a large picture book of the Portland Japanese Gardens fanned out on top. The first time I'd been to the Gardens was with my dad during the Rose Festival and in the spring when the cherry blossoms bloomed. I'd taken Mitz this year and I could still see her beaming smile at the sight. French nouveau and abstract art adorned the walls. Iron sculptures on marble stands I'd expect to see in a ritzy art gallery sat across the room.

The luxury inside this apartment didn't match the building. Kyle said Nightingale had failed to appear on a burglary charge. If the items in this place weren't stolen, the money to buy them might have been. Whatever the source of his cash, the man collected fine things. I couldn't imagine white couches and glass tables anywhere near Mitz or Floyd, let alone me.

"Helllllooo," I sing-songed again. The apartment echoed with a silence that made the hairs on my arm stand to attention. Or the lack of heat in the place caused the shiver that rattled me next. I pulled the jacket zipper up under my chin.

No one was home. Commonsense said time to go, but given he'd avoided me once, he might try to duck me indefinitely. It couldn't hurt to find out more about him and see what made the man tick before I left.

I made my way into the kitchen with its hanging rack of expensive copper pots and pans and brushed-chrome appliances. The black marble countertops were spotless. The cupboard filled with exotic spices suggested he was a good cook. I headed for the bedrooms. The first had a top-of-the-line treadmill and weight machine against a wall of full-length mirrors, and a towel flung over the weight bench. Nightingale might have recently worked out and had gone for a smoothie.

With the prospect of him returning any minute, I took long strides into the master bedroom with its black lacquered furniture, more abstract art, and the bed covered with a comforter stuffed into a burgundy velvet duvet. While some modern décor looked clean and classy, this room felt cold and sterile.

The sound of trickling water came from the master bath where the door was three-quarters closed and a light was on. I froze, expecting Nightingale to walk out and bust me. The stream remained constant with no other sounds. Nightingale had a bladder the size of a horse or he had a leaking faucet. I bet on the latter.

I shook my nerves and headed for the door. Nightingale's medicine cabinet was my next stop anyway. Dad had said if you want to know the intimate details of a person, the medicine cabinet tells no lies.

With one hand, I pushed the door open. A ball of fluff darted past me and let out a howl. My heart plunged as I swung around fast enough to catch the white tail of a cat scampering out of the bedroom. This sneaking around stuff was going to give me a heart attack. I needed to check this last room and get out of there.

I turned toward the bathroom. The smell of wet rusted metal hit my nose before I saw the source. The rigid body of a man floated in the bathtub, his chin on his chest, the water deep red around him.

Jay Nightingale, I presume.

TWELVE

THE WATER TRICKLING against the porcelain sink rever-
berated in my ears, along with my crashing heartbeat.
Nightingale's arm hung over the tub's edge, a puddle
of dark blood beneath it; bloody cat paws were tracked
all over the floor.

Bile erupted into my throat and I slapped my hand
over my mouth. If Nightingale had wanted to run after
seeing Brooke die, I understood why. Every nerve in
my body urged me to bolt.

But there'd be no opportunity to look around the
room once the police arrived. I had to understand what
had happened here. One white towel rested on the tile
edge near the tub and his clothes hung neatly over the
towel rack. A candle long burnt out sat on the tile sur-
round. A few blood droplets splattered the walls. No
knife or razor was visible. It could have fallen in the
water. I didn't plan to check.

Had Nightingale committed suicide? I hadn't seen
a goodbye letter during my trek through his place.
There were no marks on the wrist that hung over the
tub. The other one was submerged. Wasn't planning to
check that either. I'd already have to explain why I'd
been in the house. Touching the body and messing with
potential evidence would only add to my problems.

A few breaths for calm and I scanned the room
again. Aside from the pool of blood under Nightin-

gale's arm, the space looked tidy. I'd read that it wasn't uncommon to fold one's clothes before killing yourself. That went for having the bath towel nearby and ready, but it felt weird. Unless he hadn't planned for it to be his last time. Something wasn't right.

Without moving, I inspected Nightingale closer. Coagulated blood stained his chest. It could have been caused by a wire or knife wound to his throat. It would account for the red tub water. Without moving his head, I couldn't be sure. If right, however, I could be smack in the middle of a crime scene.

Before leaving, I grabbed my phone and took a picture of Nightingale. Morbid, but with this twist, having a picture of him might come in handy.

Stuffing my phone in my jean pocket, I retraced my steps out to Nightingale's bedroom, where I bent over, hands on my knees, and swallowed the golf ball-sized lump in my throat. Process serving hadn't prepared me for the grizzly scene, but I was determined to stick this out. I forced myself upright for a quick sweep to find out more about this man who hadn't shown last night.

Using my shirt as a mitt, I opened his bureau drawers. T-shirts were neatly folded in one and boxers in another. He had a few long pajama pants in a center pull out and workout shorts, running tights, and tanks in the bottom. A jewelry box contained a leather bracelet, several gold chains, and a couple of Rolex watches. After seeing the condo, I wouldn't expect anything less.

On the right side of his tri-fold closet I discovered Nightingale loved sports coats. Velour, silk, cotton, linen, and tweed. He could have opened a Men's Warehouse. Next to that hung a selection of leather pants.

Brown, suede, and black, along with a variety of dress pants. Leather shoes, boots, and even flip-flops were neatly stored in a hanging shoe organizer. I shut the closet and opened the single one next to it, finding a different story.

A collection of spiked collars, leather masks, paddles, and whips covered a holder resembling a pool cue rack. My face contorted. The man had been into some kinky stuff. Careful not to touch anything else, I shut the door and noticed a black leather glove on the floor in front of the nightstand. It no doubt belonged with the contents of the closet.

Back in the living room, nothing struck me as out of order. On the elevator down, I punched 911 on my cell and waited in my car. Floyd's ears got a thorough massage as my thoughts churned and I nursed my coffee. My hands shook. Caffeine wasn't the best idea, but the hot liquid was comforting.

Brooke Hanson and the man Georgette thought was involved was dead. Were their deaths linked? It was an awful big coincidence if not. Without more information about him, or those he surrounded himself with, however, I didn't have the answer. I could kick myself for not pressing him more on the phone when I'd had the chance.

Another thought had also snuck into my head. Where was Georgette last night?

The nausea brought on by the goriness in the tub lessened after a few minutes. The unsettling questions had not by the time a squad car and an unmarked Chevy pulled in front of me.

A burly man with a crewcut, and a short muscular man with gray hair and a mustache exited the unmarked and walked my direction. Two uniformed officers followed. I got out of my Spitfire and leaned against the door. The wail of a siren drew closer. A Toyota SUV pulled up across the street, and Kyle Jaeger, still in uniform, climbed out. I would have rather talked to him than any of them. He didn't reach me first.

"You the lady that called?" the gray-haired detective asked.

"Yes," I answered. "The body's on the fourth floor, apartment 401, master bath." I handed him my card.

The medical examiner arrived next. The detective tucked my card into his jacket and met the M.E. at his rig. They had a conversation I couldn't hear before the burly detective pointed at me. "Don't go anywhere," he said as he and the entourage followed the M.E. into the building.

"Not planning on it."

Kyle trotted across the street.

"Thought you'd be off duty by now," I said, my shoulders relaxing at seeing a friendly face.

He stepped onto the sidewalk next to me. "Was, and almost home when I heard the call on my scanner. Address sounded familiar. What's the story?"

The pounding of my heart started to calm with Kyle next to me. "Nightingale's door was open." I brought him up to the point where I walked into his bathroom. "That's when I found him floating in the tub."

"Suicide?"

The acid in my stomach tried to make a comeback at the idea of Nightingale's lifeless body. "Too much blood on his chest."

"Sliced throat?"

"Could be, and not that long ago. Which meant he was dead—or dying—about the time I expected him at the Limbo last night." I shuddered. "I'm glad I didn't arrange to meet him here."

Kyle put his hand on my arm. "Me too."

I forced down a swallow. I'd been stoic, keeping the situation compartmentalized. His touch was crumbling that wall fast. Closing my eyes for a second, I got ahold of my emotions.

He dropped his hand to his side "The boys upstairs will want a full statement. If you'll stay put, I'll see how long it'll be."

I nodded.

We went into the building. A few chairs had been arranged in the corner of the space and Kyle left me sitting. I rested my head on the back of the chair, clearing my mind, while I waited. Death scenes weren't an everyday occurrence for a P.I. We were called in by the families after the crime scene tape had been removed, not before. Thank God. Not sure I could take much of this.

Doing what my father asked for Georgette was proving to be a challenge. I'd messed up my interview with Nightingale and now he was dead. Justified or not, I couldn't shake the feeling that my poking around and asking questions had somehow caused it.

From the corner chair, I watched an officer come and go through the glass doors. Probably getting a search warrant. Thirty minutes later, Kyle hadn't returned. About to jump out of my skin, I went outside to pace. A couple of cars were parked out front, and no foot traffic. With the lack of people around, coming in and out of the building, unnoticed would be easy.

Even more so at night when traffic dwindled to nothing. Perhaps another tenant had seen something. The police would be on that.

The building door opened and Kyle approached with the gray-haired detective.

"I'm Detective Richmond," he said. "Sorry to have been short the first time. You Roger Pruett's kid?"

My dad had worked with the cops many times over the years. I shouldn't have been surprised. "You knew my dad?"

"Ran into him on a couple of cases. Good guy. Knew his stuff. Sorry to hear about his stroke."

I nodded, wishing he were here now to lend me his expertise. "Thanks."

"Were you a friend of Mr. Nightingale?"

"No. He was a witness to a death I'm investigating."

"Didn't realize you took over for your dad. Who's your client?"

I hesitated, knowing how Georgette felt about Nightingale and afraid to throw her name into the mix, but I had little choice. "Georgette Hanson."

"Brooke Hanson's mother, the woman killed a couple of weeks ago at the MAX tracks," Kyle added. Since he'd done the initial report, he filled the detective in on how Nightingale fit.

The detective listened and nodded.

"Was Mr. Nightingale murdered?" I asked.

"Can't comment on an active investigation," he said. "You find a weapon?"

"I'm going to want an address on Georgette Hanson," the detective said to Kyle, ignoring me. "I'll need to check her whereabouts of the last twenty-four hours."

Of course, and why he wasn't sharing information. He'd want the location of everyone who had reason to cause the victim harm. Georgette had been angry at Nightingale, but I couldn't believe she'd ever act on it.

"Let's get your statement," he said to me and I followed him to his sedan. We climbed in and Kyle went to his truck to wait. "You talked to him yesterday?" the detective began once we were settled.

"Briefly. We were supposed to meet at the Limbo, but he never showed and didn't answer my calls."

Detective Richmond made notes while I rehashed what I had told Kyle earlier about finding Nightingale in the bathroom. "And Mrs. Hanson, did she know Mr. Nightingale?"

"Not personally," I said. "She believed he knew more about the night her daughter died than he told the police."

He rested his pen on his knee. "Any truth to that?"

I had opinions that he'd acted strange at the scene. Supposed eye contact with Brooke in a dark bar. A cryptic conversation with him where he sounded bitter. "Nothing solid."

"What made her think he did?" He gripped his pen again.

"Intuition." He gave me a sideways glance. "I'm pursuing the angle that Nightingale did know her daughter and was holding back."

"You'll keep me posted on that investigation?" he said.

I nodded. "You do the same?" He gave me a lopsided smile. It didn't often go both ways.

"Do you think she could have killed him?" he asked. Looking out the window and tracing the vinyl trim with my finger, I recalled our first conversation. Georgette had been certain that Nightingale was guilty of something. "She sought me out to find the truth about that night. Really, she sought my dad out… I don't see the purpose if she planned on killing the guy." Unless she was creating an alibi, which I didn't believe. The image of his bloodied corpse struck me again, my stomach flipping in protest. "And the way he died…." I folded my arms over my chest. "No, I don't think she did this. Have you seen his closet?"

He shot me another look and I expected a reprimand. "He was into BDSM," he said, instead.

"BD, what?" I asked.

"Bondage and discipline."

"Sadism and masochism," I finished.

"Right."

I'd heard of its existence, but never seen it. After seeing those paddles and whips, I was okay with that. "You think that played into his murder?"

Once again, he ignored my question and went on with a few of his own. An hour later, and after another run through of my steps in finding the body, he gave me the clear to go. He handed me his business card as we exited his car and he disappeared into the building.

Kyle reemerged from his truck and joined me on the sidewalk. The smell of his fading cologne tickled my nose. He'd been up since last night and it was nearly two in the afternoon. He must be exhausted and yet he'd come to the scene for me. And stayed. He smiled.

"Thank you for hanging out during this, but I'd better be going," I said.

"Where you off to?"

"Home." Except I wasn't. Mitz and Jeff would be at

least two more hours. I couldn't tell Kyle I was headed to Georgette's house to make sure I should remain on the case with Nightingale dead.

Kyle and I had progressed into the friend zone, but he was a cop and there was an active murder investigation. Best not to give him an opportunity to tell me I shouldn't do something.

"Want to grab a cup of coffee instead?" he asked.

My inner voice screamed yes. My outside-voice won out. "Raincheck?"

He nodded. "Sure."

I'd brushed him off to push forward on my case. It was what I was hired to do; what my father would do. Jeff could be more right about me than I wanted to admit.

In my car, I felt Kyle's eyes on me as I checked Georgette's address and did a U-turn in that direction. Despite what I'd told the detective, I had one other question to be answered by my client. Where had she been last night while the man she believed killed her daughter lay bleeding out in a bathtub?

THIRTEEN

A SEDAN WITH government plates was parked in the driveway of the Hanson's newer traditional two-story house when I pulled up with Floyd snoring in the seat beside me. I'd assumed Detective Richmond would come himself and I'd have time to get to Georgette first. Instead, he'd called another team to drive straight out.

A man in his late sixties with a comb-over answered the door. His V-neck T-shirt and belly hung over baggy trousers. He had a gruff demeanor, but warm eyes. A salt-of-the-earth kind of guy who reminded me of my dad. "Is Georgette here?" I scanned the area behind him not seeing anyone.

"She's busy right now." His voice had a pack a day gravel to it.

"I'm Kelly Pruett. Are you Mr. Hanson?"

He grunted a yes.

"Your wife hired me to investigate your daughter's death. She'll want to see me. It's important."

He turned and disappeared.

Georgette emerged a moment later, wearing a silk lavender blouse and black pants, her wide-eyes and ghostly-white skin reflecting pure fear. The sedan in the driveway must have spooked her. "I assume you've heard what's happened to Nightingale?" I said.

"Yes. How do you know?" she whispered, a tremor in her voice.

"I found him."

She gaped with a blank expression. "Where're my manners? Come in. A detective is here asking questions about where we were last night."

A question I had myself. I followed her into the kitchen where a young man sat at the dinette table sipping coffee.

He stood when he saw me. "You must be Kelly Pruett." He extended his hand. "I'm Detective Rakow. Detective Richmond told me you might drop by."

"He did?" I gave him a firm shake.

He nodded. "Said you were Roger Pruett's daughter. If you were anything like your old man, I should expect you."

Because my dad kept his cases to himself, I wasn't privy to his apparent reputation for being tenacious among his contemporaries. "I'm here to see my client. Are you guys about wrapped up?"

"Just starting," he said.

"Can Kelly stay?" Georgette asked the detective. She perched at the edge of the chair across the table from him, wringing her hands.

He swished his mouth back and forth. "That'd be fine. If you want to," he finally said.

Protocol often dictated that no other people should be around during questioning. He must have decided there'd be no harm. We were both on the same side of the law, after all.

I settled in the chair next to his. Mr. Hanson reappeared wearing an unbuttoned flannel shirt and propped his elbows on the kitchen counter with his arms folded across his thick chest.

"Did either of you know Jay Nightingale?" Detective Rakow began.

Georgette and Chester shook their heads in unison.

"Did you blame him for Brooke's death?"

Chester shook his head again, but Georgette said, "Absolutely. You people let him out without pursuing every angle. How do you know he didn't push Brooke that night? How can you be sure he was merely 'passing by?'"

I gave Georgette credit for being honest about how she felt. My focus fell on the detective and what he'd make of that honesty.

He glanced up from his notepad, eyebrows raised. "Why do you believe otherwise? You know something we don't?"

"No." Georgette wilted.

He scribbled some notes. "Where were you last night?"

I perked up, leaning in for the answer.

"Playing bridge with the couple next door," Georgette said.

"Until what time?"

"Oh dear," she glanced at Chester. "What time would you say, honey?"

He hem-hawed. "Midnight, I guess."

"That sounds about right because we cleaned up and sat down to watch the end of the news."

All verifiable information. So far, so good.

"What time did you go to bed?" Detective Rakow asked.

Georgette stopped kneading her hand. "We watched *Late Night*. About one."

"Did you know where Jay Nightingale lived?"

"Not the slightest idea." Chester sounded resolute.

Georgette's frown creased her forehead. "I hope you don't think we've done anything wrong. We were furious he'd been released, but we wouldn't kill him or anyone else for that matter."

I hoped that too.

"No one's accusing you," the detective said. "We're obligated to conduct a full investigation when a murder's been committed. Anyone that would've had a motive, anyone in the area, any friends or family, they'll all be interviewed."

Georgette's and my shoulders relaxed at the same time.

"I see," Georgette said.

The detective's cell phone rang and he reached into his coat pocket. "Excuse me." He got up and walked outside.

Glad for the break in the interview, I shifted in my chair.

Chester grabbed a pack of cigarettes off the counter. "Come get me when he's ready," he said as he headed for the back door.

Georgette watched him go. "We're both such a wreck."

I waited until we were alone. "You promise you and Chester had nothing to do with Nightingale last night?"

Georgette's mouth opened, shocked I'd go there.

"I'm sorry. I have to know." A driven investigator

or not, even my dad wouldn't continue a case if he suspected his client had committed a felony.

"We were right where we said. I loved Brooke, and I did believe Nightingale wasn't being honest, but I would never…" Tears filled her eyes.

My dad always believed people had an element of bad in their good. In some ways, I believed that, too. More so after Jeff cheated. But I held out hope it wasn't always the case. I wanted to believe Georgette. Because my father had asked me to help her, I needed to. "Okay," I said. "The next question is, do you want me to continue my investigation since your suspect is dead?"

She sniffed and dried her eyes. "Of course. I must know what happened to my baby that night. If that leads back to Nightingale, so be it."

I didn't know where it would lead, if anywhere. "Let's go back to Brooke being distant. It may be she didn't want you to learn about the apartment. Can you think of any reason why?"

"No."

"Did she have any addictions?"

I expected an outright denial. Georgette hesitated. "Not that I was aware of. Although I didn't realize she drank."

Kids hiding things from their parents wasn't new. There were also things parents didn't want to see. "Brooke never mentioned being at odds with anyone?"

"Never. I can't imagine anyone upset with her. She was a good girl. Obstinate, sure, and liked to do things her way. Who doesn't?"

She and I, both. "What kinds of things?"

"Life in general, I guess. She and Chester always butted heads."

"Think, Georgette. Was there any inkling she could be into something or upsetting someone? You said when you saw her, she looked stressed. Do you think a previous relationship may have upset her and come back around?"

"Not that I know of."

"Had she talked about troubles at work?"

"She never mentioned work, other than when she paid off our house and she said they paid her a ridiculous amount."

Accountants made good money. I'd have felt more concerned if she'd told me Brooke was broke all the time which might suggest a drug or gambling problem. Georgette wasn't giving me much to go on. "Is that it?"

"I guess."

Brooke's distance could have been caused by anything from work and men troubles or having a lot on her mind. The fact she paid off her parents' house made me think she'd been a good and caring daughter. "I will tell you I believe Nightingale knew more than he shared with the police." I told her what Amanda had said about Nightingale and Brooke at the bar. "Finding out if there was a connection is where I'm at. If there is one, he'd been lying and people don't generally do that unless they're guilty of something."

"Like killing my Brooke?" Georgette straightened.

I shifted in my chair, torn between giving her some peace and not wanting to lie. "Something was going on with Brooke and I'm working to unravel what that was." Georgette looked at me with hopeful eyes. "No, I can't get there yet."

Georgette slunk in her chair.

Hating to see her deflated, I continued, "I'm not sure where the police are on finding Nightingale's killer or what their theory will be. To me, it's suspicious the only witness to Brooke's death has been murdered the same night we planned to meet. In our earlier conversation, he sounded angry at someone." Would he have told me more about that if I'd pushed? "With him dead, I'll have to find another way to find who that person was, but I *will* figure it out."

Georgette scanned my face. "Please be safe. I don't want anything to happen to you and your family. Your father would never forgive me if it did."

She gave me an opening to ask more about her and my dad. As I was about to, Chester walked into the room. "I will," I said instead. "I watched him deal with the risks of doing this kind of work. I'd like to think I'm prepared. It's more important right now that we focus. Is there anything else you can think of?" I directed the question to both of them.

"I've told you everything," Georgette said.

"Did you tell her that she never came to see you?" Chester grumbled.

Georgette's eyebrows knitted together. "Brooke called when she had time."

He blew out a breath between his lips sounding like a propeller. "We raised her better than that. When she lived down the street, we saw her more. After she left for that place in southwest, she was like a damn ghost."

She patted Chester's hand in what appeared to be a common dynamic between the two of them. The agitated and the calmer. It was a good balance. I'd seen it in my parents. My mom had been the high strung one, with my dad trying to appease her. Jeff and I were both yin and no yang.

Detective Rakow finally returned. "There's been a new development," he began. "Fingerprints were found in Nightingale's apartment that aren't his. I'd like to take you down to the precinct and have you printed, for elimination purposes."

Georgette's face dropped. "I didn't do anything."

"It's routine, ma'am."

"It's standard to ask, but you're not required to give them. And you always have the right to hire an attorney," I said to Georgette wanting her to understand her options and ignoring the detective's stare.

"Ms. Pruett's right. This should be pretty quick and easy though—unless there's some reason you wouldn't want us to have them?" the detective said.

Georgette glanced at me. "Will they take yours?"

Georgette was a reserved woman. The thought of accompanying a police officer downtown would feel like a mark of shame. To have them ink her fingers and be put in the system would be equally upsetting. Then again, her daughter's name had been all over the papers. Perhaps her shame-o-meter was maxed out. I could convince her it was no biggie. "Mine are already on file." Georgette's concerned frown remained. "It's really not uncommon for them to ask," I added.

She finally nodded and turned toward her husband.

"I'll come with you, hon," Chester said.

"We'd like your fingerprints, too, Mr. Hanson."

"That's fine."

Georgette stood and we walked into the living room where she gathered a short wool coat and scarf from the coat tree near the front door. The detective and

Chester went out ahead of us. She pulled a glove from her pocket and put it on.

As she got ready, I studied the living room with its comfortable furniture and antique lamps. Framed pictures of Brooke on the brick fireplace mantel caught my eye. One showed her at about Mitz's age dressed in pink tights and a tutu, her feet in the fifth position and both arms curved above her head. In another, she was older, probably twelve, and perched atop a black horse looking fearless and flashing a full smile. Her high school graduation picture anchored the shelf, her cap tassel draped across the front. Great memories captured in still shots showing Brooke happy and carefree. My heart ached thinking of what Chester and Georgette had lost.

I checked on Georgette's progress whose face was pinched in confusion. She turned her back to me and continued to fumble about in her coat and purse. I was about to ask if she was okay when another photo grabbed my attention. A teenage Brooke stood next to a much younger girl. They weren't touching or smiling—like two people forced to be in the same picture and wanting to be miles apart. The two girls had dark brown hair, but their noses were different, as was the shape of their face. I leaned in closer. Was that who I thought it was?

"Who's that standing next to Brooke?" I pointed to the photo.

"That's Hannah. Brooke's sister. The one I mentioned who lives in Seattle." Georgette faced me, her cheeks flush.

"That's the girl who's staying in Brooke's apartment."

"You've met her?"

"Yes. When I went there Friday afternoon. She told me her name was Trina."

Flustered, she stuttered. "That can't be true. She moved months ago. We've tried to call and tell her about Brooke. She hasn't called us back."

"She'd already heard." Had she learned about Brooke on the news, or did she run in the same circle as Brooke and found out that way? As sisters, it would make sense she'd know at least a few of Brooke's friends.

"You're sure it's her?" Georgette asked.

"Very. Those serious eyes haven't changed much. Is that normal for her not to keep in touch?"

Georgette frowned. "Unfortunately. She's a free spirit. I'm surprised she'd have been staying with her sister. They never got along."

The body language in the picture confirmed that was true and from an early age. That didn't explain why Hannah-slash-Trina had not come clean about who she was and suggested that she and Brooke only had a landlord-tenant relationship. And why not contact her mother when she came into town? Especially with a family tragedy—a tragedy she hadn't been broken up about. Or had she even left town?

Outside, I said my goodbyes and told Georgette I'd be in touch. As I got in my car and backed out of their driveway, Georgette ducked into the front seat of the sedan and Chester opened the door to the back. The base of my skull tingled. They were going to the station for a routine matter. Georgette was innocent. No reason to worry for them, right?

I shifted into gear and rolled down the road. I needed proof that Nightingale and Brooke were connected—besides Amanda's observations. And Hannah was Brooke's sister. She had to know more than she told me earlier. Including where Brooke's other house was located.

I dropped onto the highway for the drive back to Meadow Verde to find out. Perhaps I'd made the first error by introducing myself as Brooke's friend—a mistake I wouldn't make again. I was a P.I. Time to start owning that and demanding answers.

FOURTEEN

FOR THE SECOND time in two days, I parked in front of Brooke's apartment building. Already late afternoon, I was pushing the time. Jeff and Mitz would be getting back soon. With a dead body, an interrogation, and the discovery that Hannah had lied to me, I couldn't go home yet. I texted Jeff. "Something came up in the case. My witness was…." Bad idea to overshare. I backspaced. "I'll pick up Mitz. Running later than expected. Call when I'm on my way."

I hit SEND trying to wall out Jeff's words that I was like my dad. Sometimes I wore that as a badge of honor. I didn't want to admit that he'd get consumed by a case and be an occasional no show when he said he'd be there. With no intention to get that comparison, I'd wrap this quickly and pick up my girl and finish our weekend together.

After giving Floyd a pee break and making sure he was well secured in my car, I knocked on Brooke's apartment. There were no lights on, but the centered dead plant I'd seen last time had been shifted in front of Brooke's entry and recently watered. While nothing short of a miracle would bring it back to life, it was a sign that Trina, or Hannah, hadn't run off. Yet anyway.

Shuffling sounds came from the other side. "I hear you," I said, "and I have a key. The knock is a courtesy. I'm coming in either way."

More shuffling.

"You have thirty seconds. Twenty-nine. Twenty-eight."

The door swung open. "No need to get bossy." Hannah yawned, her hair in a lopsided ponytail. She wiped crust out of her eyes. "No luck finding those tax returns?"

Either she'd figured out my lie right away and was being sarcastic, or she was serious. I didn't care which. "You going to let me in?"

She rolled her eyes and walked away.

Closing the door behind me, I followed her to the living room, where she had the muted 13-inch TV tuned to ice skating.

She flopped down onto the futon. "Pull up the beanbag if you like. Who are you really?"

I stood. "Kelly Pruett. I'm a private investigator your mom hired to find out what happened to your sister."

Another patented eyeroll. "Seems obvious she fell in front of a train."

"Not much love lost between you, I see."

She shot me a sardonic look. "Perceptive."

"Why didn't you tell me who you were?"

"Why didn't you?"

Touché. "I thought you'd be more comfortable talking to a friend than a P.I. My bad. But you must know where Brooke's other place is and that's why I'm back."

"What, you and Mama don't think this place is good enough for Princess? Or is it Daddy-o?"

The entire family was the recipient of Hannah's sour attitude and I didn't want to be in the middle of their drama. "You told me yourself she'd moved out.

Where did she live?" My phone vibrated in my pocket. I silenced it.

She shrugged. "Downtown at the KOIN Tower. One of the penthouse suites. Not sure which one since I never got an invitation." The annoyance in her voice said the last part clearly bothered her.

"A penthouse?" A suite in any skyscraper in the city would have cost a million to own and thousands a month to lease.

"Yeah. Big sis had money. You've figured that much out if you're any kind of a P.I."

I didn't like this girl. "I did, which is why this place doesn't make sense. You must have kept in touch with her since you're living here. By the way, your mom thinks you're in Seattle."

She chuckled. "That's what I tell them when I don't want to feel guilty about not coming around. As for living here, Brooke and I had an arrangement. She let me stay in this Godforsaken place and I kept her secret quiet. Real gracious of her, don't you think? She lived in luxury, and I got the roach motel." She waved her hand at the room.

I ignored her sense of entitlement. "You could always go home. Your parents would welcome you, I'm sure."

She grimaced. "No thanks. At least I have freedom here."

"What secret were you keeping?"

"Her other place, obviously."

Obviously. "But why?"

"No clue and don't care."

Two minutes with Hannah made me grateful for

being an only child. "When you said she didn't have a boyfriend was that the truth?"

"Brooke would never be *owned* by anyone."

Having a boyfriend didn't mean one was owned, but I didn't feel like arguing. "Did you know any of the people she spent time with?"

She sat up. "We weren't close. I'm sure my mother told you that part."

"She did, just not the details."

Her folded arms over her chest said she didn't intend to fill in the blanks.

More touchy family dynamics. I pulled up Nightingale's picture on my phone and cropped the image to show his face. "This is a photo of a man Brooke might have known. I'm warning you now it could be disturbing."

She took the phone and squinted at the screen, then resized the image with her fingertips. "Oh shit." She flung the phone back at me like it was on fire. "Who are you?"

I tucked the phone back in my pocket. "Have you seen him before or not?"

"No. Who is he? Did you kill him?"

My turn to roll my eyes. "His name is Jay Nightingale. He witnessed Brooke falling in front of the train. However, your mother thinks he could have had something to do with her death."

Hannah grimaced. "Never seen him. How'd he die?"

"Murdered."

She shuddered. "Thanks for the image." She turned away from me and threw the bedding I'd seen in the closet over her shoulders. "I'm going back to bed. I have to work tonight."

I remembered the cocktail dress on the bedroom floor the last time we met. "You work at a bar?"

"I'm a waitress at Casa Diablo, among other things."

"Casa Diablo? Isn't that the House of…"

"The Devil. Yeah."

"That's a bar?"

"Strip joint."

I didn't have to ask what she'd meant by among other things.

She burrowed further into the covers. "Lock up when you go," she said, ending our conversation.

Her attitude had to contribute to why she was on rocky ground with her family. Had that been born into her, or created from family hurts and slights? If Mitz ever iced me out like this, I wouldn't handle it as well as Georgette seemed to. "You really should call your mother."

Hannah didn't respond.

My brain hurt from overload. Mitz and Jeff should be at his place by now. On the way down the stairs, I saw he'd called. My return call went to voicemail. I texted: "On my way." I scanned the area as I approached my car. Floyd was perked up in the seat. Down the walkway of the complex, Luke stood outside his door, smoking, and peering at me.

I waved and he raised his hand slowly, as did the hairs on the back of my neck. His having Floyd the last time bothered me. Had he been watching? Did he know about Hannah? A guy that observant wouldn't let much get past him. If he did, why not tell me that when I interviewed him? Unless he didn't know at the time or it didn't matter if the rent got paid.

As I dropped onto the Interstate, I replayed the conversation with Hannah. The penthouse, while a curious development, made more sense than Brooke living at Meadow Verde. Could Hannah, and everyone else I'd spoken with, be wrong about Brooke having a boyfriend that she lived with? She could have held onto the dingy apartment as insurance if it didn't work out. In that case, the identity of the boyfriend was the real secret.

FIFTEEN

JEFF LIVED IN VANCOUVER, WASHINGTON, directly across the Columbia River from Portland, in a light gray craftsman with white trim, rock veneer, tapered columns set on bluestone bases, and eaves lined with clear cedar. Lexus, Mercedes, and BMWs were parked in the neighboring driveways. Jeff's Subaru Outback sat in his.

A lifetime ago I had called this home. We'd been married eight years, and bought this place a couple of years in, right after Jeff took his manual writing job. We'd picked Washington because one of the best schools for the Deaf in the country was located nearby. When we divorced, the money I made for process serving didn't allow me to afford the mortgage. With Mitz's needs, it didn't make sense to sell. When the market was better, Jeff would refinance and give me my half. In the meantime, Jeff worked from home and could afford the upkeep.

I moved out, then back into my childhood home with my father. There, I had a bedroom for myself and had converted the guest bedroom into a little girl's getaway for Mitz. The bonus was my dad would get to see Mitz more than ever before. Best laid plans... I'd been there a couple of months before he died. Hard to believe that had only been earlier this year.

Returning to the scene of my failed marriage reminded me of all that I'd lost recently besides my dad and didn't conjure many pleasant memories. Even when things were good with Jeff, I had never fit in with the Suzie Homemakers or the PTA moms. Or with the corporate America types. Most of the time I had no clue where I did fit, if at all.

I rang the bell. Jeff answered with his mouth set in a hard line. "Glad to see you could make it."

I bit my lower lip. He had a right to be annoyed. "Sorry, I ran behind. It's been a day. Is Mitz ready to go?"

"Didn't you get my message? We just got back from the hospital."

My heart jumped. "What happened? What hospital?"

"Come in."

He stepped out of the way and I stood on the maple floored entryway while he closed the door. "I called you back and I texted. You should have said something then."

He led me through his kitchen and into his dining room where I set my purse and phone on the table. "I got your messages about the time we were at Urgent Care. Mitz cut herself and she needed a couple of stitches. I called you back. When you didn't answer I figured you were too busy."

"I was interviewing a witness and thought you were at OMSI. I kept in touch all day. I'm sorry I wasn't able to answer in that moment."

"No biggie. I handled it. Like usual," he said.

His tone made me bristle. "Plenty of things happen during my time with Mitz that I handle, without you."

"Right. Except today was your time and had she been with you…"

"You offered to take her because you had this theory she'd be safer with you than me."

He didn't have time to finish his response before Mitz bounded down the hall from her bedroom with a bandaged hand.

I rushed over, grabbing her in a hug. "What the heck." Letting her go I signed. "What were you doing that you got hurt?"

"Cutting an apple." She signed back with her good hand.

It would have been easy to do the blame game, except it could have happened at either one of our houses. I didn't push for more information. "I'm sorry, sweetie. Next time, make sure to ask Dad or me to help, okay?"

She nodded. "You come to my room? I want you to meet Charlie."

"Charlie?"

"Daddy got me a hamster."

I glanced at Jeff for approval, which he gave with a nod, before letting her drag me down the hall to her cotton-candy-colored bedroom. For the next ten minutes, she introduced me to her little friend, and showed me the beaded necklace and bracelet she'd been working on. I'd bought her a kit for her birthday last month.

"I can't finish it now," she signed.

"Bring it with you next weekend. I'll help you." Her smile indicated she'd like that. "Did you have fun at OMSI?"

She gave me the rundown of the exhibits they'd seen—a much better day than the one I'd had.

"That's wonderful, Ladybug. I'm sorry I had to work, but it sounds like you had fun."

She patted my leg. "It's okay Mama. Daddy said sometimes mommies have to work. I understand."

"He said that?" That was a one-eighty from the Jeff I knew.

She nodded. "Yeah. And he said sometimes even if we don't like the work mommies do, we have to be supportive." I was surprised by Jeff's words about work and my working, but it was good news.

I gave Mitz another long cuddle. "I'm going to go sweetie, and you'll stay with Dad so you can rest your hand. I'll call you later to say goodnight and I'll see you next weekend." I left her playing and found Jeff at the kitchen table, cradling his head in his hands. "I'll pick her up from school on Friday. Thank you for your help today."

He didn't answer.

"Are we good?" I prompted.

He lifted his head and thrust my phone at me. "What have you gotten yourself into?"

"What are we talking about?" I took my cell and saw a missed call on the screen. I didn't recognize the number.

"Who's the dead guy?" he asked.

"You went through my stuff?"

"Answer the question."

"You first. You sound like the private eye now."

"You had a call. Thought I'd be nice and bring your cell to you, but the caller hung up. I don't know, old habits die hard. I opened your phone and looked at the pictures. Shoot me."

"You mean you used to go through my phone when

we were married?" I'd never put on a passcode when we were together. I'd never thought it was necessary.

He didn't answer.

Heat crept into my cheeks. "You were the one who betrayed me. Even when I suspected you and Linda had slept together, you didn't see me rummaging through your stuff. If her damn earring hadn't fallen out of your pocket and you didn't turn as red as a beet and start sweating, I might never have known. I should be able to leave my things in your presence without worrying."

"Is this the case that you were working on last night?"

One of us had to be truthful. "He's the guy who was supposed to meet me and didn't show."

"How'd you get a picture of him?"

"I'm the one that found him earlier today."

He frowned.

"The police are handling his murder investigation."

His shoulders relaxed. "Because your client thought he was involved in her daughter's death and he's dead, life will go back to normal, right?"

"Well…"

He threw up his hands. "Great. You're not done."

"I haven't found out what happened to Brooke. All I'm fairly sure of is that she might have known the dead guy and had seen him at the bar before she was killed at the tracks."

Jeff's forehead creased. "He pushed her?"

"Don't know that part yet. But Brooke had been living in a penthouse in a swanky part of Portland, not in the low-rent place her parents believed she lived. Bottomline, she was not who her family thinks. Until I can give them a picture of who she was and what happened that night, I have to keep digging."

He shook his head. "Aren't you concerned? Someone has been murdered. It could be connected."

My heart pounded from having to explain this to Jeff and being reminded that this had turned out to be more than I'd thought I'd been hired for. It had to be more than my father would have imagined after protecting me from the perils of investigating while he was alive. But imagined or not, here I was. I wouldn't stop until I fulfilled his wishes. "Yes. Although his dying may have nothing to do with my case. I don't know anything about Nightingale or what he was into." Other than some bondage stuff, which tidbit I didn't intend to share. "Like I said, that's all a police matter."

"Just be careful."

"Of course…" My throat tightened. "I have to go."

"Fine. Do me a favor. Put passcode protect on your phone. If Mitz had seen that picture…"

"Already on it." I had meant to do it earlier and got distracted—something I couldn't let happen again. It was causing me too much grief.

A half hour later, I glided into my own drive and gazed up at my house. The darkened windows were a stark contrast to a couple of nights before when I came home to Mitz and all the lights on. Even after the day I'd had, I didn't want to go inside and face the quiet. If it wasn't Floyd's dinnertime, I might have driven away.

We got out of my car and I unlocked the door to my house. Leaves crunched behind me. The hair on my arms pricked up. Floyd stopped and put his nose in the air. "Arlene?" I called. No one answered.

I glanced up at her house next door. Our two

homes were situated on a slope; mine at the bottom—
Arlene's higher up. The main part of her house was
dark and the yard, including the staircase that bridged
our two properties, was quiet. The only light came
from her upstairs bedroom. Shadows of trees consumed the space between. I peered into the street.
Light mist had started to fall.

The sound of leaves crunched again, farther
away this time. I rushed Floyd through the door and
slammed it behind us, sliding the deadbolt with such
force I pinched my skin and let out a yip. Sucking on
my stinging finger, I shook the handle for good measure. It had probably been someone out walking their
dog. Sometimes I surprised myself at how brave and
forthright I could be. Other times, I cringed at my
jumpiness.

Upstairs in the kitchen, I shrugged off my coat and
fed Floyd. I swirled a heap of smooth peanut butter
out of the jar, stuck the spoon in my mouth, and went
into the living room to check messages. There were
three calls, all from Georgette.

In the first message, Georgette and Chester were at
the precinct waiting for the fingerprint technician. The
second, that the police were questioning Chester and
she wondered what could be taking so long. The final
message had come in ten minutes before I got home.

"Kel-Kelly, they think I ki-killed Nightingale. I
tried to call you on your cell, but you didn't answer.
My God, I can't believe this is happening. Call me
Kelly. Ca-call when you can. I'm at home. For now."

I plopped down on the couch and stretched my
neck. The Hansons had gone in for simple fingerprinting. Had the detective interrogated Georgette further

and something else came up? I wanted to believe in her innocence. There'd be no reason to involve me if she'd planned to kill Nightingale all along. I dialed Georgette and pulled the spoon out of my mouth. Chester answered.

"Bunch of bull." His low voice cracked. "Don't know what those jerks are thinking. She's too frail for this nonsense."

"Can I talk to her?" I asked.

The clank of the phone being set on the counter was followed by his muttering that became fainter. A minute passed before Georgette came on the line.

"What's going on?" I asked.

She repeated her earlier message. "They told me not to leave town." Her voice trembled.

"Why? What do they have on you?"

"They found a woman's glove in Mr. Nightingale's bedroom."

I'd seen that glove on the floor and thought it was connected to the paraphernalia in the closet. Earlier today, Georgette had reached into her pocket retrieving only one glove. I hadn't noticed whether she put it back or left the house gloveless because I'd been distracted when I saw Hannah's picture. I'd even dismissed Georgette's confusion as she dug in her pockets as being a nervous wreck. What if it wasn't confusion, but panic?

Georgette read my mind because she said, "I have a similar pair, but I swear the one they found isn't mine."

"You have that pair at home to prove that, right?"

"I've misplaced one, but we'll find it."

I closed my eyes. "Georgette, please tell me you were never at Nightingale's apartment."

"Absolutely not," she said, quickly. "It'll turn up."

What were the odds of this being a coincidence? "Start looking for it right away."

"Chester's been tearing the place apart since we got back."

"Keep me posted."

"I will. And Kelly, I am innocent. I wouldn't hurt anyone."

I wanted to believe her—despite the glove. I also knew better than to take people at their word. "Everything will get better once you find the glove." At least it would go a long way in shoring up my belief in her.

I laid there, sucking the peanut butter off the spoon. There were now three possibilities to who killed Nightingale. A mother full of rage who wanted vindication, someone else he'd pissed off in his life that was unrelated to my case, or someone scared enough to kill the only witness to Brooke's murder. Which one was it?

Thinking about Georgette and the glove, and who else might have been in Nightingale's apartment, had my head in a spin. The day's events had left me exhausted and frazzled. I wanted someone to talk it out with.

At one time, that person would have been my friend Linda. Having known her since I was in middle school, we shared everything, which later meant my husband. We hadn't spoken since the day after I learned of the affair. Even now I wasn't sure what hurt more—Jeff's betrayal or hers.

I pressed the heels of my hands into my eyes. Who could I share what I was going through and who wouldn't shut me down, tell me I was wasting my time, or complain about my parenting? Someone who might get it. That person was Kyle.

I'd been wanting to update him about Brooke's penthouse and to hear his voice again. I sat up on the couch, smiling at the thought of him.

I reached for my cell. My finger hovered over the numbers when a thump, followed by a scraping noise came from the living room windows.

SIXTEEN

TREE LIMBS AROUND my house often hit the upstairs bedroom glass if the wind was howling outside. Which it hadn't been when I arrived home. And the sounds I'd heard had come from this main level.

Floyd trotted in the room and stood rigid at the window. If he was on high alert, the noise hadn't been my imagination. I shouldn't have dismissed those crunching leaves earlier. My eyes darted around the room. All the blinds were down.

With the swoosh of my heartbeat in my ears, I rolled off the couch and crawled next to Floyd. He'd laid down, but hadn't moved his focus. Willing my inner racket to quiet, I strained to listen.

The scratching sound came again. Floyd jumped up and barked. Since my house had three stories, the backyard was at basement level. The only way that anyone could be near my living room window was to be in the oak tree right next to the house. Which meant that they could be peeking through the downward slant of my blinds, watching me.

My first instinct said run. The second said, hell no. No one came to my house and scared me like this. Commonsense also made a comeback. I could call the police, but what if it was an animal in the tree? I had to check it out first.

Creeping to the light switch, I smacked it off and

darted to the kitchen where I traded my spoon for a meat cleaver. I gathered my wits and marched to the offending window, lifting the blind an inch to see out. Rain splatters on the glass distorted the view. With lack of light in the backyard, I couldn't see anything else.

There was only one way to know if someone was back there. Leaving Floyd in charge in the living room, I tucked my cordless phone into my waistband and slunk down the basement stairs. My dad's gun was locked in his bedroom. Having it with me would require that I go into his room. Thumps or no thumps, I wasn't ready for that. I'd been licensed to carry since I was 21, but I'd never gone out armed as a process server and hadn't been to the range for over a year. For the moment, it was safer locked away.

Cleaver at my side, I peered out the small glass panel of the basement door that led into the yard. Nothing moved. Nightingale's murder had me on edge. A raccoon could have run through the tree. Or I'd misjudged the wind and a gust had hit the limbs.

I only needed to convince my racing heart, which meant going outside. The back door creaked as I pushed it open wide enough to squeeze through. From the cement slab, I turned on the flashlight app of my cell phone and scanned the beam from left to right.

Through the October rain, I directed the light onto the swing set—the one I used to play on and Mitz still used. It stood sentinel in the back corner, the lone swing moving back and forth. Leaves on the oak and maple trees rustled overhead. The wet cold grass permeated my tennis shoes with each small step I made further into the yard to inspect the surroundings. There were no odd sounds. Only the leaves and the protest of the rusting chains from the rocking swing.

Good thing I hadn't called in reinforcements. Dad would've never let a few branches on a window throw him into a panic. I turned back to the door when a man toppled out of the oak twenty feet away and hit the ground with a grunt.

My breath caught as I leapt into a defense pose, meat cleaver raised in front of me, adrenaline flowing. "What the hell are you doing out here?" I demanded.

The intruder wore a bulky black thermal jacket, ski mask, and blue tennis shoes. He scrambled to his feet and sprinted towards the gate on the other side of the yard.

"Stop," I yelled. He didn't slow. I took chase, my mind at full speed. Every nerve ending pinging like a pinball machine. Muddy patches slowed my progress. A gopher hole sucked the shoe off my right foot. The distance grew between us. I refused to stop. With the knife clenched in my hand, I must've looked like a character out of a cheap horror flick. I felt like one.

By the time I'd gimped to the gate, the guy had cleared my side yard and disappeared. My heart pounded so hard I thought it might come out of my chest. The thought crossed my mind to go house to house and check my neighbors' yards, but I wasn't equipped to hunt anyone down wearing a light jacket and only one shoe. And this time of night I could end up being the one chased with a meat cleaver or worse, shot.

To the right of my yard, Arlene's house was dark. If she'd heard anything, her house would be lit up like a Christmas tree. Part of me wanted to confirm. The rational part didn't want to scare her. Or to explain, since I didn't know why someone had been here in the first place.

Wet and freezing, my body trembled, as much from raw nerves as the cold. I secured the gate and rescued my poor shoe from the mud. Before going back in, I studied the oak tree the intruder had dropped from. A large lower branch was bent near the living room window. My back muscles tightened. Whoever it was had seen me look out, even though I hadn't seen him. Not anticipating I'd come out to investigate, he'd started to leave and got clumsy.

Back in the house, I dead-bolted the back door, left my filthy shoes and socks on the landing near the laundry room, and punched the thermostat up to seventy-five. On the couch, Floyd jumped up and leaned his body against mine. I hugged him close and dialed the police. There could be a string of burglaries in the neighborhood I wasn't aware of, or I'd been followed home. Having a report on file either way, was the smart thing to do.

With my face buried in Floyd's fur, I waited for the police to arrive. The cell phone rang. I jumped, startling Floyd. Jeff's name flashed on the screen. He could want to continue his lecture about Nightingale's photo. It could also be about Mitz's hand.

I answered. "Hey."

"Were you in bed?" Jeff asked.

"No. In another room."

"Everything okay?"

I couldn't tell Jeff what happened. The picture of Nightingale already had him freaked out. "Everything's fine. Mitz okay?"

"She's good. You sure? You sound tense."

He knew me too well. "Positive. What do you need?"

Jeff hesitated. "I was thinking about what I'd seen tonight."

I should have known. "Not now, please."

"I'm concerned. Not only for you, but for Mitz."

"I understand. Like I'd said, the police are on the Nightingale murder part, and I've made some progress on Brooke's case." If knowing she didn't live where her records said she lived was progress.

"That's good. However, I think Mitz should stay with me indefinitely. We can talk about it more after your case is done."

"I hoped you'd support me in my first real investigation that I'm doing at my father's request. And I'm doing this for our daughter—we both decided that my working would be necessary." Had what he told Mitz been a lie? Things you tell your kids so they don't feel like they're being slighted when mom is late?

He cleared his throat. "Yeah, I know."

My pulse raced again. "There are plenty of women cops who find dead bodies and investigate murders every day. I'm not some anomaly."

"True. But you're not a cop, and I didn't and wouldn't have married one."

I wanted to be indignant and continue the argument, but after the intruder, I couldn't. Mitz was safer at his house for the time being. "I'll admit it's been a weird weekend. But this case will be wrapped up by Friday."

"If the case is done by then, cool. If not, Mitz stays with me."

Jeff's need to control things wasn't new. His desire to have everything neat and tidy. No waves. Not even ripples. We had both lost one parent at a young age and dealt with those losses very different. I walled off the grief and kept plowing through regardless. He tried to control everything around him. I wasn't one of those things anymore. Our common ground of a childhood experience didn't equal our lives working well together. Divorced or not. "The case will be done by Friday, and you don't get to redo our Parenting Agreement."

"I don't want her coming in second to your expanding career."

"She's never been second to anyone. My choosing to keep my dad's business alive and doing as he asked hasn't changed that."

"Let me know when you're through."

"You got it, Jeff. I'll let you know." I white-knuckled the phone and forced the frustration down. "Let me say goodnight to Mitz."

Ten minutes later and confirmation her hand wasn't bothering her, I hung up, my thoughts returning to the night's events and whether I was cut out for this kind of work. Every nerve impulse had jetted through me like fireworks. I'd been terrified. Most people in their right minds would have run like hell. I grabbed a meat cleaver.

When necessary, I had my dad's fearlessness. For the first time I understood his thrill of investigating. Since the divorce and the death of my father, I had wondered what would inspire me and give my life a different purpose. Taking on new and different investigative cases could be the answer.

One purpose I wasn't going to give up, however,

was being a parent. I loved Mitz without question. I wanted her with me and back to the joint custody arrangement that had worked well up until this week. The quickest way to accomplish that was to solve this case. Which brought me to my visitor. It could have been a pervert checking me out, or a kid scoping the joint for a future break-in. It could also be someone wanting me to stop nosing around. Which one?

The doorbell rang. "It's the police," came from the other side of the door. I'd give them a report and find out.

SEVENTEEN

THE NEXT MORNING, I woke sprawled on the couch, drool running out of my mouth. I'd given the patrol officers my account while doubting they could do much with it. Other than describing the guy's clothes, I couldn't tell them the color of his hair or eyes. Nothing about the way he ran stood out, except he was fast. If I was going to embrace being an investigator, I might want to rethink the coffee and peanut butter and get my butt back to a gym, and to practice using firearms.

The police had looked around the place to make sure my house was secure and left around ten. Listening for weird sounds and thinking about the case and whether Georgette had found that glove, I'd tossed and turned in bed for a couple of hours. About midnight, the adrenaline faded and I'd traipsed into the living room, feeling safer with Floyd on the floor next to me, and passed out.

With my T-shirt sleeve, I swiped the slobber from my cheek and rolled off my makeshift bed onto all fours, coming nose to nose with my dog. He yawned before inspecting me. He always looked like he had a rough night with those sad-sack eyes and droopy jowls. I wrinkled my nose at his bad breath and kissed his snout. "Morning, boy."

My home phone rang. Mitz was already at school. Hopefully, it wasn't Jeff wanting to resume last night's conversation. I got upright enough to grab the cordless on the end table. The caller I.D. read *private*.

"Hello." I stifled a yawn.

When no one answered, I clicked off and flipped the phone onto the sofa. All that effort for a wrong number. I inched myself up to my feet. Sprinting through my yard had awakened long-forgotten muscles. A few stretches later, I went into the kitchen for coffee. In mid-pour, the phone rang again. I shoved the pot into the coffeemaker and made my way back to the phone.

"Hello."

At first, only silence, until the caller panted into the receiver.

After last night, I couldn't afford to be naïve and think it was a kid pranking me. The two calls could be meant to intimidate me. Like the guy in my backyard hadn't been enough.

I hung up, fear prickling at me at the notion that someone wanted to scare me. Getting my number wouldn't be that difficult, but who had I met so far that could outrun me or wanted me off the case? While Hannah didn't like her sister, she had told me about the penthouse when I came clean. The waitress, Amanda, had fed me the information about Nightingale in the first place. Georgette and Chester, no way. She'd hired me, number one, and neither could run that fast. The bartender, Derek, had changed his statement to the police, and had a thing for Brooke, except he'd only gone on a short break after Brooke left. Other than not liking questions in general, I didn't see why he'd bother me. There was the apartment manager, Luke, who I suspected had a thing for Brooke too. Other than creepy for having Floyd far away from my car, I didn't see how he fit in either.

I stared at the phone, expecting it to ring again and trying to come up with a pithy retort for when it did. The phone was stubbornly quiet.

Staring at it all day was an option, or I could give Floyd a much-needed break. I opted for the latter and took him out front, instead of the backyard. It was broad daylight and overcast. My eyes darted everywhere, scanning the street and the bushes. As soon as Floyd had done his business, I hurried him inside. We were on our way in when the phone rang.

Swooping up the receiver, I only waited a beat to respond. "What do you want?"

The panting started.

I thought of my dad, not recalling that he ever dealt with this kind of crap. I'd be damned if I would. "You've screwed with the wrong person."

"No, you have," a deep voice said and clicked off.

For a second, I hesitated, having not expected an answer, before I punched *57, the phone company's code for call trace. I wouldn't be privy to the results, but Kyle might be able to make an inquiry and see who the caller was.

With the phone back in its holder, I peered out the front windows looking down at the street and my yard where Floyd and I had been. Leaves rolled down the road. A jogger wearing earbuds ran by. Arlene's car sat in her driveway, her outside light off. Nothing out of the ordinary. Same in the backyard. Everything looked fine—but it wasn't fine. Who had I riled up?

I didn't have time to contemplate with Friday approaching sooner than later. My dad's words played in my head. *The fastest way to the other side was straight through the middle.* Brooke's penthouse was next up, and with it being Monday morning, her employer. Hopefully, both visits would gain me a much clearer picture of her life.

In the shower, the hot water pelted the knots out of my shoulders. Wearing my hair down, I dressed in black jeans, a smoky grey mock turtleneck, and black loafers. I wore my charcoal warmup jacket and zipped it to my chin. Since it shouldn't be a long day, and Floyd looked comfy in his cedar bed, I left him behind.

At my Spitfire, my breath hung in the air as I got in and turned the key. The engine whined and sputtered. A few foot pumps on the gas later, fumes filled the car. I squeezed my eyes closed and hung my head. I'd flooded the damn thing.

No surprise given the way the morning had begun. Odds of my car starting any day were 70/30. Most days I didn't care if it took an hour before it cooperated. This morning I didn't want to wait.

The thought of Arlene's car snuck into my head causing my jaw to clench. The last time I'd seen her, she'd looked in my purse and got Jeff in my business. I'd almost rather chew on glass than ask her. Unless I wanted to sit around and waste time, however, no other alternatives came to mind. The sooner I got the answers I needed, the sooner my life would go back to some semblance of normal. Whatever that meant.

I climbed the stairs that connected Arlene and my properties and rang the doorbell. She answered wearing a zippered blue housedress with white stripes. Her blonde hair was tucked behind her ears. Even without makeup, her skin was smooth and more flawless than mine. Her love of the sun clearly hadn't been as great as my obsession over the years.

"Sorry to bother you," I said.

"No bother. Coffee's brewed. Come in." Leaving the door ajar, she walked away.

In the foyer, an antique mahogany buffet lined the wall. A Victorian bowl and pitcher set, along with pictures of Mitz and Jeff's and my wedding picture, were placed on top. "I can't stay long." I followed Arlene into the kitchen I'd been coming to since childhood. Several years ago she'd done a full renovation with sleek stainless-steel appliances and granite countertops. The layout had remained the same, as had the small oak dinette set. Jeff, Arlene and I at one time had played Trump around that table. I'd fed my daughter some of her first meals there.

"How's Mitz?" she asked.

"Her hand will be tender for a few days, but she'll be fine."

"Good. What a scare. Too bad you weren't around to go to the hospital with them."

"I missed the call or I would've been."

Arlene nodded. She poured a cup of coffee with her back to me, taking her time.

"I'm actually here because I need a favor," I said. Since my asking her or Jeff for anything were rare, she knew asking was hard for me.

"Sure you don't want any coffee? You're always in a hurry," she said.

"Thank you. It's not always this crazy. I'll take half a cup...."

"How's the case going? Any *earth shattering revelations*?" She turned, handing me a full mug.

I had to face it—Arlene would never let up on judging my life, job and relationships. I put the coffee down and turned to go.

"Don't," Arlene said. "I mean…" She turned and opened the refrigerator, grabbing a half-gallon of milk from the door. "I'm sorry."

I stopped and focused as she poured milk into her coffee, not looking at me.

"Please stay," she said.

Why did it always have to be hard with Arlene? One minute she annoyed the hell out of me, the next she threw me off by being pleasant. "What I'd really like is to borrow your car. Mine won't start and I have to get downtown."

"Oh." She sipped from her steaming cup. "For how long? I have a dentist appointment this afternoon."

"I'd have it back by noon."

Arlene set her coffee down. "Guess that would be fine. Not a minute later." She shuffled to her bedroom and returned with the keys. She slipped one off and handed it to me. "While Jeff is here this morning, I'll have him look at your car."

"No thanks. It flooded. My fault."

She stared at me. It had been enough to ask to borrow her car.

"Suit yourself. Be careful and drive safe," she said.

With my mom dying in a car accident, there wasn't a moment I didn't drive safe. Could this be what it would have been like to have a mom when I started driving? Is this what mother daughter relationships were like? Arguing in one breath, helping each other the next. It was something to think about as Mitz was growing up.

"I will. By the way." I hesitated. I was ninety percent certain last night's visitor had been related to the Hanson case and it wouldn't cause her any problems. If it wasn't… "Some kids were messing around on my property last night. If they come back, or if you see anything around your house or mine, call the police. That'll scare them off."

She slid into a chair at her dinette table and unfolded the newspaper. "Sure," she said, not reacting like I thought she might—a bit worried.

"Okay. Well, thank you again."

When I reached the door, she called from the kitchen, "It's really okay to accept help from family, Kelly."

"I know," I stopped. "I mean…"

"I know what you mean." She appeared in the doorway. "Yes, you're borrowing my car. Yes, you accept my help with Mitz and Jeff's too, but you don't lean on us. Like those boxes still in your garage. Are you ever going to get to those? I could come over and help you."

I hadn't been able to face those boxes. Bringing them upstairs would mean admitting that everything about my life was different. That Dad was gone. "Thank you, Arlene, but I just haven't had time. And I can't lean on you anymore. I'm divorced." I hadn't expected to share that with her.

She rested her shoulder against the doorframe. "When Jeff's father and I were married, we were separated for a full year. Did I ever tell you that?"

"What? No." My hand slid off the knob.

"He had…an indiscretion."

I looked at her. "What?"

She had a sad smile. "When I talk to you about Jeff, don't think I don't understand."

It took me a moment to gain my composure. "That must have been horrible. I'm sorry, Arlene. I had no idea."

She waved me off. "Of course you didn't. I didn't talk about it. We never told Jeff. Jack and I played it off that he was on extended business trips."

"Why did you let him back in?" I asked.

"Because I loved him and I didn't know anything else. I'm not like you. I never had the opportunity to work and I couldn't afford to go on my own. But I did stay, and in the end, I was happier for it. That's why I've been disappointed that you didn't."

I hadn't realized why she wanted Jeff and I back together. Why she'd judged me for leaving. Now it made perfect sense. "You came from a different time, which I respect Arlene, but it's more than the affair for Jeff and me."

She waved me off again. "Oh yes, and the career path you seem to have chosen."

"Working for my father was important to me then, and continuing his legacy is now. If you two want me to *lean* on you, then stop being critical of that."

Her eyes narrowed. "You realize your father never intended for you to take over the business."

"That's absurd. He left it to me in his will. We were about to start training before he died. And he left me the letter to help my current client."

"He only left you the business to sell it. As for training, if he'd been serious, he would have started earlier."

"We wanted Mitz to be older."

"That doesn't sound like your father since he had

you by his side from early on. I don't know about the letter, but I'm certain he thought you'd have sold the business by now."

"I don't want to sell."

"You're not listening. He knew the burden of being a P.I. Why do you think he didn't give you any cases? Why do you think he drank? Why he never remarried? He didn't wish that kind of life on you."

"He told you this?" I folded my arms over my chest.

"Several times." Her eyes were on mine.

My dad's will didn't say anything about that. Nor had he ever indicated to me that he didn't want me to take over. "It doesn't change anything. I want the business. I love the business. Please try to understand that this is all I have left from my dad."

I'd only come to borrow her car. Not for revelations about Jeff's father's affair or my father's secret wishes. My dad had primed me for years to take over. Or had he? He'd kept most of the investigations to himself. He promised me more, but never delivered. Had we run out of time or was Arlene right? She couldn't be. Dad had left me the letter to help Georgette, whether I understood that connection or not. Unless it was a backup plan that was never meant to transpire. I didn't want to go there at this moment. I hadn't even adjusted to him being gone.

"I'll be back by noon." I walked out the door.

She didn't say goodbye.

HALFWAY BETWEEN THE KOIN Tower and the law firm, I pulled into a lot and parked Arlene's green Oldsmobile Cutlass next to a Smart Car before finding my way back to Second Street and Brooke's supposed second home.

The massive KOIN Tower lobby floor was covered in rose marble and the place echoed like a mausoleum. A stone-faced woman with bifocals scanned her row of monitors at the security desk before greeting me. "Can I help you?"

"Good morning." I gave her my sweetest smile. "Can you tell me if Brooke Hanson lived here?"

Her eyes went back to the monitors. "No."

"No, she didn't live here, or no you can't tell me?"

She pointed her nose down and peered over her glasses with an arched eyebrow. "Exactly."

The woman was security, not the welcoming committee, and my disruption of her duties clearly wasn't appreciated. "She recently died," I continued, handing the woman my business card. "I'm working for her family and it's important to confirm whether she lived here or not."

She pushed her glasses up onto the bridge of her nose and read my card. "While I'm sure it is, the privacy of our tenants is our top priority."

I dug in my purse and pulled out a twenty. "What would it take for you to answer the question?"

The woman studied the money and then me. "A search warrant."

Bribes must work better in the movies. Tucking the money back in my purse, I stared at her. "I understand you can't let me into Brooke's place without proper paperwork. Could you at least verify the information?"

She didn't look up.

"I'm willing to disturb the grieving mother to come down here with whatever you need, but no one likes to be yanked out of their home only to be told they're in the wrong place." Ms. Stone Face took guarding the palace quite seriously. I had a 50/50 chance she'd be sympathetic.

She studied my card again. "She lived in a penthouse suite. And you're right. You won't be getting in without the appropriate documents."

"Thank you. I'll be back."

Outside, I pulled out my cell and punched in Kyle's number. When his voicemail picked up, I asked him to call. Since a search warrant required hard evidence, I doubted he could do much. My next call was to Georgette. As the executor of Brooke's estate, she'd have the power to get us into that apartment. And after our phone conversation, I wanted to hear the status of the missing glove.

The beep sent me directly to voicemail for her too. Did anyone ever pick up their phone? "Please come to the KOIN in downtown right away and bring anything giving you authority over Brooke's estate. Call when you're on your way."

A wave of apprehension washed over me. Georgette should be up. Had the police come back for her already? I could only wait to hear from her, or Kyle who might know the status as well.

Until then, I focused on my next stop to see what kind of law firm paid their accounting staff enough to afford a penthouse suite.

EIGHTEEN

ANDERSON, HIEFIELD & PRICE'S area of expertise was international and business law. I stepped onto the fifth floor and into the carpeted lobby of the law firm and saw immediately their practice was lucrative. Maple walls with redwood accent panels. Fresh orchid bouquets in modern vases on pedestals in etched nooks. Two receptionists sat at a long low counter. The blonde, whose name plaque read Wendy Johnson, smiled at me first.

With my card extended, I approached. "Hi Wendy. I need to speak with someone in your accounting department."

She scanned my card. "There are several. What's it regarding?"

"Brooke Hanson." Wendy's smile faded. From the corner of my eye I watched the other receptionist turn and stare at her.

"I'll have to call and see if anyone's available," Wendy said.

She punched an extension and I surveyed the reception area and the office beyond it. At nearly ten o'clock, people had settled in at their neat little cubicles. A few employees dressed in suits passed by, coffee cups in hand, nodding politely at me.

"Hi Rachel, it's Wendy. There's a Kelly Pruett here inquiring about Brooke Hanson. Can you meet with her?" Wendy paused. "One moment." She covered the mouthpiece with her hand. "What exactly do you need to know?"

"Can I talk to Rachel? It'll be easier."

Wendy's mouth opened and closed before she handed me the phone and I introduced myself. "I have a few questions about what Brooke did here. The family hired me to look into the circumstances around her death. It shouldn't take much of your time."

Rachel paused. "I'll be right down."

"Thanks," I said to Wendy, handing her the phone. "She's on her way."

Wendy directed me to the waiting area with low slung leather chairs and a coffee table covered with several international newspapers, along with current issues of Forbes and Time. Their firm's diverse and wealthy clientele probably ate that stuff up. I was more a People girl.

I'd just sat down when the elevator opened and a woman emerged. In her late thirties, she dressed in a pencil skirt and body-hugging suit coat. She was athletic, taller than me by a few inches, and wore thick framed glasses, her light-brown wavy hair pulled away from her sparsely done face into a stern bun. I wouldn't call her ugly by any stretch, but she was shy of pretty.

She looked familiar. Someone I might have seen around the courthouse. Which made sense with her working for a law firm. Her stride and demeanor reminded me of a cop. When she reached me, she introduced herself as Rachel Mosley and I handed her my card which she inspected.

"Nice to meet you. Let's go into the conference room for some privacy."

We walked into the space off reception. A cherry wood credenza lined the half-wall under the picture window, and a matching round table for six was centered. I took a chair to the left of the door. She chose one opposite me.

"Please send our condolences to the family," she said when we were settled.

"Absolutely." I reached into my purse and pulled out my notebook.

She sat with her shoulders back. "How can I help?"

I placed my forearms on the table. "We can start with what she did for the firm."

"As an accounting clerk, Brooke handled mostly billing, and some receivables."

Having the inability to balance my own checkbook, any accounting skills were impressive. I checked my scribbles to confirm what Georgette had told me. "I have down that she was the firm's chief accountant."

"Not hardly. She was the head of Billing."

Georgette could have been confused on the actual title. "Is that a large department?"

Rachel shook her head. "It's a department of one."

Or not. Why would Brooke tell her mother something different? Then again, why wouldn't she. Being honest with her parents didn't appear to have been Brooke's highest priority. "Is there a head accountant?"

"Not per se. We have an accounts payable position. An outside company handles our quarterlies, year-end, and tax prep."

I tapped my pen on the notepad. "How much did a position like that pay?" While I hadn't been to the penthouse, it didn't seem probable she could afford it on a clerk's salary.

A sardonic look crossed Rachel's mouth. "I can't disclose that. The laws are strict about what I can say, really."

Determining the source of Brooke's cash would help me understand her more fully. I tried another route. "Who did she report to?"

"The firm's CFO and managing partner, Dave Anderson, is everyone's boss." Rachel skimmed her cheek with the palm of her hand.

She might have an itch, but her fidgeting told me she didn't like talking about Brooke. Or was it her boss that made her uneasy? "What exactly is your role here?" I asked.

"Human Resources."

"Did Brooke report to you as well?"

"Yes and no. I oversee. Mostly I handle benefits."

"What's your monthly salary?"

She cleared her throat and picked at the edge of a bandage on her hand. "I'm not going to discuss that with you. How's that relevant?"

For a split second, I thought she might spit at me I'd offended her that much. "I wanted to gauge her income."

"For what purpose?"

I leaned back in my chair, ignoring the question. "Do you know where Brooke lived?"

"Southwest, I believe. It's in her file, I'm sure."

I would have thought she'd at least update her employee file. Unless it was a temporary move. "Did she have a boyfriend?"

"No idea."

"She ever talk about anyone, or go to lunch with someone in particular?"

Rachel shifted. "No, and not that I saw."

I always figured office girls talked to each other more. Unless... "How'd you get along with her?"

She frowned. "We worked fine together."

"I'm sorry. I know it must be hard to have a co-worker you saw every day die so brutally, and so young."

She nodded, a flicker of pain in her deep-set eyes.

"Did Brooke get along with the other employees?"

Her gaze rested on the door before returning to me. "She was always a hit with the men."

There were no signs of jealousy as she said that. "Not with the women?" She shrugged.

"Does the name Jay Nightingale sound familiar?"

"No." She shifted in her chair. "Brooke and I weren't that close, as you can tell from my not having answers to your questions. And I didn't have the impression she had many friends. Work took up a lot of her time."

Georgette had said the same thing. There might be one way to confirm that. "When you cleaned out her desk, were there any personal items?"

"Not much to speak of."

"Her cell phone perhaps?"

Rachel shook her head slowly and glanced at her watch. "Are we done?"

My hope of ever finding that phone was fading. "Almost. A couple more questions."

Rachel brushed at the imaginary bangs again.

Her body language said she had somewhere else to be, so I hurried. "Did she ever seem depressed?"

"Never."

"How about stressed? Were things here at work bothering her?"

Rachel's mouth set in a hard line. "You wanted to know her duties, which I've answered, and then some."

I leaned in. "You have, thank you, but anything you can tell me might help the family understand what happened the night she died."

Rachel fidgeted with her hands. "What do they think happened?"

"That she was murdered."

Rachel tensed. "You can't possibly believe anyone here had anything to do with her dying?"

"Of course not," I said. "I'm trying to piece together that night. The family said she'd been different and distant in the past year. Had you seen that as well?"

She scrunched her mouth. I'd seen the look when serving papers. I'd ask for positive identification, and my about-to-be-served would decide whether to tell me the truth or not. She had the look of weighing options. She opened her mouth. The conference room door flew open and banged against the wall.

I flinched, still on edge from last night's intruder, and turned to see a short, stocky man with slicked black hair filling the doorway. Easily in his mid-forties, he was dressed in a dark suit and red power tie.

He scowled, a vein pulsing at his temple. "Rachel. Introduce me to our guest." The smell of mint on his breath mixed with the spiciness of his cologne.

She shot out of her seat, almost knocking it over. "Mr. Anderson. This is Kelly Pruett."

Wendy had briefed him because I sensed he already knew my name. Despite his stature, he had presence. I stood slowly and extended my hand. Rachel had injected plenty of drama into the room without me amping it up. "I'm a private investigator."

His eyes narrowed and he left me hanging. "Brooke's accident has been a terrible loss."

"The family's devastated as well, except they don't buy the accident part."

He sniffed, reminding me of a bull about to charge. If he started pawing the ground with his foot, I was out of there. "What are you looking for here?" he said.

"Gathering background information. That's all." I tried to sound harmless.

He turned to Rachel. "Did you tell Ms. Pruett what Brooke did for the firm?"

"Yes, Mr. Anderson," she said, a balance of fear and resentment in her tone.

He smiled, as only a lawyer practiced at making a good show could. "Then I'd be happy to escort you out."

Why the rush? "I was also inquiring whether Brooke had appeared stressed prior to her death."

Anderson squared his shoulders and rested his fist into the palm of his hand. "Brooke was a fine employee and person. Everyone loved her. But we have a policy that our employees' information is private. This conversation is over."

As he talked, his hand moved, flashing a pinky ring on his left hand. My eyes locked onto it. I broke my gaze to scan his face. "Even if the employee is deceased?"

He met my eye. "All of our employees, past and present. We can't help you any further."

Amanda had mentioned that Brooke spent time with a man at the Limbo who had a pinky ring.

Rachel stared at the floor. "I'm sorry Ms. Pruett. Mr. Anderson's right. Our policy prohibits us from disclosing anything further except by court order or if you're with a legal authority. You understand, I hope. As a law firm, we have to protect ourselves."

Maybe, but she had been about to tell me something before Dave Anderson had busted in. He stood to the side of the door, twisting his pinky ring. Goosebumps stung my skin. He rotated it over and over. Amanda had said the man with Brooke might take his finger off by the way he worked his ring so much. How many people in the city had the same gesture? Or that ring? And Dave Anderson matched Amanda's description, right down to the slimy part.

I stuffed my notebook in my purse. I was shaken, but that wouldn't stop me from asking what needed to be asked. "You been back to the Limbo lately?"

Anderson's eye twitched. "You need to go." He stopped twisting his ring and waved me out like a construction flagger.

I didn't move. "What were you doing with Brooke at the bar? I have witnesses that say you joined her often. You two have a thing going?"

He snorted. "Because drunk witnesses are so reliable."

He didn't say no. "Did you know Jay Nightingale?"

"Out." He appeared stoic, but his face reddened.

Rachel's eyes were wide. I reached out my hand to her and she shook it, limply. "Thank you for your help."

She didn't answer.

Sweeping past Mr. Anderson, I ambled through the

reception area mouthing *thanks* to Wendy who inspected her manicure.

On the elevator down, my mind ticked off questions. Why was Dave Anderson spending time at the Limbo with Brooke? Were they only catching a beer after hours? Or was there more to it? Amanda had said the man had appeared to have a thing for Brooke, but she didn't return the infatuation. If it was an affair, it didn't sound very amorous. Unless they were hiding it in plain sight. Which would only be important if Dave Anderson was married. That might explain why he didn't want to admit being at the bar to me, especially with Rachel in the room.

What I didn't know was how Nightingale fit into any of this. Any more than how Brooke could afford that penthouse. Or why she had a low-rent apartment on the other side of town.

As soon as the doors opened, two uniformed security guards met me. Talk about overkill. "I can find my way out," I said.

"Here to make sure you do," a guard replied. They fell in behind me to the revolving door. Outside, I stared at them staring at me. There'd be no getting back inside today.

Finding a park bench across the street, I shook the tension out of my body before checking my phone. Nothing from Georgette or Kyle. Arlene needed her car back by noon. I had time and didn't want to leave Portland without getting into the penthouse where Brooke had lived. The place might offer a clue of how she could afford to live there, since the law firm hadn't given me much.

As for Dave Anderson hanging with Brooke at the

Limbo, Rachel might have some insight, or at least have been privy to office gossip she could share. While Amanda had said Pinky Ring-slash-Anderson wasn't at the bar the night Brooke died, she'd also said Brooke had appeared to be texting and waiting for someone. That person could have been Anderson. I had to find a way back into those law offices to push Rachel for answers.

My phone chirped. Georgette would meet me at the KOIN Tower in fifteen minutes. There were so many questions and so few answers. Would the real Brooke Hanson please stand up?

NINETEEN

WHILE I PACED the sidewalk in front of the KOIN Tower waiting for Georgette, Kyle texted asking what was up. He was in the middle of a briefing and taking a break.

I sent a quick note recapping where I was and why. Since Georgette was on her way, I didn't tell him I'd initially reached out, hoping he had a suggestion to get past security.

"Can I catch you later?" I asked.

"I'd like that," he replied.

So would I.

As I tucked my phone in my purse, Georgette and Chester walked up the street. Chester's serious expression and Georgette's tired eyes had me worried.

"How're you holding up? Any luck on that glove?" I asked, afraid to hear the answer.

She fanned out her fingers to show me both on her hands. "Indeed. Thanks to my sweet husband."

Chester nodded with a self-satisfied grin that softened his whole face and made his eyes dance.

Relief flooded through me. "Thank God. Where'd you find it?"

"It had dropped between my car seats. That's why I didn't answer earlier. We were touching base with the detective to let him know." Georgette waved the legal documents. "You going to tell us what this is for?"

I led them into the building. "We need to get into Brooke's apartment."

"She didn't live here," Georgette said.

"Yes, she did."

"I don't understand."

"Me either, not yet." We approached Ms. Stone Face. "Look what I've got," I said, handing her the papers.

She didn't smile, and barely glanced my way as she read the will naming Georgette as the executor. The woman would be a real hoot at a party. She picked up the phone and called the building super, Ms. Matson, who arrived a few minutes later.

After explaining the situation, the four of us rode the elevator to the top floor in silence. Ms. Matson unlocked the double door to a penthouse suite, one of four on this level. Much of the home was visible from the entry where limestone led to plush carpet, which led to bamboo floors. The wall of windows extended floor to ceiling and framed a snow-covered Mt. Hood shrouded in clouds. The pink leather couches in the living room were adorned with silk pillows and chenille throws and surrounded a big screen television. The place had a wet bar, a massive filled bookshelf, and an atrium with an empty hot tub.

Georgette and Chester's wide-eyed expressions mirrored my own. We all were in awe of our surroundings and said nothing at first.

"How much is this place?" I finally asked Ms. Matson.

"Ten thousand a month," she said, standing back at the door.

Too much for an accounting clerk. "Who signed the lease and pays the rent?"

"Ms. Hanson, of course."

"From her own checking account?" I asked.

The landlord looked at me like I was from outer space. "Yes."

Brooke's monthly income would have had to be verified to qualify. "Any chance I could see the application and lease documents?"

She walked to the row of light switches and flicked them on. "I can scan and email the file to you later today if that works."

I nodded and gave her my card. "Did Brooke live alone?"

"As far as I know."

"Any boyfriends visit?"

She made her way back toward the door. "Not that I know of. I don't see the tenants though unless they come to my office. She moved in about a year and a half ago and always kept to herself, never complained about anything, and paid her rent on time. She was a landlord's dream."

Ms. Matson was a very hands-off building manager and didn't have much else to offer. She didn't hover long after that and asked us to lock up when we left.

The thirty-five-hundred square foot suite was immaculate, but like Brooke's other apartment, there were no personal pictures or mementos leaving the space cold and void of life, despite the money poured into it.

Georgette broke the silence. "My Brooke lived here?"

"You had no idea at all?" I asked.

Georgette didn't answer. It was a lot to process.

We walked through the rooms together. The kitchen cupboards had plenty of cookware. However, based on my own pantry that lacked certain food staples and spices, it didn't appear Brooke cooked much. The guest bathroom was beige and basic.

"There's nothing here that proves this is Brooke's house," Georgette said. "I haven't seen anything I recognize."

"Nothing?" I would've expected a piece of furniture, a kitchen appliance, or even a bath towel to stand out for her.

"No."

They followed me to a large bedroom filled with workout equipment similar to Nightingale's place. Anyone could have a workout room. I noted it anyway.

When we found Brooke's bedroom, I entered first. I flipped on the light and knew immediately why Brooke hadn't told her parents about this place. Deep red paint covered the walls and heavy velour curtains hung over the windows. Two leather whips were crisscrossed and mounted above the king size bed. Fur-lined handcuffs, a blindfold, and a silk gag lay on the nightstand, along with a basket of candles. A black dog crate, large enough to house a human, but not large enough for that human to stand, sat in the corner with a black-mat inside. Restraints were bolted into the bed and on the wall.

I moved to block the doorway so Georgette couldn't go in a second too late. She came through, Chester right behind her.

Her face turned the color of the walls. She swayed and Chester gripped her arm.

"Let's go," he demanded.

"No." She held steadfast and batted his hand away.

With a huff he turned back to the living room. I had pegged Georgette as passive and frail. When she was determined about something, even Chester didn't question her. It was like she'd prepared herself to find out something shocking about her daughter before she'd come here.

"You okay?" I reached out to steady Georgette.

"I'm fine." She straightened and strode to the nightstand, her gaze locked onto the items on top. She reached to open the drawer, then pulled away. If I were her, I wouldn't want to know, either.

Georgette turned to the large walk-in closet and disappeared inside.

I inspected the paraphernalia on the walls. The whips were like the ones I'd seen at Nightingale's. They both had fancier homes than one would expect and dabbled, if were not completely immersed, in the same unconventional lifestyle. I opened the nightstand and found oils, gags, and clips.

After seeing Nightingale's place and now this, I didn't believe that he and Brooke's first meeting was on the night she stumbled down the street. He knew her, like Amanda had said. That didn't mean he'd pushed her. He may have not wanted to admit their connection because it would have invited more questions from the police. Would that have led them to a different conclusion?

I gave Georgette a few minutes before I joined her in the closet. She stood in the middle, her head buried in a blue angora sweater.

"Brooke's?" I asked.

"I gave it to her for Christmas last year," she whispered.

Her raw emotion caught in my throat. "I'm sorry."

She inhaled through her nose and hung up the sweater. "I didn't want... I had no idea about any of this."

Brooke had wanted it that way. "Let's get out of here."

Georgette followed me until we found Chester. She dropped onto one of the pink couches next to her husband, who had one leg flopped over the other and bounced his foot like a ball on a paddle. She placed her hand on his leg. "I'm so confused," she said.

"Well," I began, my attention drawn to the coffee table where books on Japanese Gardens and Asian architecture like the ones in Nightingale's house were fanned out. My heartbeat quickened.

"Kelly?" Georgette said. "What's going on here?"

"I have a couple of theories." Neither of which I wanted to unload on Brooke's parents all at once. "Here's what I'm certain of. Brooke's job as an accounting clerk at the firm wouldn't have been enough income alone to live here."

"Chief accountant," Chester corrected.

I shook my head. "Clerk."

They both frowned at the realization they'd been told another lie.

Georgette's eyes welled. "Who was my daughter?"

Good question. "A woman who lived two very different lives. The one she told you about, which is why I suspect she kept the Meadow Verde place, and this one." I stopped short of calling her a dominatrix, but that's what the room implied. Even though Nightingale didn't have as much in the ways of tools of the trade, he might have been a dominator. There could be varying degrees in this arena. I scanned the books on the table again. If they were servicing clients, those clients must have something in common.

"What's all that stuff in there used for?" Georgette's voice cracked.

Chester rested his hand on Georgette's back. His eyes said he knew. He didn't answer her question.

"They call it BDSM," I said.

Chester searched my face. "Please."

He didn't want me to go on, but side-stepping wasn't going to make it go away. "Essentially, it's sex play, with a twist."

"Anyone who'd want that is a sick bastard," Chester said.

Georgette squeezed her eyes closed. "My Brooke was such a loving and gentle girl. All that in there looks violent."

"It can be, I think." I'd need to do more research. Or Kyle might know more about it. "However, it is consensual."

"I can't believe that of Brooke," Georgette said. "Next thing you'll tell me is she was a prostitute and Nightingale an unhappy client."

"I'm not convinced Nightingale was a client, but based on both of their bedrooms, they had to be into the same things and perhaps even working together in some capacity. If she was getting paid for that, it would explain being able to afford this beautiful home."

I thought of Dave Anderson and Brooke spending time together at the Limbo. Did he know Brooke was into this lifestyle?

"Do you think whoever killed Brooke killed Nightingale?" Georgette asked.

There was no question that Nightingale had been murdered. Was the fact that Brooke had been telling lies proof she'd been pushed that night? "Something took her down to those tracks. Nightingale being there was no coincidence. Whether they were meeting, arguing, meeting someone else…don't know. Because she was drunk, she may really have stumbled." My mind went to my intruder and the phone calls—clear signals for me to back off. "But something else could have gone down that night. Something Nightingale witnessed or at least knew about and was going to tell me before he died." I just needed to figure out what that *something* was.

Georgette frowned. It wasn't the answer she'd hoped for. "I can't believe this is real," she said. "She'd never tell me what the firm paid her, but Brooke saved. Even as a little girl, every cent went into a gallon jug." A smile touched Georgette's lips at the memory. "She was always good with money."

She was grasping at anything that would extinguish the possibility of her daughter getting paid for sex. No matter how good a saver Brooke was, paying off the Hanson's newer home and living here wouldn't have been doable on her law firm wages. "I'm going to look around again before we go."

"I'll sit with Chester." Georgette melted into the leather sofa.

I couldn't blame them for not wanting to see more. My gaze rested on the spectacular view of the Willamette River and Waterfront Park. In the summer, the park and river would be filled with people boating, sunbathing, and listening to concerts. Now only a few pigeons perched outside on the ledge, the gray view as barren of life as Brooke's condo.

I walked back to her bedroom to make sure I hadn't missed anything. Inside a smaller closet, I found Brooke's leathers, and more tools of the trade. Gags, lubricants, clothes pins, paddles, and spiked collars.

The more selection I found, the clearer it became that this was not all for personal pleasure. There must be clients. Were they connected to Nightingale's? The similar books suggested they were. But how did they find them? There could be a website where people mingled. Portland could also have a BDSM scene where connections were made by word of mouth.

My hand was on Brooke's dresser drawer when the front door opened. Ms. Matson must have come back to check on us or to bring the documents I'd asked for.

"You two found the place, I see." I'd heard that voice before. It wasn't Ms. Matson.

Georgette said, "What are you doing here?"

"Where the hell have you been?" Chester added.

I walked back into the living room and crossed to the sofa where Georgette and Chester sat. Hannah was dressed in jeans and a burgundy sweater, her dark hair resting on her shoulders, and far more put together than the last time I saw her curled on the futon.

"Hey." Hannah grinned at me.

"What *are* you doing here?" Having spent time with Hannah, I didn't suspect she'd shown up because she cared about seeing her parents.

"Didn't want to miss the show."

My jaw bunched. Had I been used to get her parents down here? "I think it's time we all talked. Don't you agree, Hannah?"

"Yes, Hannah, please," Georgette said. "We need to talk."

"Sit down for God's sake," Chester boomed.

Hannah glared at them. "I'll give you five minutes." She flopped into the big chair directly opposite us.

TWENTY

HANNAH SAT WITH her arms over her chest, one leg flung over the other, bouncing the same way her father had, earlier. Tension hung in the room like the haze of cigarette smoke at the Limbo.

Georgette's face scrunched. "Where have you been? We're family. We need to stick together."

"Please, don't start. I've been here and there," Hannah said.

Chester glared at his daughter. "Your mother's been worried about you. How dare you do that to her?"

Hannah wouldn't meet her father's eyes. "Whatever."

I was witnessing the dynamic I'd sensed earlier when I'd met Hannah. Hoping to redirect the conversation, I said, "Hannah, as you know, your mother thinks your sister was murdered."

She rolled her eyes. "Don't know anything about that. But I've been around, Mom. I've been at Brooke's pad at Meadow Verde. Big sis lived here, and I got her discards. A pretty accurate reflection of my whole life, don't you think?" She clamped her hand over her leg to stop the bouncing action.

Georgette's mouth gaped open. "You always knew about this place?"

Hannah inspected the cuticles of her right hand.

"Were you ever going to tell us?" Georgette asked.

Hannah looked at me with a raised eyebrow. She had told them, with me as a conduit.

My shoulder muscles knotted at the confirmation of being used. "Why two apartments?"

"Have you seen the bedroom?" She sounded almost hopeful.

I nodded. "If you've never been here before, how do you know what's in there?"

"Oh, she loved to brag."

"Thought you two didn't talk?"

"I didn't define *her* bragging as *us* talking."

We were into semantics. Nice. "What was she into exactly?"

"She was a dominatrix. Isn't it obvious?"

It had been to me, but Georgette's face turned crimson again.

"That's right, Mom, Brooke was no angel, despite what you believed."

The contempt Hannah leveled would have toppled a mountain, but I sensed there was something deeper going on besides jealousy even if I couldn't put my finger on what.

"She was a prostitute?" Georgette whispered.

"What do you think? Look at this place." Hannah lifted her palms in the air for emphasis.

Georgette crumpled further into the couch. "Why would she do that?"

"Maybe she liked the attention," she said. "Everyone needs that sometimes."

I detected more hurt in her tone this time.

"Don't spout this crap to your mother and me about your sister," Chester snapped.

"You girls couldn't get along for two seconds. Ever." Georgette's voice strained.

"Wonder why."

"Stop." Chester's voice raised a notch.

"I never believed she was perfect." Georgette grabbed his hand.

Hannah sagged into the chair. "You sure treated her as if she was. I'm your flesh and blood, and you treated me like I'm the genetic reject."

"That's not true." Georgette shook her head. Chester wrapped a shielding arm around her.

Sitting ring-side could give some a headache. I found myself hanging on every word. At this rate, however, they'd keep going in circles. Hannah knew far more than she'd shared with me earlier. If I could get her alone for an hour in a well-stocked bar, I could only imagine what I'd learn. But she was flighty, and I didn't know how long I'd have her attention. "Chester, why don't you take Georgette out for some fresh air."

He hesitated; his brow wrinkled.

Hoping to play on his protectiveness of his wife, I gave him a pleading look that she didn't need to hear any more.

He finally nodded. "Good idea." He shot another glare at Hannah, who shifted in her seat.

Georgette stood. Her legs wobbled. The color had drained from her face leaving her skin blotchy and pale. Chester maintained his grip on her as they went out onto the balcony. He slid the glass door closed behind them.

"What?" Hannah said, tearing her gaze away from the balcony door and refocusing on her cuticles.

"Who were Brooke's clients?"

"Rich bastards, can't you tell?"

"Why are you so angry with her?" I asked. "Minus the sarcasm please.

She stared at me. "You don't have a sister?"

"No." And never happier about that fact.

She tilted her head like she was thinking. "Right... Then you wouldn't understand."

I didn't bite. "Since she loved to brag, did she tell you who those *rich bastards* were?"

"Not specifically."

"Do you know anything about her work at the law firm?"

"She did some stuff for them and had me help sometimes, you know, more breadcrumbs. That's all I can tell you."

"She had you helping with accounting?"

She pushed a strand of hair out of her face. "No. Entertaining."

"Like what's in Brooke's bedroom?" I didn't hide the shock in my voice.

"Hell no," she said. "That kinky shit isn't for me. Just going out."

"Out?"

She looked at me like I was dense. "She once set me up on a supposed blind date with a firm client who was in town for the week and wanted some company in the evening. I was down, until she said I could make double my pay and sleep with him. I told her she'd lost her mind."

"Aren't you a stripper?"

She frowned. "I'm a cocktail waitress. Give me a break."

"You told me you did other things there."

"Yeah, like night deposits and backup payroll. For the record, being a stripper doesn't make you a slut."

She was getting me off track. "Sorry." I shouldn't have assumed. "Back to Brooke—she lined you up with law firm clients?"

"A few."

"Is it possible the men who wanted more than dinner were her clients then?"

She gnawed on her thumbnail. "Would make sense because I certainly wasn't going to do them."

Being a partner in the firm, Dave Anderson had to be in the know of what was going on. Unless he was oblivious, he'd be privy to what was happening in his own firm, even after hours. He didn't come across as the non-observant type. That could be why he hung out with Brooke at the bar. "Were you telling the truth about Brooke never mentioning Jay Nightingale, the guy's picture I showed you?"

She grimaced, perhaps recalling the image. "Yes."

How was it that he was at those tracks that night? "Is it possible Brooke upset one of her clients?"

"No clue."

"You think there's a chance her death had something to do with this secret life she was living?"

"No idea. But secrets have a way of catching up."

That sounded interesting. I held her stare. "What makes you say that?"

"Experience. That's all. What goes around, comes around." She checked her watch. "I have a lunch date."

Glancing at my watch, my heart jumped. Eleven thirty. Arlene would have my head if I didn't get her car back by noon, but I couldn't stop now. "What came around for Brooke?"

Chester slid open the glass door. Hannah looked at me. "Why don't you ask the married man she had an affair with?"

I straightened. "Who was that?"

"A guy she worked with. She liked to brag about him. Said she had him wrapped."

"Was his name Dave Anderson?"

"Never said. But she enjoyed having control over all of the men around her."

"You mean the clients? The married man? Were there others?"

Hannah smiled. "There were plenty. Besides the married guy, she also talked about one she tried to be normal with, and another she tormented like nobody's business."

"Brooke had to give you names at some point." I pressed again, already concluding Dave Anderson had to be the married guy from work.

Georgette stepped inside and had overheard our conversation. "Brooke would never date a married man." She said it without conviction. Her belief that Brooke had been a good girl had dissolved like sugar in water.

"Unbelievable," Chester said.

"Brooke did a lot of things, Mom." Hannah threw her hair back again.

Hannah was slipping away and I had to get her back on topic. "I'm confused. Were these other men, like the married man, clients or lovers?"

"In her world, they might be all the same. Married Guy could be a creep, though. One night I'd called and Brooke answered, drunk. She told me she wanted to dump him but wouldn't."

"Or couldn't?" I asked.

"Probably both."

"When was the last time you saw her?" I asked.

Hannah didn't answer.

"Hannah," Georgette said. "When did you see Brooke last?"

"The night she died," she blurted.

That put a new twist on things. "Where? At the tracks?"

"Oh please. I'd met up with friends in Portland and I was late for work. I was headed down from Sixteenth when I saw Brooke leaving some bar. When she spotted me, she yelled for me to stop."

"Did you?" I asked.

"No. My shift was about to start, and I was over a block away from her. She started toward me, then stopped to talk to someone."

"Did she stop or was she standing and talking to someone when you saw her?" Derek had said he'd escorted Brooke out, so the latter would make sense.

"No. She was definitely walking my direction until someone reached out."

The skin on my arms tingled. Someone had been outside the bar. Were they waiting for Brooke to come out? "Can you describe who it was?"

Hannah nibbled on her thumbnail again. "No."

"Are you sure? Could it have been Dave, I mean Married Guy?" I punched up the law firm on my telephone and went to the About Us page.

"I'd never met him and I was too far to tell much."

I handed her my phone.

"This better not be another creepy picture."

"Just look." The MAX tracks were north of the

Limbo. If Brooke had been running to catch up with Hannah, that would explain why she'd been headed that direction. Georgette looked my way and nodded. She caught that fact as well.

Hannah shook her head and set down my phone. "I can tell you she did break away from whoever it was and kept coming even though I kept going."

"Why didn't you wait?" Georgette asked. "She was your sister."

"In name only, Mother. We were fighting and I didn't want to get fired for being late."

"Did the man follow?" I asked.

"Didn't pay attention. I was out of there."

A heavy silence hung in the air. My next question wouldn't lighten the mood either. Hannah had admitted to being in Portland the night Brooke died. "Where is Casa Diablo?"

"Over on Eighth and Stark. Why?"

"You'd have to go past Ninth and cross Morrison to get there."

"So…"

"Are you certain you didn't see her at the tracks that night?"

"Why would I see her? I ran ahead."

"You have someone who can attest to that for you?"

She met my gaze. "Whoa."

Chester and Georgette shut their eyes, perhaps bracing to hear an answer they couldn't bear.

"There wasn't much love lost between you," I said. "Did your fight get physical? Did you wait for her there—to confront her?"

"Hannah, you didn't?" Georgette said.

"Mom," Hannah said. "This is crap. You know me better." She folded her arms over her chest.

"You seem vested in destroying her image with your parents. Otherwise, why not tell me this when I saw you yesterday?"

"Because you might not have believed me if you didn't see it for yourselves," she said. "But I certainly wouldn't have admitted to being in Portland and seeing her if I'd killed her. Give me a break."

"Except the case was deemed accidental," I said. "You could have banked on it never coming out."

She didn't hear me. "You guys are crazy." Her voice squeaked. "I already told you I didn't even talk to her that night. I saw her, and she got distracted by someone. I never saw her again." Her chest turned red and the color crept up her neck. A sign of distress, and a trait I shared. "Okay I'm a horrible person because I didn't wait." She continued. "Not much I can do about it now."

Every time I'd seen Hannah, some new detail came out about what she knew of Brooke's life. Now to find out she'd been downtown at the same time, going the same direction as her sister? I wasn't sure I bought her story. "How about Nightingale? Are you telling me the truth you don't know him? How does he fit in? Did you see him on your way to work that night?"

"Your five minutes are up." She stood.

I stood with her. "If it wasn't you, Hannah, then tell me what you saw."

Hannah strode to the front door.

"Hannah, don't go," Georgette shouted after her.

She walked out, slamming the door behind her.

The three of us were silent; my heart pounded. I

turned to Georgette. "What did she mean Brooke was her sister in name only?"

Georgette stared at her hands. "Brooke was adopted."

I rubbed my eyes, trying to dispel the headache that had come on. "Why is Hannah so angry?"

"Jealousy, I suppose. Hannah's always had a problem with Brooke, who was ten years older. When we couldn't get pregnant, we adopted. We only planned to have the one child. Then I got pregnant with Hannah."

Shouldn't they have been thrilled to conceive? "Why would you treat Hannah differently?"

"She's not mine," Chester said, his body rigid. He yanked his arm from around Georgette, stood, and marched out the front door.

Some of the puzzle pieces dropped into place with a thud. I'd seen no resemblance of Brooke to her parents, right from the start. As I'd stared at Hannah, I hadn't seen Chester in her at all. "Chester treated Hannah different than Brooke. Why did you?"

A tear rolled down her face. "I didn't. I love Hannah. When she found out early on that Chester wasn't her father, she used every slight and opportunity to say she was treated different because of that fact. She would get vindictive and I started to withdraw. I never meant to hurt Hannah or Chester, but I did." She lifted her gaze at me. "The affair with Hannah's father didn't go on long. At least Chester forgave me, for the most part." She searched my face, like she was looking for something. Understanding? Forgiveness?

"Does she know who her father is?"

"She knows." Georgette jumped up from the couch. "We should go. Chester's waiting for me."

Her abruptness threw me off. Obviously, this was a touchy subject. "Of course," I said. "But do you think Hannah could have hurt Brooke?"

"I don't want to think so."

For some reason, I didn't either. If only wanting something, and the truth, were the same. I thought of the Nightingale connection. If Hannah had killed her sister, wouldn't he have told the police that? Why protect her? Especially if Hannah was telling the truth that she didn't know him. "Any other siblings or bad blood I should be aware of?"

Georgette shook her head and started for the front door.

When we got to the lobby, Georgette approached the guard for keys to Brooke's place. The guard disappeared to make a copy of the will and returned with two sets of keys. Georgette handed one to me in case I needed to get back in.

Outside, we found Chester pacing. Georgette clutched his arm and offered him a sad smile. I promised I'd call her later and started to run to Arlene's car, when I realized I'd left my phone in Brooke's penthouse.

ARLENE EXPECTED ME in twenty minutes, but I couldn't be without my cell. I found it right where Hannah had set it down on the end table. Hannah's arrival had interrupted my going through Brooke's place. If I made it fast, I could make it back to Arlene on time.

In Brooke's bedroom, I flicked on the light again. Dressers, like medicine cabinets, could tell a lot about a person and it's where I'd left off.

Opening each drawer, I noted how every piece of

underwear had been rolled into tubes except one had been pulled out and laid on top. Similarly colored socks were also rolled and placed together. This time a couple had been yanked from their place and shoved back in. In the next drawer, T-shirts were crisply folded and in color succession from light to dark. Several looked lifted. In each drawer, something was out of place. Brooke clearly had issues with needing things nice and tidy. It was odd she'd left some items in disarray. Or had she? I walked into the walk-in closet. When I'd gone in before, I'd focused on Georgette. This time I noticed every shoebox had its lid popped off and tossed on the floor. I sifted through the boxes. They all had shoes in them. I had the distinct impression that someone had gone through Brooke's things already.

I fingered the fabrics of her beautiful and stylish clothes. Silk blouses. Wool slacks. Linen scarves. Conservative. A stark contrast to the leathers I'd found. A navy wool coat caught my eye. I turned the coat on the hanger toward me, the overhead light catching the iridescent buttons. Mother of Pearl, to be exact. One was missing. What were the odds?

I unzipped my jacket pocket and pulled out the button I'd found in Nightingale's lobby. I pressed it against the coat. It matched. More confirmation that Brooke and Nightingale did indeed know each other. She'd even been to his apartment to see him.

I had to keep moving if I didn't want to be late. In the living room, I scanned the massive bookshelf that took up an entire portion of a wall. Brooke had a definite taste in books. *The Vampire Diaries* by L.J. Smith filled half a shelf. Anne Rice novels the other half. *Some Girls Bite* by Chloe Neill struck me as funny. The other shelves were filled with crime novels from Patricia Cornwell and horror by Stephen King and Dean Koontz. Brooke had liked the dark side, for sure. Several books had been taken off the shelf and stacked, causing many of them to shift onto their sides.

They told the same story as her bedroom. Things may have originally been in order but had been messed with. Had someone been through her things? How did they get past the gatekeeper or through the front door? What were they looking for? My search had offered no answers to those questions.

I needed to get back to the law firm and corner Rachel Mosley. Besides wanting her take on Dave Anderson and Brooke's likely relationship, she might know what Hannah had been talking about with regards to entertaining firm clients.

While something about the space didn't feel right, I was out of time. Locking up, I stepped into the elevator and punched Lobby. Before the doors closed, a woman stepped in with me.

TWENTY-ONE

THE WOMAN HAD silver shoulder-length hair with a youthful bounce. Her yellow oxford shirt, brown tweed blazer, and riding pants the color of buckskin tucked into black English riding boots made me think she'd come off the cover of a Ralph Lauren catalogue. Her soft leather purse with gold buckles hung from her shoulder and she pressed it against the front of her body, revealing French manicured hands. While not rail thin, she looked fit enough to outrun me in a second.

"Quite the view from the penthouses," I said. "You live in one?"

She nodded, smiling with no eye contact.

Not one for small talk. "It's a beautiful place. Do you know your neighbors?"

"Not really." She glanced at her watch.

The body language said leave me alone. Luckily, I wasn't easily dissuaded. Process serving had taught me persistence if nothing else. "Brooke Hanson?"

The smile froze, but her eyes dimmed. "Can't say that I did."

"She lived down the hall."

"I'd seen her, but I didn't know her."

I could buy that since my own neighborhood had residents I only recognized by the car they drove. "Did you hear what happened to her?"

Her smile melted. "Truly unfortunate."

Truly. "Have you lived here long?"

"I moved in with my daughter less than a year ago."

Brooke would've already been living here, if the timeline provided by the landlord was correct. "You wouldn't happen to know if Brooke had many visitors, would you?"

She pursed her lips. "My time is not spent in the elevator lobby."

Even Brooke's neighbors didn't have details about her. That girl had been good at keeping her life private. The elevator opened. The woman threw me a quick glance that read *I'm done with you* and darted out, making a beeline for the revolving door. I gathered my coat around me and did the same.

To shave off time, I took a shortcut to the parking lot. My brain ticked through my interaction with Hannah and whether Brooke had caught up with her sister near those tracks as I passed a self-serve lot and recently demolished building across the street. And who had stopped Brooke outside the bar? More importantly, did they follow her when she broke free?

On the corner of Third and Columbia I waited for the crosswalk to change and examined the fenced-off rubble. Derek had left Brooke on the street and gone back inside. If someone had been waiting outside the door, he would have seen them. Knowing that Dave Anderson was the pinky-twisting man who'd been with Brooke at the Limbo, I needed to go back and find out what more Derek had to say on both of those subjects.

When the WALK flashed, I stepped into the street. The accelerated roar of an engine hit my ears first.

The road rumbled. Headlamps raced toward me. I leapt back when the car swerved toward the curb. A wall of wind smacked my face. The heel of my shoe caught. Arms stretched behind me, I crashed and skidded on the concrete before rolling out of danger. My purse catapulted into the air and dropped next to me. The lone driver of a black Cadillac gunned the motor, shooting loose dirt and gravel in my face. The smell of oil and EPA-violating exhaust filled my lungs as I scrambled off my ass and onto my feet. "Son of a bitch," I screamed, limping after the car to get the license plate number.

Smoke concealed the entire backend as it fishtailed another block, took a right, and disappeared.

Dazed, a shiver of cold and rage whipped through me. My head throbbed. The sting of my scraped palms and the ache in my low back yanked me back to what had happened.

On the sidewalk, I searched for my elevator buddy or anyone who might've seen this near miss. No one. A tingle climbed up my spine, more from intuition than a pinched nerve. This was no accident. I had no proof, no witnesses, and suffered from an overactive imagination. After the intruder last night and the calls this morning, my gut said I was supposed to have been permanently taken out of this investigation.

My poking around had touched a nerve. I'd either poked someone hard enough to get them to come after me, or someone was afraid I'd be coming for them next.

At 12:01 p.m. I came to a hard stop in front of Arlene's garage. I'd called on the way to let her know I was driving as fast as I could legally but she didn't answer. She rushed out her front door. Her pinched lips and rigid stride left no doubt about her state of mind. Dodging the speeding car in Portland again would have been more desirable than facing Arlene.

My chin dipped to my chest as I got out. "I'm sorry. I'd have been early but had to go back for my phone." Nearly being killed might have been a more sympathy-inducing lead in, but neither of us had time for the lecture that would follow.

She gave me an icy glare. "You promised to be back. *I'm* going to be late."

"I'm…"

She waved me off. "Save the excuses."

I could only watch as she hustled into her car and swung the Oldsmobile out of her driveway. She must still be annoyed with how our conversation had ended earlier and that I hadn't relented about giving up my dad's business. It had been a hard year of grief and loss, but this case had given me focus. I felt closer to my dad, and I didn't want that to go away. But at what cost? My life? Mitz being kept away from me? No doubt Jeff would get an update. Another card he'd use against me on why Mitz should live with him full-time.

The scrapes on my hands stung in the cool air. Deflated, I hobbled down the stairs adjoining our property where my Spitfire waited. Next time I'd be kinder and not flood its engine. Inside, Floyd greeted me. After giving him a long break, I checked the phone. No messages. With my jacket off, I paced around the living room before moving into the kitchen where I gulped down a glass of water and spread a heap of peanut butter onto bread and sliced a banana, layering it on top. Floyd trailed me as I went room to room making sure no one had tried to break in. All clear.

The house echoed with quiet. Back in the living room, I forced myself to plop on the couch. Rolling my stiff shoulders, I ate, ripping pieces of sandwich off for Floyd, and trying to relax; to shake the adrenaline that had shot through my body. The near-death experience downtown had me amped, and my muscles were as taut as guitar strings. Emotions rotated in my head. I should call the police and file another report. At least if something happened to me, the authorities would have a paper trail. They already had blue sneakered masked man. Adding heavy breather and black Cadillac weren't much else to go on.

Calling the cops would be back-burnered for now. I had a list of things to do on the Hanson case anyway, except all I wanted to do was see Mitz, hold her close and tell her I loved her. But school wouldn't be out for a while and if she saw me, she'd know something was wrong. I didn't want that.

What I needed was distraction. Upstairs, I changed into jeans and a sweatshirt and gathered a few clothes to take to the laundry room. Arms full, I headed for the stairs with every intention of going down them. Instead, I stood in front of my dad's door, the lump from earlier expanding in my throat.

My reaction caught me by surprise. Once the grief took hold, it wouldn't let go. The clothes tumbled from my arms. I pressed my forehead against the door and drew in a breath—and cried. The ache of missing him made my heart hurt with every wave. He'd raised me. It didn't matter what Arlene had said, that he drank too much, or wasn't always around. He was around enough for me. He loved me and I'd loved him.

He'd told me countless times what all fathers told their children—I'm here for you. Always. But he wasn't anymore and he'd asked something of me that he hadn't prepared me for. Process serving only scratched the surface of what it meant to be a P.I., and he'd protected me from most of that.

Uncertain, I didn't know where to turn. I'd been running in circles finding clues. I was on the verge of figuring out the connections. Or that's what I kept telling myself. All I'd seen for my troubles were threats from Jeff, another dead person, and nearly getting myself killed. What would you do, Dad? I said with my hand on the door, heart pounding, hot tears streaming down my face.

If what Arlene said about my dad not wanting me in the business was true, I was supposed to quit. And do what? I wasn't built for a desk job. Besides, he'd left me the note to help Georgette even if he hadn't envisioned what the case was costing to solve. Or what the case would be at all. Regardless, I'd never be able to look myself in the mirror if I didn't see this through. Dad had been many things. A quitter wasn't one of them. If I planned to step into the life he lived, solve this case, or even take over his business and become a full-fledged investigator, I needed to step in all the way. That meant acting like a P.I. With Mitz to raise, it also meant making sure no one took me away from her.

A calm settled over me like a warm blanket. I knew what my dad would do. He wouldn't let any son of a bitch cause him to stand in front of a locked door and weep. He'd defend himself. It was time I did the same.

The key to his bedroom was in a locked drawer in my nightstand. I retrieved it.

Another wave of sadness came through as I unlocked the door and gave it a small push. It creaked open. The cool mustiness of the room combined with the scent of his musky cologne wafted out. My legs shook when I stepped inside. Dad had made his bed, like he had every day. Aside from a cobweb clinging to the ceiling, the space was as he'd left it that last morning. An old quilt that his mother, my grandmother, had made was draped over an armchair. He used to put his shoes on from there. A Nancy Drew book he often read to Mitz before bed rested on the cushion.

The morning he died, he hadn't felt well. I insisted he stay home and rest. He reminded me that before I'd moved back in, he'd lived alone for years and he was fine, thank you. He insisted he come to work. In the end, it wouldn't have made a difference. What I didn't know was hours spent on stakeouts had taken a toll on his body and his right leg had felt hot for some time. He had a blood clot, and it broke loose. It chose that day to do it. I'd learn later that a congenital heart defect created the perfect storm for that clot to wreak havoc and led to the stroke that killed him.

Nothing I did could save him. In retrospect, I was glad he hadn't stayed home, or I wouldn't have been there to hold his hand in those last moments. A fresh wave of tears streamed down my face as I brushed my fingertips on the comforter.

Turning to the closet, I wiped my tears with the palms of my hands. Being a P.I. was my way of honoring my dad's memory, and everything he meant to me and Mitz. Moving closer to finding out what had happened to Brooke and solving this case would make him proud. I had to believe that. I did believe that.

In the closet, I knelt to the gun safe and punched in the lock code, Mitz's birthday, and the latch released. Dad's 9mm Sig Sauer was inside and secure. My gun rested next to his. I reached for my Glock.

There was no turning back. This was the real deal and I was all in. If upsetting people wasn't a sign of being a true P.I., I didn't know what would be. It was also a sign that Brooke had not fallen on her own in front of that train. Attacks were amping up to get me off the case. If I was someone's target, it meant whoever was at the root had plenty to lose. I had to be ready for anything.

After relocking the safe and the bedroom, I went downstairs. Once the wash was started, I secured the Glock in my purse and sat down to make notes of my time on the case so far. I'd started a short list of next steps when my phone made the sound of a train whistle. Email. As promised, Ms. Matson had scanned over the documents for Brooke's penthouse. To make it easier to see, I ran into Mitz's room where we kept the Mac and pulled up the message on the larger monitor.

On the application, Brooke listed twenty-grand as her monthly gross and the source as the law firm. I didn't know of any clerk positions that paid that kind of money. However, when it required two months of pay stubs, there was a note: *Waived/See Verification*, along with the words, *Guaranteed*. It didn't say by whom. There also didn't appear to be a separate guarantee in the materials. I replied to Ms. Matson asking for that information and hoped she'd respond soon. Since people didn't guarantee debts for mere acquaintances, the document could be telling. There had to be some level of trust, or commitment involved.

Next, I opened the verification documents, curious who would be willing to verify her bogus income. The form was signed by Dave Anderson, Chief Financial Officer of Anderson, Hiefield & Price.

He was willing to confirm her income, but neither he nor Brooke were willing to provide proof. He wouldn't want a trail of compensation for the kind of extra work Brooke was doing. My guess, if Brooke was seeing multiple firm clients, or other men as Hannah had suggested, her compensation far exceeded what she put on the application.

My phone blasted a train whistle again at the same time as the email alert scrolled across my screen. The guarantee was attached. I opened it. As I'd begun to suspect, it too was signed by Dave Anderson.

I jumped out of my chair. I wanted back in that law firm to finish my interview with Rachel Mosley. If I had to, I could wait outside until she left for the day. I'd work on the details on my way. If I hurried, I'd miss afternoon traffic. Keys in hand, I swung open the front door with Floyd on my heels when a familiar Toyota 4-Runner pulled into my driveway. I leaned my shoulder against the doorjamb as Kyle Jaeger climbed out of his truck.

TWENTY-TWO

"WHAT'RE YOU DOING HERE?" I asked Kyle from the front door, trying not to smile so much I looked stupid.

"You said you'd catch me later. Is now a good time?"

"To be caught?"

He smiled, his eyes bright as he climbed the stairs. "Perhaps. I was also coming with some info. You heading out?"

Yes, but I wanted to hear his news and get his opinion on what I'd found in Brooke's place. "I can spare a few minutes. Come in. You want something to drink?"

I led him to the kitchen where Sunday's dishes were in the sink. I cringed and moved to put them in the dishwasher. Kyle reached for my hand. I'm pretty sure my heart skipped a beat.

"Let's sit down," he said.

If he kept holding my hand, he could direct me anywhere.

Floyd shuffled into the kitchen, Mr. Beasley hanging out of his mouth. He dropped it at Kyle's feet and sniffed every inch of Kyle's shoe.

"Inspector Gadget, I presume?" Kyle said, letting me go.

"He thinks so." I tucked my hands in my front pockets. "Floyd, meet Kyle. Kyle, Floyd."

Floyd's nose moved up Kyle's pant leg like a vacuum cleaner.

"You think he approves?" Kyle asked.

"He hasn't peed on you."

Kyle took a step back.

"Yet." I kept a straight face.

"He pees on people's shoes?"

Kyle's stricken face was priceless. "Only if provoked, or if he doesn't like you." Floyd met my gaze with his droopy eyes. "Don't you boy?" His backend wiggled in reply. I looked up to find Kyle watching us and I held back a laugh.

"I promise not to upset him," Kyle said.

I grabbed two Cokes from the fridge and led Kyle into the living room. He sat straight on the couch. I curled on the other chair across from him with Floyd sprawled on the carpet below my feet.

"How are you doing after finding Nightingale yesterday?" Kyle asked.

His lifeless body floating in the red water had crossed my mind a few times. Along with the image on my phone that had me in trouble with Jeff. It bothered me. Having my gun in my purse was helping a little. "The shock is wearing off. Slowly."

"How'd the visit to Brooke's place go?"

I sunk into the chair. "Eye-opening. What do you know about BDSM?"

His eyes narrowed. "Brooke was into that?"

"Yeah, there were more signs of it there than at Nightingale's place."

"Portland does have a pretty active subculture."

Did he blush a little? "It's perfectly legal, right?"

"The quick answer is if it's done between a couple who consents, yes."

I scanned Kyle's face for tells that he found that

appealing and hoping he didn't. "You see a lot of this stuff?"

"Not me, but Vice does. The dark side anyway. I've heard a few locker room stories. There are plenty of men and women who are willing to give up total control and pay well for it, and people who are thrilled to wield that control and take their money."

"That brings up my other point. What if someone is paying for it? No way Brooke got her penthouse on her salary. Doesn't that cross the legal line?"

"Depends. BDSM doesn't always mean sex is involved. But if someone is paying for sex, then that's prostitution. And in Oregon, that's illegal."

I nodded. "That's what makes the next part hard to understand." I told him about the identical books in both Nightingale's and Brooke's place. "The firm Brooke worked for handles international law. Hannah said Brooke had paid her to entertain a few of their clients. Nightingale must have been doing that, too. Why would a law firm put itself into jeopardy like that?"

He rocked his head back and forth, contemplating. "Was Hannah entertaining or having sex with them?"

"Brooke asked her to do both at one point, but Hannah insists she only entertained."

"Did she confirm Brooke was having sex with clients?"

"She assumed."

"Assumptions don't mean much without proof. If she wasn't, then Brooke, and the law firm, technically weren't doing anything wrong."

I played with the pull tab on the Coke can. "I wonder how Dave Anderson fits into all of this. I'm guessing he and Brooke were having a relationship based on Hannah saying Brooke was seeing a married guy from the firm. And the waitress at the Limbo told me about a slimy guy with a diamond studded pinky ring who hung on Brooke at the bar."

"Let me guess. Anderson wears a similar ring."

I nodded. "He's also as slimy as they come. The clincher for me is that he signed a guarantee for her penthouse and verified her income so she could get that penthouse. People don't just do that."

He stretched. "Seems like a sound conclusion they were more than friends."

I relaxed into the chair feeling good that he agreed and took a drink of pop. "The only thing is the waitress also said pinky guy was more into Brooke than she was into him."

"If they were into BDSM, that doesn't sound off base."

"Do you think he'd be aware of the other men?" I thought about it for a second. "Of course he would. Because I can't forget the connection of the law firm and her entertaining clients. He couldn't have liked that."

"Depends on their arrangement."

"I've never known a man who's okay with sharing his woman. I mean, how would that work, juggling multiple men and multiple relationships?" In their world, it might not be considered unusual. It sounded exhausting to me. And complicated.

"In the subculture, the dominatrix rules everything and there are agreements in place ahead of time. If her world is all about domination, they weren't dating in the traditional sense, and he wouldn't have much say."

"He hardly seems the submissive type. Do people change their minds?"

"All the time. Including the dominatrix. She can release people if she's done with them."

"Interesting." I shifted in my chair. "Hannah told me that Brooke wanted to dump the married guy or Anderson, but said she wouldn't, or couldn't because he was a creep about it. If she was in control, why couldn't she?"

"You said yourself that if she's in with the law firm, and he's signed and guaranteed her penthouse, there's a lot on the line for her. In her situation, it might not have been as easy as telling him to go away."

"You may be right."

"And I'm going to add to why that could be true. When you texted you were at the KOIN Tower, I got curious whether there was any connection between that place and Nightingale. There wasn't. What I did find though after scanning the tenant list is that Dave Anderson and his wife, Cindy, live on the same floor as Brooke."

My mind spun. That fact would have made it harder for Brooke to get away from him. "That explains a few things." I told him of my observation that Brooke's place looked gone through. "I kept wondering who could make it past the gatekeeper downstairs. Without documentation, I couldn't. With Anderson living that close, the fact he guarantees the penthouse, not to mention the relationship they apparently have, he'd have a key. He had to be the one that went through her stuff." I didn't have a clue what he'd be looking for, but how convenient to be neighbors. And messy if they ever broke up.

"Except you don't know who else she may have given a key to."

Kyle was a master at punching holes in my theories. "Right. The other men."

"Or friends."

"I haven't seen evidence of those, and the issue remains of getting up that elevator."

Next, I brought him up to speed on Hannah being downtown that night and someone stopping Brooke outside the Limbo. "She couldn't I.D. the person, but whoever it was, stopped Brooke abruptly and she had to break free."

"Any ideas of who it was?"

I drew in a breath. "Not yet."

"Did Hannah see the guy follow Brooke?"

"No. She took off."

"Which means Brooke could have stumbled and fell in front of a commuter train."

"I don't believe that at this point."

"Why?"

I didn't want Kyle to be worried or to shift his focus from this conversation, so I couldn't tell him about my near miss today that had me believing otherwise. "Let's just say too many elements are starting to come in. The alternative lifestyle. An affair with the boss. Entertaining clients." And my brain had started to go another direction. "I also keep thinking about the train conductor, Mr. Foley. He said Nightingale kept repeating 'Goddamn her' at the accident scene. What if he was wrong? What if he meant him, and the him was the person that killed Brooke?"

Kyle lowered his chin and raised an eyebrow like I was cracked.

"Hear me out." I could be onto something and didn't want him to go devil's advocate on me. "What if whoever stopped Brooke, followed her. They could have argued and the argument ended at those tracks. What if Nightingale witnessed it go down and the killer knew he'd been seen."

Kyle leaned forward. "I'm with you so far. Nightingale witnesses Brooke being murdered. The killer sees Nightingale. Then what?"

I rubbed my face. Thinking. "Perhaps the killer knows Nightingale. He convinces Nightingale to stay behind to talk with the police and create a cover story that Brooke was drunk and fell. With an eyewitness, and no other evidence, the police would deem it an accident. Case over."

Kyle cocked his head. "Who would have the clout to do that?"

"In that scenario, I can only think of one person. Anderson."

"Okay. I'll bite. How would he have convinced Nightingale?"

I bent down to pet Floyd. "The man was into BDSM. No, both men were into BDSM. For all I know, they could have dossiers of secrets on each other. Anderson could have leveraged one of those secrets. You tell me. You know more about the subculture."

"Okay. We'll put a pin in that one. We aren't sure what kind of dirt Anderson had on Nightingale, but enough to leverage him to stay behind at a crime scene and report false information to the police. Did I miss anything?"

For the first time, I felt like a legitimate investigator talking murder and motivation with Kyle. My dad would have liked him. "Nightingale does this under duress. That may have eaten at him because he was upset when we talked. Thinking back to our conversation, he had sounded like he he'd been covering for someone."

"Anderson?"

It was my turn to rock my head side to side. "It's a possibility. Based on what I found in both of their apartments, Nightingale was working for Anderson's firm and entertaining clients. Anderson and Brooke are having a thing. Brooke and Nightingale were into BDSM. It doesn't take a rocket scientist to see the dots."

"It's whether they connect or not. If you're right about him doing work for the firm, Anderson would have some clout to get Nightingale to stay, especially if the arrangement was lucrative."

"Based on the art alone in Nightingale's house, it was."

"Of course, that scenario assumes a lot. Someone going through Brooke's things and the person in front of the bar arguing with her could be different people. Not to mention she could have run into someone entirely different near the tracks."

I leaned back. "Right. And I don't know who was outside that night. It could have been one of her other men. Or a firm client." I sighed. "Have you been kept in the loop on the Nightingale investigation?"

"Some. It sounds like he had a steady stream of male visitors and an occasional woman or two."

I thought of the pearl button I'd found. One of those women visitors had been Brooke. "Would that be normal to have a male and female master have cross-over clients?"

He stretched his legs out in front of him. "Sure."

My head started to ache at going through the possibilities. The first question I needed to confirm was who had been outside that bar waiting for Brooke. Derek had escorted her out. He'd held back that he liked Brooke. He could have held back on telling me who he saw when he left Brooke on the sidewalk.

"You're looking a little intense," Kyle said, bringing my attention back. "How about a break?"

I gave him a smile. "Yes." I enjoyed how it felt to brainstorm with him. Whether premature or not, I could see myself doing this more often. I liked entertaining Kyle as my future. "There is one thing I could use your help on though."

"Anything."

I kneaded my hands. Now would be the time to tell Kyle about my intruder, and the guy who'd nearly run me down, except I'd already filed that report and had the other handled. I didn't want him to get all cop show and be protective of me. But I couldn't get information from the phone company without the proper authority. "I got a few hang-ups this morning. It's probably nothing, but I punched in the trace code. Any chance you could check with the phone company and see who's behind the calls?"

He frowned. "Doesn't seem like a prankster would cause you concern."

"It's the timing, I suppose."

"I'll check it out. I am more than a pretty face."

"I like your pretty face." The words had slipped out and flush crept up my neck.

His face matched my shade of red. "I'll see what I can do. After this conversation, I'm starting to wonder if we closed out Brooke's case too soon."

"You believe she was murdered?"

"I think there's more to the story. I'll need to keep my superiors updated."

If the case did re-open, my involvement would come to a halt. Not that I didn't want Brooke's death to be solved in any way possible. I just liked the idea of being a part of the resolution.

It was 5:30. We'd talked the afternoon away and the room took on a dimness as the sun set. My revisit to the law firm would wait. I got up to flick on the lights. "You hungry?"

"I am, and I'm a good chef."

We went into the kitchen and scrounged around. It'd been a long time since I'd cooked with another man besides Jeff. After my grocery delivery, I had a good selection of food in my house, including the fixings for spaghetti. Ground sausage and onions in the fridge, noodles and marinara sauce in the pantry, and a loaf of French bread on the counter.

Kyle found my only bottle of Merlot stashed in a cupboard and poured us a glass while I stood at the stove browning the onions and sausage. He set a glass down on the counter next to me.

I looked up from my cooking duties and smiled. "Thanks."

He gathered me in his arms. He kissed me, gently at first, and then with meaning. A warm sensation swept through my entire body, including my toes, making me dizzy. He pulled away to look at my face, still holding me. Waiting for my reaction. My one hand held a wooden spoon, my other one around his waist. I felt clumsy, silly, hot—and speechless. He let me go and backed away, catching my shocked expression.

"I'm sorry," he said.

"No," I said in a small voice. "Don't be."

"I thought we should get that out of the way. I mean, I thought you felt…"

"I do."

"But?"

"No *but*."

He smiled, broad, making his dimples even more deep and sexy. Sign me up to wake every day next to this man.

Setting the spoon down, I leaned into him. This time I kissed him hard, making the point that we felt the same.

The doorbell rang and I jumped back, flustered at the disruption. The bell sounded again. "Hold that thought." I craned my neck to see him until I rounded the corner into the living room.

Flipping on the outside light, I opened the door.

"Mama," Mitz said, darting straight into me and squeezing me with the fierceness of a bear cub.

My heart raced. With both arms wrapped around my little girl, I pulled her close and stood in the entry. Jeff didn't catch the hint. He maneuvered around us and came in.

"Hey guys. What's up?" I said, casual, my shoulders tense.

"Mitz wanted to see you."

The feeling was mutual. I held her tighter. "How'd you know I was home?"

"Mom mentioned you were here and we wanted to check on you."

Arlene had probably seen Kyle's truck in the driveway and was curious who it belonged to. "*We* did, huh." Or it could be that after our conversation of keeping Mitz away until after the case, Jeff's over protectiveness of me had won out. The dilemma was Jeff and I hadn't dated other people since the divorce. We hadn't prepared Mitz. It didn't feel like the right moment to spring that on her. I backed up from my daughter and signed, "I thought about you all day. Is your hand better?"

She nodded.

"She's fine," Jeff said before raising his nose in the air to sniff. "Are you cooking?"

"This might not be the best time, guys. Can I come by later? We can go for ice cream."

He ignored me. "I'm hungry. What's for dinner?"

"Jeff, please. You should go. You saw the truck in the driveway…"

"Oh?" Jeff said.

"I have company." I tried to not move my lips and nodded to Mitz, hoping he got my meaning.

"Who?" Jeff's eyes narrowed. He made no move to leave.

"It doesn't matter, Mitz doesn't…" I started.

Kyle walked into the living room with a kitchen towel thrown over his broad shoulder. He towered over Jeff by at least four inches. Jeff shrunk another inch when Kyle reached out his hand. "I'm Kyle Jaeger."

"Nice to meet you." Jeff shook his hand with added force.

Mitz stared up at Kyle, her eyes wide, before she glared at me.

"He's a friend," I signed, but she frowned, turned, and ran out the front door. "Ladybug," I said to her back, knowing she couldn't hear me.

"Good one, Kel." Jeff followed her.

"You should've called first." I trailed, stopping at the front door, aware of Kyle.

"You should've told me you were seeing someone else. At least then I would have *known* to call."

"We're not seeing each other. We're just...." I didn't want to scream at Jeff and Mitz running down the stairs, his protective arm around her small frame. He put her in the passenger side. When he slammed her door, he whipped around. "Leave it alone tonight. I'll explain it to her."

"But Jeff..."

"Really. I'll make sure she's okay." I thought he also said under his breath, "I always do."

He hopped into the driver's side and started the engine. A lump caught in my throat as Mitz, refusing to look at me, rode away.

TWENTY-THREE

WATCHING MITZ AND Jeff drive out of sight, I thought of Hannah and Georgette, and how distant they were from each other. I wouldn't let that happen to me and my daughter. But there was a chance with Jeff and me not getting back together, Mitz would judge me the unreasonable one, and over time drift away. My heart squeezed. I'd have liked the opportunity to warn her about the prospect of someone new in my life.

Inside, Kyle was in the kitchen finishing up the marinara.

"So, that was my ex-husband and daughter." I tried to lighten the mood, but my voice was tight with annoyance at Jeff for putting me in this situation, and with sadness.

"Gathered that." He didn't look my way. "Would you like me to go?"

"No."

He stirred the sauce. "Your daughter has your smile."

"Look—" I started.

"It's okay, Kelly. Like me, you've only been divorced a year. I get it's a stickier situation when kids are involved."

He'd been married before? "Like most kids of divorce, I'm sure Mitz wants us back together, so seeing you…"

"He seems like a nice guy."

That was up for debate at present. "Generally. There are reasons we're divorced."

"I don't want to interfere."

"You're not."

He wiped his hands on a towel. "Your dinner is ready, Madame. I should go."

"Please don't." I stepped into him, put my arms around his neck, and resumed where we'd left off before the doorbell. He pulled me to his chest and kissed me back. There were no tingles this time. I tried to remember the first kiss. Nothing helped. Guilt over Mitz had taken its place. Pulling away, I patted his chest before turning to the stove.

"Another time," he said.

Disappointed at how the evening was ending, I nodded and turned off the stove. A moment later, the front door closed. Kyle's truck thundered to life, followed by a distant rumble. Head down, I stood in my kitchen alone fighting the wave of self-pity near the surface.

No longer hungry, I poured the sauce in a bowl and set it in the refrigerator. There was only one way around feeling sorry for myself—action. It was how I'd survived the losses of this past year. I couldn't sit around and do nothing. The way to get this case over with, and my life back in order, was to keep moving.

The Limbo should be cranking to life about now and not too crowded yet on this Monday night to get some questions answered from Derek. And Amanda. I wanted to update her on the identity of pinky man and get more details from her.

Thirty minutes later, Floyd and I parked nearby as the happy hour customers thinned out. Stepping out of my car, I scanned the street for any crazed drivers or blue shoed joggers, and clutched my purse tighter. With my gun close, I felt safer, but being lax was not an option. My dad wouldn't be.

Inside, I climbed onto a barstool. Derek was serving. No sign of Amanda. "I'll have a wine spritzer," I said.

"Coming right up," he said, popping a bubble with his gum. He turned away to grab a glass and a bottle of chilled pinot noir and a club soda. I caught his glance through the mirror lining the back-counter wall. He set the glass down in front of me. "Weren't you in here the other night?"

"Yeah." I took a quick sip. "Kelly Pruett. A friend of Brooke Hanson's family."

"Right. The ambience bring you back, or more questions?"

Perceptive. "The latter."

"I told you everything last time."

"Except that you had a thing for Brooke."

He wiped down the counter with some added pressure. "I liked her. That a crime?"

I took another sip. "Odd you didn't mention it. You seemed angry at her before."

His nostrils flared. "People who can't hold their liquor are annoying. What are you really, a cop?"

"Private investigator."

He stopped wiping. "Not a family friend?"

"I'm both." Not a lie. I liked Georgette.

He tossed the rag in a nearby sink. "You are working with the police?"

"Nope. The family. They don't believe what happened to Brooke was an accident. Quite frankly, neither do I."

He lifted a glass from the back counter and dried it with another towel. The man didn't stop moving. "You think I'm involved?" He smacked his gum.

"Didn't say that, but the police report and your statement doesn't jibe. Why'd you backpedal about someone following Brooke out?"

"It's hard to keep track of things in here when it's busy."

I cocked my head to the side. "You're an astute guy. I'm surprised you'd be confused."

He relaxed some at my observation. "I am. This time, I got it wrong. I thought someone went out for a while, but one of the waitresses corrected me and said I had it wrong. The person had come right back in. Figured it was rude to get people involved who weren't and that's why I changed my statement."

I saw his point. "Who's the waitress?"

"Amanda."

She hadn't mentioned that when I'd spoken to her in the alley. An easy check when we spoke shortly. "What did you see when you left Brooke outside the door."

"Nothing."

"No one was even smoking a cigarette?"

He shook his head, picking up another glass to dry.

There was at least one person out there—the person who stopped Brooke. "Tell me more about the guy who used to hang out at Brooke's table. You know his name?"

"No. He was just some chump who was interested in her."

He'd said that before. He had to know something about him. "How often was he here?"

"Occasionally."

"More often than not?"

He shrugged.

I'd take that as a yes. "Did he touch her? Kiss her? Argue? Did you get the impression they were a couple?"

The questions made him tense again, making me think he didn't enjoy watching someone hanging on Brooke. "I don't pay attention to the floor."

Back to that excuse. He noticed enough to dole out bits, yet not enough to be helpful. I drew out my phone and pulled up the law firm's website and showed him Dave Anderson's picture. "Is this the guy you saw with Brooke?"

He barely glanced at the screen. "Never seen him."

My bullshit meter went into overdrive. I took a drink and set the glass down a little too hard. "You said you saw the guy that sat at Brooke's table."

"And?" He wouldn't look at me. "That's him. Slicked back black hair and a pinky ring."

He shrugged. "Can't help you."

Why was he lying? I pulled up Nightingale's picture next, cropping the photo to focus on his face and thrusting it in front of him. "How about this guy? Jay Nightingale."

He winced and shook his head. "Don't know him and never saw him. You asked me about him last time. But, wow."

That summed it up. Deleting his image would be the first thing I did when this case was done. "And you're sure no one was outside when you left Brooke?"

"Yep."

I tucked my phone back in my purse. Derek was being evasive. Was there some guy code where men didn't talk about each other? Or had this all hit too close to home? "Tell me more about your attraction to Brooke?"

"We've gone over this."

"Did she like you back?"

His inched up shoulders said I'd hit a nerve and my suspicion was no. "Were you aware she was into some interesting stuff?"

He huffed. "I wouldn't know."

His body language and words were off. "Was it hard on your ego to have such a beautiful woman reject you?"

He gave me a half-smile. "It was nothing serious, lady. Ask anyone. I flirt with a lot of women in this bar."

"Some people think it bothered you."

"Then they're wrong." Derek went to a container of limes and a knife. When he returned, he shifted gears. "I feel like you're getting the wrong impression of me. I'll admit Brooke was cute, but she didn't like me. It was no big deal."

For many men, that was always a big deal. "You cut her off that night. That's what took her outside the bar and on her path to her death. You ever think about that?"

"Every day." His mouth twitched. He quartered the lime with the sharp blade. "Only the law says I can't serve someone when they're intoxicated, whether they like that fact or not. I do feel bad about what happened to her though. If I can help, I want to."

My skin tingled. While I didn't believe him, I reached into my pocket and drew out a card. "You can help by calling me when you remember who was outside that door."

He took my card and tucked it into his vest pocket without another word.

A man walked up and sat down three seats over. The conversation had ended. Whether Brooke and Dave Anderson flaunted their relationship in public, Amanda had seen them together. I might have believed Derek didn't pay attention, except he denied ever seeing Anderson after telling me he'd seen Brooke's tablemate. I could keep pushing at him to find the truth. I could also get myself ousted from the premises.

Purse in hand, I slid off the barstool and laid a ten on the bar. "Amanda working tonight?"

He shook his head. "She was supposed to. She's been a no-show. I expected her at three yesterday and today."

My stomach tightened. "Is that normal?"

"No. I tried to call, but no answer."

"Could I get her address or number?"

"I can't give employee information out like that."

"Will you text her and tell her I'm trying to get a hold of her then. It's important."

"When I have time. Or I'll have her call you next time I see her."

Not convinced he'd do either, I'd find her myself.

It was after nine when I crammed myself into my Spitfire and ruffled Floyd's head. I didn't feel like going home to an empty house, and it was too late—or perhaps too soon—to call Mitz and see if we were okay. I sent Jeff a text asking him to tell her goodnight and that I loved her. I didn't get a response.

I hadn't been back to my office since the case started. If I swung by there, I could prepare the proof of service I owed Carla at Baumgartner & Sokol for their divorce petition served yesterday. Despite my "expanding business," as Jeff had put it, I did have other clients I couldn't neglect. Even more pressing, I could do a Google search on Amanda and try to make contact. One day of missing work wouldn't have concerned me. But two? Something didn't feel right.

TWENTY-FOUR

AFTER STOPPING AT my favorite Mini Mart for a refill of steaming hot, thick black coffee, I checked my rearview mirror a dozen times on the way to my office. My nerves were frayed from the earlier events of the day. Wondering where Amanda was didn't help. But my paranoia had me feeling foolish until glance thirteen spotted a pair of halogens keeping pace with me. Tapping my blinker, I shifted into the left lane. The car followed. When I drifted into the right lane, it drifted with me.

My shoulder muscles bunched. In the movies, people were followed all the time. Not so much in reality, and never to me. Of course, lots of *firsts* had occurred since taking on the Hanson case.

Dad liked to outsmart and outwit his opponents—which is how he viewed every target of an investigation. In this situation, he might pull over and confront the person. Out-muscling someone was not among my options. Nor was whipping out my gun. A more practical solution would be to drive to the police station a mile from my office.

Before letting my imagination go crazy, I took the exit into Northeast, to see if this guy could keep up through the maze of streets that I could traverse in my sleep. The car crowded my bumper, its lights on bright, as I turned on Broadway. With the light bouncing off my rearview mirror, I couldn't make out the license plate or if it was the black Cadillac that had tried to take me out.

Without another thought, I punched the gas and skidded right onto Seventh. Left on Wygeant, right on Ninth. The headlights faded to a safe distance. Even so, to humor the practical part of me poking its head out, I drove past the police station and slowed below the speed limit. Floyd had perked up at my maneuvering. "Sorry boy." When I glanced in the rearview mirror, my follower, imagined or not, was gone.

Letting out a shaky breath, I shook my head. "Am I losing it, Floyd?"

He rested his chin on the seat and let out a heavy sigh in reply. He thought I'd lost it a long time ago.

Circling back to Hancock, I parked in front of my office. The sole streetlight in front barely illuminated the sidewalk. I'd always liked the character of this old building with its worn brick, glass doors, and green striped awnings. Now it looked daunting and barren. The muscles in my back tensed. The tenants in the building had been gone since sundown, as expected, and their windows were dark. My insides decided to have a party. In the future, I'd leave a nightlight on inside.

"Let's do this." I bounced my car door open. Floyd stretched out and I scanned the street while turning the key in the lock. Once inside, I threw the bolt closed.

A pile of mail had been shoved through the slot, which I gathered and went into my paneled office. Dropping the keys in my purse, I flicked on the desk light and settled down at the desk. Bills and junk made up most of the mail. A couple of checks for process serving had made their way to me. While Floyd sniffed around the floor and found his bed, I listened to messages.

Watts & Watts had four subpoenas for an upcoming trial. Bailey & Rider had an interview for me to conduct of a traffic accident witness. Baumgartner & Sokol was confirming I'd served the divorce papers. I could cross that off my list. After the computer powered up, I retrieved a blank Proof of Service form. My friend since grade school, Jessica, called to see if I wanted to do lunch. She worked as a social worker now and an email had come through on getting together earlier and I hadn't responded. I would as soon as this case was done. I missed talking with her about life and raising my daughter. I'd let even my friendships falter this past year.

In the confines of this little room, with messages droning, and Floyd in his usual spot, my muscles began to unwind. I slunk into the chair and typed in the information on the Proof. I'd spent years in this building with my father. This was my territory. I hit the print button and entered Amanda's name into the Google search field. The tension in my body continued to ease as a series of options populated the screen.

An all too familiar clicking sound changed that.

Every hair on my neck stood at attention and Floyd's eyebrows raised. The back door at the end of the hall had opened.

I shut off the desk light and sat in the dark, not breathing, waiting to hear footsteps that didn't come. But certain of what I'd heard, my office felt like a cave with no way out.

Purse in hand, I crept to the corner of the room on

the same side as the door and crouched, pulling out my gun. From that vantage point, I would be able to see the intruder before being spotted.

I sat in the black silence. Heart pounding. Every sense on high alert. The internal party upgraded to a rave as I listened. Not a breath. Not a creak. Not even the slightest breeze from an open door, which I'd never heard close. Floyd was unconcerned with his head back down on the bed. Five minutes passed before I decided I'd given into paranoia again.

To be sure, I called out. "I know you're in here. I've got a weapon, and I'm licensed to use it." I sounded very *Hawaii 5-0* and ridiculous.

Of course, no one responded.

It could be I'd forgotten to secure the door on Friday afternoon and the wind had blown it open. I stood, shaking the tension out of my arms and strung my purse over my shoulder. "C'mon Floyd. Let's lock it better this time." With gun in hand, I walked through the door into the main office. The flash of a closed fist barreled toward my face and connected with my jaw.

The exploding force dropped me sideways to the floor and had the gun flying out of my hand, skittering away from me. My purse crumpled at my feet. Dazed, it took me a beat to realize what happened and survival mode to kick in. I had to get out of there. As I tried to get to my knees, my attacker's vice grip encircled my ankles and yanked me flat like he was going to pull me down the long hall. Floyd's frantic barks echoed in my ears.

Panicked at being trapped, I twisted onto my back to see my assailant. Only the smallest amount of light seeped in from the street; enough to make out a familiar black mask. This time I had to remember details. A visceral fear swept through me. More than details, I had to get away. Arms close for protection, I rolled, scrambling to get on my feet. A solid kick dug into my rib, flattening me. I doubled over against more blows and patted my hand around me in desperation to find my gun. My attacker was near me, stepping on me. He could be searching for the same thing. I couldn't let him find the gun first.

TWENTY-FIVE

WE BOTH SEARCHED with a frenzy for a gun we couldn't see. He gave up first and stood upright. With my life on the line, I couldn't give up, but only found my purse strap instead.

Another kick rushed at me. "Stop it," I screamed and realized the barking had stopped. Where was Floyd?

There was no time to contemplate. My attacker's foot aimed at my head loomed in my peripheral. When it came hurling at me, I clutched his shoe with both hands. A moan rivaling my last push when having Mitz poured out of my mouth and I ignored the piercing pain of what had to be a cracked rib. I lifted his foot and my body at the same time. The man crashed down onto his back.

The urge to find out who this jackass was felt strong. But in my injured state, I was defenseless. I had to get into the open. With a death grip on my purse, I tugged it toward me, wrapping the strap around my wrist.

"Floyd come," I yelled on all fours, crawling to the door. The man recovered and tackled me. A bit of light came through the front blinds giving me a glimpse of him. Narrow angry eyes glared through the knitted slits. I tore at his face and Floyd must've been tearing at his pant leg because I heard, "Shit, get off me," in a deep voice.

The man kicked. Floyd let out a yip.

"Don't you dare touch my…" The intruder wrapped his hands around my throat cutting off my airway. Desperate, I clawed at his hands to loosen his grip and fought to detangle the purse to get to the pepper spray.

Sheer panic hit as pressure built behind my eyes. I gasped for breath. My vision clouded. Dread welled up in me. My strength fading; searching for that spray. He drew in close and spat on me.

Tears stung my eyes at the indignity as my hand wrapped around the spray. Holding my breath and squeezing my eyes closed, I aimed for his face.

He jumped off with a high-pitched scream and sprinted down the back hallway and out the back door. If every breath didn't shoot a sharp current of pain through my body, I would have followed.

I laid there panting and wincing, struggling to swallow, and to breathe. Floyd trotted over and laid down on my arm. I patted him gently to make sure he hadn't been hurt. After a minute, I managed to prop up into a sitting position, using Floyd for leverage. My cell was hiding at the bottom of my purse. I called 911. Once I was on my feet and the light was on, I found my gun in the corner. Lot of good being armed had done. The only danger I posed was to myself. If I kept at it, Mitz would be living without a mother. The pity party of one continued until the police unit arrived and I swiped some wayward tears from my cheeks with my sleeve.

One of the officers was a young rookie. The other I recognized as Gerry Soucy, an old timer who'd helped my dad out a few times.

"Do you need an ambulance?" Gerry asked the minute he saw me. I must have looked as bad as I felt.

"No. I'll get to urgent care when I'm through here."

We settled in my office and they bombarded me with questions. I answered with what few details I'd picked up about my attacker's physical description. His build was a little bigger than my size, but he doubled me in strength. And he'd spit on me. The thought rankled me. "He'll also be washing his eyes out all night." That gave me some satisfaction. I proceeded to tell them about the intruder report I'd filed the other night and how I figured it was the same guy. I added to that a vague description of the black Cadillac, who might have followed me here. They had finished the report when Kyle walked in.

"We seem destined to be together tonight," he said from the doorway.

"Hey Kyle," Gerry said. "You know Kelly?"

"We've met." He gave me a small smile.

"Your police scanner?" I asked.

Kyle nodded.

"We're done here," Gerry said, and the two officers rose to leave. Gerry handed me his contact information. "Call us if you think of anything else."

"I'll walk you out," Kyle said to the officers.

He wanted their take on the situation before talking to me, and I didn't mind waiting to fill him in on my side of the story. Adrenaline had begun to fade, exhaustion and intense pain taking its place. An overwhelming desire to sit and cry came over me. I sucked it up.

When Kyle came back in, he looked at me long and hard. "Anything you want to share?"

"I needed to do something for another client."

He folded his arms over his chest. "I could have come with you."

"I didn't decide to come here until after I'd left the Limbo."

He pursed his lips together. I didn't know Kyle well, but signs of irritation are universal.

"I'm fine, Kyle." I just had to be fine to be able to work and take care of my daughter. And depending on anyone else would feel like a failure. Dad had never depended on anyone.

He nodded. "That's why you flinch every time you take a breath. Why didn't you tell me someone's been stalking you?"

"I wouldn't call it stalking. I filed a report." I pushed myself gingerly into a standing position to defend myself. Another jolt of pain had me leaning against the desk. "And I told you about the prank phone calls."

"Right. You only neglected to mention the guy in your backyard and nearly getting run over this afternoon—and thanks for not bothering to clue me in on the last one since I saw you right after."

I'd felt so confident at conquering the world at that point. "I should have. I'm not a fan of being told I can't handle things on my own."

"Obviously." He frowned at me. I frowned back. Damn him for being right.

We stared at each other for a long minute, until I had to relent and sit. "Are you going to drive me to urgent care or what?"

He touched my side. "Pretty bad, huh?"

I nodded. His touch put me back on the verge of crying. Feeling battered and broken was not something I relished. In fact, I down right hated it.

"Come on. We'll take my car," he said.

The idea of Floyd and me climbing into his 4x4

made me wince. "Floyd likes the Spitfire. Let's take mine and you drive."

With some slow maneuvering, we made it to the car and Floyd wedged behind my seat in the small space where he immediately passed out. Nothing phased that boy of mine. I wish I could do the same. We drove to the clinic in silence. I didn't know what else to say. My jaw hurt from the punch and my throat was tender from the hold my attacker had on it. I wouldn't have been able to say much anyway.

For the first time, in a long time, I rested my eyes, content to let someone else take care of me. I shrunk into the seat and tried not to breathe deep.

At the hospital, they took x-rays. I walked out with a prescription for Tylenol with Codeine and bed rest for the next few days. While nothing was broken, I did have not one, but two bruised ribs that should heal in a few weeks. My jaw would look like I'd lost a UFC fight and the pinkish marks around my throat promised to be sore and turn purple and ugly soon.

Two Tylenols were down my throat the minute I filled the prescription and headed to meet Kyle in the waiting room. I froze when Kyle came into view. Jeff sat in the chair next to him. Had they been comparing notes?

Jeff hopped up from his chair. "You okay?" he sounded panicked. "What happened to you?"

"I'm fine. How'd you know I was here?" I scanned the room. "Mitz isn't here, I hope." I didn't want her to see me like this.

"She's with Mom. I got a call because your medical file lists me as your emergency contact. They wouldn't give details though. So?"

There was no way around avoiding his question. "I'm getting close to finding out what happened to Brooke and someone isn't happy about that."

He shook his head and pressed his lips together. "I'll take you home," he finally said. "We can talk about it more there."

Kyle had appeared at my side and put his hand on my shoulder.

"I appreciate your concern," I said to Jeff. "But let's talk another time." Hopefully never. "Right now, I need to go to bed." Kyle gave me a sympathetic smile, probably feeling awkward at being in the middle. "Kyle brought me in my car. He'll take me home."

Jeff nodded. "Whatever." He turned to go.

"Is Mitz okay?" I asked before he reached the door. "I mean about earlier?"

"She'll survive. We both will." He left without saying another word.

This night kept getting shittier by the minute.

As I climbed back into my car, Kyle told me he'd called his desk sergeant for someone to cover his shift and he'd stay the night. We could pick his car up in the morning.

I didn't argue.

At home, he tucked me into bed. "I'm going to check out the house and then bunk on the couch."

In the dark, I reached out for his hand. He grabbed it and pressed his lips against my palm. He disappeared from the room, leaving me alone. The medication had kicked in and my eyelids felt like weights. The sharpness in my ribs and jaw muscles dulled to an ache rather than a stab.

Kyle wandered through the downstairs checking

windows and doors. A creaking sound five minutes later said he'd settled on the sofa where he tossed and turned. I wanted to sleep, but couldn't. Kyle Jaeger was in my house. He cared about me. Didn't mind my profession. And he'd become good at picking up my pieces. If I had let Jeff bring me home, he would've harped on me to quit for the rest of the night. Not that I would blame him. That's what people who cared about you did. They wanted to keep you safe. Make sure you come home at night. Though Kyle hadn't said as much, I sensed he cared that I come home—and he hadn't asked me to stop being who I was. He hadn't asked anything of me.

"Kyle," I said, as loud as I could manage.

He bounded up the stairs to my call. "You okay?" he asked from the doorway.

"I'm fine, but…" I pulled back the covers and patted the mattress beside me.

"The couch is fine," he said.

"Please."

He hesitated before walking into the room and slid under the covers fully clothed. He laid on his back next to me. His warmth had a healing power. Instead of feeling nervous, the tension drained from my body like air from a balloon. He held my hand as we both stared up at the ceiling.

"You know who attacked you tonight, don't you?" he asked.

"I didn't at first. I keep reliving the moment and seeing that masked face so close to mine, his eyes. The smell of his breath." My stomach roiled at the memory of his spit on my face. The outrage I'd felt. The smell of mint…like the day I'd met him in that conference room. "Dave Anderson fits the description of my attacker. Even those few minutes I'd spent with him, I'd seen the same hate in those eyes."

"I'll have an APB put out."

I rested my hand on his arm. "I understand your position, but to be honest, between the dark and his mask, I couldn't see his face or tell you the color of his hair or his eyes."

"We can still question him."

I nodded. "The police are better equipped for this, especially if he is a killer. But can you give me at least another day to confirm one way or another?"

"How do you plan to do that?"

I was too tired to figure that out. "I don't know yet. Just one more day."

He didn't answer.

"Please."

He let out a long sigh. "That's it."

"Thank you."

He held my hand. "Before I forget, the calls you got, they came from Brooke's apartment."

Despite my tender ribs, I turned to face Kyle. "You're kidding?"

"Nope."

Brooke could have given her key to anyone. Only Dave Anderson had direct access. As Brooke's neighbor, lover, and boss, I was certain. Which only convinced me that he had been my attacker and Brooke's killer. I moved onto my back again.

Anderson could have been concerned about my investigation even before I went to the law firm and asked him about the Limbo. If Nightingale was working for him, as I suspected, he could have alerted Anderson that I was asking questions early on. Anderson would try to get me off the case and he was smart enough to know I could trace him, so he didn't dare make calls from his own phone. His mistake was he didn't realize I'd uncover his connection to Brooke's condo. Or that I wasn't going anywhere. I needed to figure out my next step. Despite my effort to think more, the pain meds swallowed me whole.

TWENTY-SIX

WHEN MORNING CAME, my eyes flew open as if I'd been rejuvenated—at least my mind. My body had been steamrolled and aged fifty years in one night. Neck muscles I didn't know existed were sore from the blow to my face. My ribs ached from the kicks. My lip stung and puffed like an overinflated balloon. I could only imagine what I looked like.

Too stiff to roll over, I shifted my eyes to find Kyle gone and no sounds indicating he was nearby. The nightstand clock read nine. Yikes.

With gritted teeth, I flung back the covers and swung my right leg across my left. I gained enough momentum to flip over, groaning the whole time. My arms, head, and stomach ended up flat on the bed; my knees on the floor. I gathered enough strength to push away from the bed and wobble to my feet.

Drenched in sweat, I shuffled to the bathroom. The visual assessment exceeded my worst expectations. The impending bruises on my throat were red, dark circles shadowed my eyes, and my hair stuck out in odd and disturbing directions.

After a thorough brushing and a few douses of water to calm the nest, I went downstairs. Kyle had made coffee and left a note on the counter.

He'd caught a cab back to his truck and gone home to feed a cat I didn't know he had. He wanted me to

sleep and he'd call later. I'd seen my face in the bathroom. I needed more than sleep.

Details of Kyle's life showed themselves in small
bits. At some point after this case we needed to have
that dinner we started and learn more about each
other—like normal people. Standing in the kitchen
alone, I wished he were here to talk to about the case.
Or to get a gentle bear hug from.

Floyd trotted into the kitchen, tail swaying behind
him, and dropped a red ball at my feet. I squatted,
wincing every few inches, and nuzzled his saggy face.
Nothing like the smell of dog breath and a wiggly
body to draw me out of feeling sorry for myself. After
a session of tummy rubs and wet kisses, and tending
to his other needs, I poured a large cup of coffee and
went up to Mitz's computer to finish what I'd begun
at my office.

I typed in Amanda Dixon's name and searched
Google and Facebook, finding her profile. It didn't
provide contact information, and she didn't have any
public updates. I direct messaged her and asked her
to call me ASAP. Getting her a message made me
feel better. I'd be happier when she responded—or if
I saw her.

On one of my go to *people finder* sites, only one
26-year-old popped up who lived in Portland with relatives in Idaho and Colorado. The age was about right.
I paid the fee with my credit card to get more info.
The results only provided what appeared to be a cell
number, no street address.

I dialed and six rings later, a voice came on. "You
know the drill."

The young woman sounded like Amanda. I left

my name and number. For good measure, I texted the same message with the addition of *we need to talk*. She should at least see that if nothing else.

After last night, my concern for Amanda had grown. If Anderson was my attacker, his being at the bar with Brooke meant he knew who Amanda was. If he suspected she'd talked to me, she could be at risk.

While I waited to hear from her, I had a law firm to get back into.

In the shower, the warm water smarted on my skin, but loosened the muscles. An empty hot water heater later, I emerged a different woman.

With an extra layer of concealer to cover the bruising, and a bit more blush to draw the eye away from my jaw, I dressed in black jeans and a black warmup jacket over a black turtleneck. Going for the serious *don't give me any bullshit* look for my conversation with Rachel Mosley. While confident Brooke was having an affair with Dave Anderson and handling some extracurricular activities for firm clients, I wanted her take on it. She couldn't be oblivious to what was going on around her.

With a list of questions ready for Rachel, I only needed to figure out how to get back in.

On the sixth floor of Anderson, Hiefield & Price, a frosty glass wall ensconced one end. Through the clear door that read AHP Admin and Accounting was a hallway and various offices. Rachel had come from the elevator for our last meeting. A scan of the building roster as I rushed through the lobby, along with the vinyl letters on the door, confirmed I was in the right place. What I hadn't expected was the keypad security system that stood guard. With my only option to wait it out, I hung casually by the ladies' restroom.

A few minutes later a couple of women emerged from the offices. I rushed over before the door closed. "Hey, I'm a friend of Rachel's. Reception sent me up and I wanted to surprise her. Can I sneak back?"

"Oh sure," the blonde held it open for me. "Do you know where she sits?"

"Yeah, thanks." I smiled, having no clue where to begin.

"She moved last week, you know."

"I didn't."

"She's in the north corner. If the name plate hasn't been changed yet, it'll be the one that reads Brooke Hanson."

After thanking them again, the glass door closed behind me. The women stepped into the elevator and were gone. Not sure how I'd managed that, there wasn't time to question. The bigger issue was to figure out which side faced north.

It took Interstate 5 for me to get my bearings. Oregon's main highway traveled north through Washington and south to California and ran along the backside of the building. Rachel's office had to be on the left.

I followed the hallway to find Rachel in a large corner space chewing gum and chuckling lightly with the phone to her ear. Before she saw me, I stepped inside and shut the door.

She cleared her throat. "What the—I need to go. I'll call you back."

"Busy?" I ignored her shocked expression as she hung up. She wore her hair in the same stern bun, but had more makeup on today, with a dark shade of plum on her lips. The makeup did little to soften her strong angular features.

"How'd you get in here?" She had a box of Kleenex next to her. She swiped one and blew her nose.

"I walked in. I apologize for the surprise, but after our last meeting, I got the impression you had more to tell me. Thought this would be the easiest way to chat without interruption."

"You're mistaken. I had nothing more to say." She gave me the once over. "What happened to your face?"

My concealer must be fading. "Had a run-in last night."

That placated her. "I should call security. No one's supposed to just waltz back here."

I crossed one leg over the other. I could have misjudged her wanting to be helpful, but I wasn't prepared to leave empty-handed. "You could. Of course then I'd have to tell everyone how Brooke had been screwing the boss and entertaining firm clients. Might not look great to have this shady firm on your resume."

The tissue she tossed missed her wastebasket. "What're you talking about?"

"Brooke Hanson and Dave Anderson lived in the same building. On the same floor in fact. Were you aware?"

Another tissue in her hand, she shook her head. "I thought she lived somewhere south."

She had said that. "Did you know about their affair?"

Her chair creaked as she straightened. "How would I know that?"

"The fact you're sitting in her very nice, spacious

corner office would be a clue. What kind of billing clerk gets this kind of setup?"

She didn't answer.

She wasn't giving me any signs that I was on the right track. Riling her up might get her talking. "One sleeping with the boss, I'd suspect. Didn't that bother you that your underling had, I assume since you moved, a much nicer office than you did?"

She shifted and her eyes flashed. "She didn't deserve or earn this spot. I'm the college graduate. The one that put in the long hours. When she was here, she barely did her job half the time."

My gut had been right about the affair. I empathized with her frustration. No one liked to be passed up because someone was better looking, or in Brooke's case, putting out. "Did you know about Brooke's unconventional tastes as well? Because when I say she'd entertained firm clients, I'm not talking about throwing a dinner party."

She sniffed. "Did I know that the law firm takes its clients out for leisure activities and dinner when they're in town? That's hardly uncommon in business."

"Again, not talking dinner here. Did you entertain those clients, too?"

"Please." Her tone was matter-of-fact. "I don't have time to go out after work. I have a child at home." Rachel lifted her chin.

With no family pictures on her desk, I hadn't realized. "I'm sure you don't want to rock the boat, but anything you can tell me helps the family."

She met my gaze and grabbed another tissue. "Allergies." She dabbed at her nose. "The entertaining is not what you think."

"Enlighten me."

Rachel picked up a pen and tapped it on her desktop. "We handle a lot of foreign clients. When they're in town for an arbitration or trial, there's often a lag time when they're stuck in the city. With the attorney busy working on the case, Brooke would arrange to have them taken to dinner and a show."

A show was one way to describe it, I guess. "I've been in Brooke's apartment. Eating was the least of what they did there. Which clients did she handle?"

"I wasn't privy to her personal life, but she entertained those high touch clients who wanted special attention."

High touch was accurate. "When those clients wanted more 'special attention' as you say, which I'm going to call sex, were other people involved with that? Perhaps Jay Nightingale?"

She dropped her pen. "Really, Ms. Pruett. What's been happening is quite innocent. I can show you the restaurant receipts if you'd like."

I waved her off. "Everyone eats. They could be doing stuff after."

"Not that I've been aware of."

"Okay—but you were aware of Jay Nightingale being an associate of Brooke's."

"Where'd you get that idea?"

"C'mon Rachel. If you saw the receipts, then you saw who was with who and when."

The way she checked her hair and dabbed her nose, she looked to be buying time and thinking about what she wanted to divulge. "Rumor had it that some clients preferred the company of men."

That matched what Kyle had said. "I'm assuming

Brooke and Nightingale decided how to coordinate that?"

"I wouldn't know."

It made sense, and would explain their unique communication, although I didn't understand why they were so secretive and all cloak and dagger with their eye contact and touching the table to meet outside. I also had a hard time believing Dave Anderson would be okay with Brooke giving those clients *special attention*. "The Anderson angle confuses me. If he and Brooke were a couple, wouldn't that get messy if she had sex with clients? Didn't he mind sharing?"

She licked her lips. "You're asking questions I don't have answers to, Ms. Pruett. My boss's opinion on his lover had nothing to do with me."

She'd confirmed the affair and Brooke's connection to Nightingale. She could be playing along. Her obvious dislike of Brooke made me think she enjoyed showing her in a bad light. But none of what she said was moving me closer to finding Anderson's motivation. Or proof he had killed Brooke or Nightingale for that matter.

I had to get more out of Rachel. "I understand your hesitation. He's your boss, but at this point, it'll come out eventually."

Rachel stood; her chair rolled back. "I've told you all I know. Please go now."

By standing, I'm sure she expected me to take the hint. I leaned back in the chair. "Here's the thing. You make it sound innocent and it wasn't. Here's how it's going to go down. The minute I leave, I'm calling a friend at the police station to tell him about this prostitution thing you have going on here."

"Prostitution?" Rachel's eyes widened.

"I'll also tell him I have proof because I have someone who would be happy to attest to being hired by the
firm and asked to perform sexual acts."

"That would be a lie."

"I don't see it that way. Even if I'm completely off-
base, you can answer questions from the cops instead
of me, who is only trying to help a grieving mother."

Rachel sat back down and picked up the pen again,
tapping it on the desk, perhaps weighing whether I was
serious or not. She bit her lower lip.

I pressed. "How much is Anderson involved when
these clients come into town?"

"I don't want any trouble from you or my boss. Obviously, Brooke wouldn't have known who to arrange
for without being told who was here. If she or her associate were doing anything with those clients, I don't
believe he condoned any of it. That would have been
Brooke's doing."

No way Anderson was innocent. "He clearly knew,
whether he approved or not."

"I can't say what he did or didn't know."

She wasn't helping me with motive. How could he
have been jealous about Brooke's activities if he sent
those men her direction? "Did he try to get her to stop
with the clients at any point and she wouldn't?"

"No idea."

"Was Mr. Anderson in love with Brooke?"

Her face turned deep pink. She didn't answer. Her
phone buzzed and she picked up.

"You got a minute?" a man's voice said as clear as
if she'd had him on intercom.

Her voice lightened. "Yes, I'll be right in."

"Or I could come to you?" He sounded like Dave Anderson.

"No, no. I'll finish up and be right there."

Rachel straightened a pile of paperwork on her desk. "I've answered your questions. You must go." She pulled open a drawer and grabbed a fresh stick of gum and popped it in her mouth. She and the bartender had a thing for gum. I didn't get the attraction.

"Is he trying to get you to take Brooke's place in every aspect?"

A wry grin covered her face. "That will never happen." The resentment I'd heard in her voice in our first meeting had returned.

"You do know what he's into." It was a statement; not a question.

She drew in a breath and let it out slowly realizing she'd been caught.

She could stonewall all she wanted. I wasn't leaving yet. "The truth will come out."

"He can be into whatever he'd like. I'm not Brooke."

Not every woman was keen on the idea of having a whip in bed with them. Sitting in Brooke's office had cost her. Even if Rachel didn't give in on the sexual role play Anderson and Brooke may have had, she was at his disposal. Which begged a question.

"I know Anderson is married." Rachel hadn't made a move for the door. "Did Brooke ever threaten to tell his wife?"

She was rigid. "Brooke liked control."

That sounded like a yes. "Why didn't he fire her if their relationship had turned?"

"I'm sure he wanted to," she retorted. "Rumor has it she demanded higher raises, more cuts of the pie.

However, if he'd tried, she would have made good on her threats to his wife and..." she stopped short.

I could guess how it ended. "And proceed to talk about the firm's activities, sparking an investigation."

She looked away. "It would have ruined everything Mr. Anderson worked for. It was Brooke that made it into something it wasn't—not Mr. Anderson."

Getting her angry at Brooke had her talking even if she had a way of not being specific. Years of being around lawyers, no doubt. "Do you think Brooke would have followed through?"

"I don't know."

I thought back to my conversation with Hannah. "Is it possible that he was the one in control? I have info that Brooke tried to get out and he wouldn't let her. She could have tried to leverage herself away from him. After all he'd invested in her, could he have been angry enough to kill her?"

Rachel's head snapped back. "Kill Brooke? Is that what you think? There's no way."

Her strong reaction prompted one of my dad's old sayings. *Thou doth protest too much.* "Are you protecting him?"

"No."

"Then how can you be sure?"

She rounded her desk and looked me square in the eye. "Because I was with him that night."

Her stiff body language suggested she wanted to drive that point home. "Seriously?"

"Yes. Dave and I were at a restaurant across town talking about employee benefits."

Dave now. What happened to Mr. Anderson? "What restaurant?"

"The Chop House. And in answer to your question, being a stupid male, he probably did love her at one point. Not that it mattered. After a while, everyone caught on that Brooke was unattainable."

Rachel's phone buzzed. She hit the button. "I'm on my way." Her voice was light again.

"Good," Anderson said.

Despite the lilt in her voice, Rachel's eyes were tired, and that had little to do with her allergies. Having to be her boss's new sexual conquest might make her weary, whether she'd admit that or not. My guess—she hadn't bet on any of this when she itched for Brooke's office. I felt sorry for Anderson's wife and, despite her rough edges, for Rachel.

"Woman to woman," I said, after she hung up, "you don't have to do this. You could bring these bastards down. Sue them for everything they're worth. You'd win."

"Or lose everything I've worked for. What then?" That fear kept her in the cycle.

Rachel could quit, but people did all kinds of things to keep the money rolling in when they had kids. That truth hit close to home. She'd helped me untangle the picture of what Brooke had been doing. I wasn't fully convinced she'd told me the whole truth. Discussing employee benefits at a restaurant across town sounded too convenient. If Anderson murdered Brooke because he didn't want firm secrets out, and Rachel knew, she may not see any way out for herself.

"If it wasn't Anderson, who else would have wanted her dead?" I asked.

She shook her head and sniffed. "Don't know and

don't want to know. I'm alive. Brooke and Mr. Night-ingale are not. I'd like to be kept out of it."

I nodded. "Understood."

Rachel stayed in her office and I walked myself to the elevator.

Once outside, the gunship gray sky hung heavy with dark clouds. I ducked into my car feeling naïve to the ways of big business. I didn't realize obtaining international clients would require special services to lure them in and keep them happy. Tropical island junkets would've been enough for me.

One thing still bothered me though. While Rachel suggested Brooke was blackmailing Dave Anderson, I didn't have physical proof of that. Brooke must have had something she was lording over Anderson—that could be pictures, or even video tapes. Is that why her place had been gone through? Was Anderson search-ing for that evidence that could destroy him? I needed to get back to Brooke's place and scour every inch this time.

First, I wanted to check on Amanda. My phone showed no calls, texts or Facebook messages. A sud-den wave of nausea swept through me. Both from stress and because I'd pushed too hard. Sweat seeped through my jacket. I'd done more than I should have, but until Amanda's safety was certain, I couldn't rest.

On my cell, I pulled up her name again. I'd missed that she had an Instagram account. I scanned her posts for any clues. One picture three months old was of Al-berta Park. I'd played there as a kid and took Mitz sev-eral times to play on the green play structure that was the center of her photo. But it was Amanda's hashtags that gave away where she lived. #lovemypark #rightnextdoor #playtime #summerfun. Google Maps gave me a view of the area near Killingsworth and the park.

Three homes had cars in their driveway. I didn't know how long ago Google had taken the images, or whether I was onto anything, but I jotted the license plate numbers down. I logged into a website linked to the Department of Motor Vehicles. Five minutes of punching in the various plates and a Visa number later, I had Amanda's location.

Once I confirmed she was safe, I had some questions for her. If she'd been holding out on me, I needed to know why.

TWENTY-SEVEN

AMANDA LIVED A mile from the Washington state line, near the Portland International Raceway and an elite golf course. Dad had taken me to a Grand Prix race at the track once when I was about ten, but he detested golf—something about wasting time chasing a white ball with a stick. Despite the two popular destinations nearby, topless bars, pawn shops and repair garages anchored the business community.

The hub was surrounded by old homes built in the 1930s and '40s. Manicured lawns, pastel siding, and white picket fences resided between homes with dead grass, chipping paint, and assorted car parts in the front yard.

I parked in front of Amanda's two-story bungalow and next to the Honda Civic that helped me find her. Although the light-blue house paint needed a fresh coat, an artistic and colorful rock garden made up her front yard. A Spiderman skateboard rested near the front steps. Red, orange and pink chrysanthemums bloomed in pots near the front door. I rang the bell and waited. After the second ring, noises came from inside the house.

"Amanda, it's Kelly Pruett. You spoke with me at the Limbo." The noises stopped. "I know you're home." I raised my voice loud enough for her to hear and inspected the peephole to see if she was looking out. I couldn't tell.

A little boy laughed.

"I'm not leaving until we talk." I crossed my arms over my chest to show I meant business if she was watching.

A minute passed before Amanda finally answered, the crease in her forehead saying she wasn't happy to see me. "What do you want?"

"To make sure you're okay. Where have you been the last couple of days?"

"You following me?" Her cheeks colored.

"No. I tried to catch up with you at the Limbo. When they said you didn't show, I was concerned."

Amanda scanned the road behind me, fear flashing in her eyes. She flung the door open. "Get in here, before someone sees you."

Her intensity made my heart pound. I stepped into a tidy country blue living room. A young boy curled in a chair was immersed in a handheld video game. The furniture had a yard sale vibe. Ruffled dust covers had exploded all over the room, consuming the sofa and chairs. It reminded me of my late grandmother's place.

"Randy, go play while I visit," Amanda said to the child. "But don't go outside that fence, got it?"

"Yes, Mom." The boy jumped up, dropping the game on the chair cushion, and darted out of the room. The distinct smack of a back door said we were alone.

"You have two minutes," she said to me.

I frowned. "I sent you a Facebook message, left you a voicemail and texted. If you'd answered any of them, I wouldn't be here."

"I didn't open them."

Facebook, I could buy. Not the rest. "Why not?"

"I expected you to get the hint and leave me alone."

"You're the one that sought me out to tell me about Brooke and Nightingale in the first place. Why avoid me now? And why did you lie to me?"

Her eyes widened. "About what?"

"I saw Derek's statement in the police file about someone going out after Brooke. Then he changed his mind. When I asked him why, he said you'd told him he was mistaken. That's not what you told me. Which one is it? Did someone follow Brooke out or not?"

Amanda pursed her lips and her hands shook. "I should've never gotten involved."

"But you did." What had happened to freak her out?

She splayed her hands and then curled them into fists a couple of times to dispel tension in them. "I have a son to protect."

"Protect from what?"

She hung her head.

"I might be able to help if you'd tell me what you're afraid of," I said.

"I can't."

"You have to trust someone. If for no other reason than if something happened to you and your son, I'd at least know where to begin."

She shifted in her chair, the idea of that clearly making her uneasy. Her eyes darted around the room.

"Think of your sister. Remember, that's why you talked to me in the first place. You wanted to help Brooke's family understand what happened."

"It was me," she blurted. "I followed Brooke out."

I stared at her, stunned, and let out a heavy sigh. "Let's sit down."

She nodded and I followed her into the living room where I took the armchair and Amanda lowered herself onto the opposing couch.

I gathered my thoughts. "You're the person that Derek was talking about?"

"Yes." Her gaze locked onto the floor.

"Why did he phrase it as if it was some random person?"

"Who knows why Derek does anything." Amanda wrung her hands. "I was concerned that he'd involved me at all. I didn't want to get questioned by the police."

"That's why he changed his story?"

"Yes. I told him if he didn't tell the officer my name, it didn't matter, but he called to change his story anyway."

I tucked my leg under me. This might take a while. "What happened after he walked Brooke out?"

"Derek came back in and I saw that Brooke had left a scarf at her table. I went out to give it to her, but she was calling after somebody."

Looking for confirmation, I said, "Was she yelling for Hannah?"

"That sounds right. I didn't see anybody out ahead of her though. Anyway, I came back inside and Derek clocked out."

One mystery solved, but… "Wait. What did you say about Derek?"

"He left."

"He went on break?"

"No. Another bartender finished out the night."

Derek's lying never stopped. "Why didn't you mention that before?"

"Slipped my mind, I guess. Derek often didn't finish shifts. It wasn't unusual."

Except that night, the woman he'd kicked out ended up dead. If it was no big deal, then Derek should have put it in his statement. Unless he didn't want to implicate himself. "I'm missing something. You went outside and Brooke is calling someone's name and you came right back in without giving her the scarf? You didn't see anyone else out there?"

Amanda's body tensed. "No."

I didn't believe that. "Amanda, the truth. Please."

She sighed and wrung her hands again. "A guy stepped out from a doorway on the side of the building and grabbed her by the arm."

My pulsed quickened. I had confirmation that Brooke stopping wasn't voluntary. "Was it Nightingale?"

"No." She shifted in her seat.

I leaned in. "Who, Amanda?"

She shook her head.

"I'm not leaving until I know."

She closed her eyes and stiffened. "The man with the pinky ring."

My heart raced. "Are you sure?"

"Positive."

I pulled up the law firm website and brought up his picture. "Is this him?"

She nodded and shuddered. "Who is he?"

"Dave Anderson, Brooke's boss." Son of a bitch. "So he stops her and they talk?"

She shifted again. "They did more than talk. He was screaming at her."

"What about?" Excitement rushed through me, wanting to hear the motive.

"He kept saying he couldn't believe she wanted to destroy him. She denied it, but he didn't believe her. When she broke free of him, she ran. I hid in the bar's doorway and watched until she disappeared."

"Any idea what he was referring to?"

"No."

That's not what I wanted to hear. "How far were you from them?"

"Barely close enough to make out what I did of their conversation."

"Did Anderson follow her?"

"I assumed so because he stepped out of his spot and went the same direction. I didn't hang out and watch."

Assuming wasn't what I wanted to hear either. "Did he chase after her?"

"No." She brushed her hand on her chin. "He was messing with his coat at first. He wore one of those long trench coats and he popped up the collar and walked her direction."

Despite Amanda not seeing it, he certainly could have caught up with Brooke. The tracks where she died were ten blocks away. But I was confused. "What are you so afraid of then? You'd seen him before with Brooke inside the bar, right? That's how you knew who he was in the first place…"

"Yes. Of course. But I'd never seen him fight with her or the extent of his rage. And he turned and saw me as I went back into the bar, which makes me a witness."

I moved, causing a sharp pain in my ribs. I winced.

"A witness to what? You didn't see him kill Brooke, right?"

"No, but who else would have? He was so furious when they were arguing, and he was the last one with her."

Amanda and I had the same theories, but I needed more concrete proof.

She tilted her head, noticing me for the first time. "What happened to your face?"

I grimaced. "I was attacked in my office last night." Not wanting to freak her out more, I held back on who I believed it had been. "Why didn't you tell me this at the Limbo? You were so cryptic. You even told me the guy with the pinky ring wasn't even there at the bar that night. Why all this *feeling* crap?"

"I didn't want to be directly linked. Something did happen to Brooke. I hoped if I got you pointed in the right direction, you'd discover the rest. Brooke and Mr. Nightingale did know each other, I was certain of that."

"And you were right." It would have been nice to have known up front about the rest of it. I was starting to need some pain medication and feeling a little cranky. "I still don't get why you didn't respond to my messages today."

"Right after we spoke that night, I got a phone call telling me to keep my mouth shut. If Randy answers, whoever it is hangs up."

"A man's voice?"

"I think so."

Dave Anderson wanted us both to leave what happened to Brooke alone. "I had some prank calls myself that originated from Brooke's place. I think your instincts to be concerned are right on."

She nodded again. "I want my life back. That's why I avoided you."

Touching my lip, I couldn't blame her. "It might be a good idea for you to get out of town for a few days, at least until Brooke and Nightingale's killer is in jail."

"I'm ahead of you. We're leaving this afternoon."

A bag was leaning against the dining table. I thought of the relatives I'd seen listed for Amanda. She was either headed for Idaho or Colorado. Both were a good distance away. I stood to go and she walked me to the door when my phone rang. It was Kyle. His voice sounded tight. "What's going on?"

"They've arrested Georgette," he said.

Dread marched across my skin. "For what?"

"Jay Nightingale's murder. They found her fingerprint on the front door."

"How is that possible?"

"I don't have the details yet," he said. "Where are you?"

"At Amanda Dixon's. My source from the Limbo. I'll be leaving soon. Can I get in to see Georgette?"

"I'll arrange it and pick you up at your place in a couple of hours."

I clicked off and locked eyes with Amanda. "They've arrested my client for Nightingale's murder."

"Wow. Did she do it?"

I didn't want to believe so. "I'll need to see what they have before I decide. But this case keeps getting weirder and weirder. Why don't you get on the road sooner rather than later."

She nodded and crossed to the back door, calling for Randy. He didn't answer or come running.

"Randy," she screamed.

He came hopping up the steps. Amanda visibly relaxed. I let out my held breath.

"Get whatever you're taking to Grandma's together. We're leaving." He disappeared down the hall to his bedroom. "He's a good kid," she said.

An image of Mitz filled my head. "He seems like it. I have a daughter too." A daughter I'd give anything to hug in that moment.

Randy trotted out from the bedroom. I waited until they were in their car and trailed them to the Interstate and north a few miles. The thought of them being followed like I'd been set me on edge. I scanned the street for anything suspicious. Amanda had concerned Dave Anderson enough to get threatening phone calls. If he learned I'd been asking her more questions, that might put a bigger target on her back. I didn't want anything happening to Amanda or her son on my head.

Amanda kept on and I took my exit for home. My hands clenched the steering wheel, igniting a burning sensation in my shoulders. Being injured was really getting on my nerves. Literally. I stretched my neck from side to side, trying to relax. My bruised ribs ached instead. I needed the time before Kyle arrived to take some pain medicine and to think.

Dave Anderson and Brooke might have had a lovers' quarrel, or a full-on blowout. Whatever the topic, it had driven him out on a Saturday night to ambush his lover. Why was Rachel covering for Anderson? If Amanda could put him at the Limbo shortly before Brooke's death, he couldn't be across town having dinner. Rachel would do anything to protect her job.

Derek's omission that he'd left early was disconcerting. Or did it matter? Amanda didn't say anything about seeing him outside with Brooke. And I had the same problem with him as I did Hannah. Why would Nightingale protect either of them if they were involved in Brooke dying?

But Georgette's arrest made me nauseous. I was so gung-ho to believe that Anderson was Nightingale's killer. What if he and Brooke's death weren't connected? What if it was a mother's rage that had done him in?

I'd almost made it home when my phone rang. I didn't recognize the number.

"Ms. Pruett?" a man said when I answered.

"Yes."

"This is Chris Foley. The MAX operator. There's something I haven't told you."

TWENTY-EIGHT

I stood on Chris Foley's country porch and rang his doorbell. With my bruised face and deodorant failing, I couldn't look—or smell—appealing. He didn't seem to notice when he answered, fully dressed this time and appearing to have made it to the other side of that cold he'd been battling. He invited me in.

The living room décor belonged in a log cabin. A black woodstove blazed, and a couple of worn recliners were stationed in front of a 40-inch TV screen.

"Thank you for coming back." He gestured me toward a red plaid couch as he lowered himself into a leather recliner adjacent to it. "I should've been up front with you the first time. I hope you understand I didn't want to get into trouble."

I sat down and made a face which had more to do with my ribs than what he'd said. "Why would you get into trouble?"

He bounced the heel of one foot on the ground. "I heard on the radio a bit ago they arrested that girl's mom for murdering Jay Nightingale."

"Georgette. Yes. I just found out about that," I said, surprised it'd already made the news. But it was newsworthy. With a bad case of tunnel vision, I didn't always think of how the world's wheels spun outside my own hamster cage.

"If I had come clean, it might not have come to that." Mr. Foley hoisted himself up and paced.

Anxiety built in my chest. "Come to what?"

"Her killing that guy. I mean, I don't think he did anything wrong. If she knew the whole story...."

The whole story would be nice for a change. "Let's start at the beginning."

He ran his hand over his thinning hair and stopped in the middle of the room. "When I saw that Nightingale fellow on the corner—after I'd stopped the train—he wasn't alone. At least I don't think he was. See, that's why I hadn't said anything before."

I leaned forward. "Walk me through what you saw."

"Shit." He paced again.

"Had it been raining?"

He shook his head.

"Were you at a bad angle when you first saw Nightingale?"

"No."

He wasn't giving me much. "Whatever it is, it was important enough for you to have me drive all the way out here. Tell me why." A snarky tone had crept into my voice. Pain had a way of doing that to me. And I was tired of getting the run around.

He scrunched his face like he'd swallowed nasty medicine. "I'd been drinking, okay? I hadn't felt good. My throat had been bothering me all week so my thermos was filled with hot tea and whiskey that night. Working the night shift can be a real bitch. I did what I needed to get through it, you know?" The words came out like a torrent.

The steaming mug on the end table and the faint

scent of whiskey said they weren't limited to when he didn't feel good. "I'm not judging."

He ran the palm of his hand over his head again and held the back of his neck before dropping into the chair next to his mug. "It's not like I'm driving a car. The tracks are laid out, and—shit."

"Let's say you did see someone talking to Nightingale. Describe that person to me."

"He was wearing a long raincoat, with the collar up."

I scooted my butt to the edge of the sofa. Amanda had Anderson wearing a raincoat that night. "Short and stocky?"

"Not really. That Nightingale fellow stood about my height. The person I saw came up to about his shoulder and thinner."

Thin didn't fit Anderson. It might have been hard to tell with him wearing a raincoat. Anderson's picture was on my phone and I showed it to Mr. Foley. "Is this who you might have seen?"

He squinted at the screen. "It happened so fast; I could've imagined it. I'm not sure."

One of those hot toddies would be nice about now. "Let's go back to when you got off the train. You'd said Nightingale was about to run off."

"Right. That's why I'm confused. I see Nightingale, I think he's with another witness who's wearing a long raincoat. I glanced away to check on the victim, and suddenly he's by himself."

"The other person disappeared?" Wouldn't he have seen the tail-end of someone if they were running away?

"Exactly. One minute I see two people, and then it's

only Nightingale." Mr. Foley scratched at his cheek and tilted his head in confusion.

"What did he say when you got to him?"

"I asked him where the other person had gone off to. He says, what are you talking about? I said, you were talking to someone. He says I'm seeing things."

"How far away were you?"

"Fifty feet or so. But see, I got distracted when I checked on the young woman. Because I'd been drinking, I thought he could be telling the truth and it got me off kilter. I'd looked around at that point and didn't see anyone else on the streets." He dropped his chin to his chest. "I shouldn't have been drinking the whiskey."

You think? "Did you push him on it? See if he was lying?"

He nodded. "Until he started acting cagey and accused me of being drunk. Then he repeated what I'd said before. That he'd called out to her. He muttered 'Goddamn her' more than a few times."

The previous theory that I'd shared with Kyle popped into mind. "Are you sure he didn't say 'Goddamn him'?"

He shook his head. "That I felt certain about. He directed the comments at that poor woman, as if she'd died to ruin his day. Perturbed me at the time, but trauma does affect people different."

If Mr. Foley was as drunk as he indicated, how could he truly be certain about what he'd heard? And I had to concede, what he'd seen… "Why were you so concerned about telling the police about the potential second witness?"

He shifted in his seat. "Because I *had* been drinking. If my bosses suspected that, I'd be screwed."

"You believe Mr. Nightingale knew that? Saying someone is drunk can be a way to deflect the conversation."

"Couldn't afford to find out. Because he jumped right to that, I thought he smelled the alcohol. I backed away and let the authorities take over. Didn't want to have to pee in a cup."

"Don't they want that after an accident."

"Only when there's a question of operator error. Her falling onto the rails had nothing to do with my operation of the train." He looked away, trying to control his emotions.

"Of course not."

He sniffed. "If they had taken me in and I failed, I'd have lost my job. My pension. I'm set to retire…."

I understood the mentality, but it sure sucked for Georgette who wanted closure. My body hurt all over. I wanted to go home and take some pain meds. "Can you remember anything else about who you saw with Nightingale?"

He shook his head. "Just the long coat." He took a long drink of the steaming mug. "You going to tell my boss?"

"I'll have to update the police. I can't promise what will happen after that," I said, hoping he hadn't thought I could protect him.

He took another drink. "I understand. Just couldn't live with myself anymore. Especially with that mom being arrested. Broke my heart." He jutted his chin out. "Whatever happens, happens."

He didn't have to tell me any of this. He was braver than most would be with the potential of losing everything they worked for. While I didn't condone his drinking on the job, I felt for him. "It might not matter with Nightingale dead."

"There's no one to point the finger at me for the drinking, but I didn't report my suspicion of a second witness right away. That won't go over well with the powers that be."

I thanked Chris Foley and left him with his hot toddy to get home to meet Kyle. After seeing Amanda, I was certain Anderson pulled Brooke aside that night. A more confident I.D. from Mr. Foley that Anderson was the one standing next to Nightingale would have been nice. Even with it, I'd need more concrete proof putting him at the scene. Perhaps finding what Brooke was using to blackmail him could offer enough circumstantial evidence given the other piece. I needed to find it.

My brain was mush for the second half of the drive. The pain in my ribs radiating into my low back had me shifting every which way to get comfortable. I needed my painkillers. But when I pulled into my driveway, Jeff was waiting.

TWENTY-NINE

"Wow." JEFF SAID, when I levered myself out of my car. I must have looked worse than last night, now that the bruising had time to set in. "We need to talk."

This wasn't the right time, but I didn't argue. Jeff followed me inside and headed straight for the freezer. Floyd greeted us in the kitchen and I loved him up while Jeff grabbed a package of peas. "Put this on your lip. It looks horrible," he said.

Tell me how you really feel. I took a pain pill and pressed the package to my mouth. "Thanks. What did you want to talk about?"

He didn't make eye contact. "Are you going to be okay?"

"I know how a punching bag might feel after a workout, if that's what you're asking."

He frowned. "Why are you being glib?"

"It keeps me from coming unglued." It wasn't a fact I'd intended to share, but it slipped out. The one thing I'd always been good at was stuffing down my emotions. This case had stirred them all up.

"Then why do this at all?"

"We've been over this before." Okay, not the whole concept of my physical jeopardy. When I decided to honor my dad's request to help Georgette, being a target had not been in the plans. I stretched to relieve tension in my shoulders, craving a nap I couldn't have since Kyle would be there soon.

It might have been the way I winced at almost every move, but Jeff softened. He came over and wrapped an arm around my shoulders. I stood there, one hand holding frozen peas to my face, the other pinned against my side. It was easy to let him comfort me. I just didn't want that anymore.

He squeezed me tighter. I yelped.

"Sorry." He let go.

I cleared my throat. "Did you come by just to see if I was okay?"

He tensed and I sensed something bad. "I want full custody of Mitz."

My muscles pinched up my spine making my head hurt. Too much. I'd hit my limit. "That's bullshit," I said with a detached calm. "You're upset because you saw me with another man and because of these injuries. Don't play games like this. Not with our daughter."

"You're moving on and dating. You're taking on more in-depth cases, with way more danger than I'm comfortable with. You can't guarantee it will never happen again as long as you're a P.I. Mitz doesn't need to see that. I can offer a more stable environment."

"Like you'll never date or work again?"

"You know what I mean."

I did. With the Hanson matter amping up, Mitz was safer with Jeff. But I didn't intend to lose custody of my daughter. "This is a long conversation we need to have and not something to be acted on with emotion. It would only upset Mitz and everything we've worked for to keep continuity. At this moment, I'm not up for that discussion. Let's set up a meeting to talk about my work, your work and Mitz." We'd never approached our marriage or our parenting with that much formality. As I was coming out of my grief and entering new territory, it was time we did.

He cocked his head. "When will that be, exactly?"

"Give me some dates when you're available and I'll do the same. We can get this to happen in the next two weeks. Will that work?"

He nodded.

The doorbell rang. Thank God. "I'm getting to the end of this. Please don't do anything until we can have that meeting."

"Fine."

"Good," I said. "That's going to be Kyle."

"I'll wait for you to open the door and make sure." He put his hands on his hips and stood firm.

I attempted to march to the entry. My expression dropped as I opened the door. "Arlene, this isn't a good time."

She stepped around me. "Hi Darling," she said to Jeff. "I was looking for you. The kitchen spigot is dripping." Only then did Arlene really look at me. "What happened to your face?"

"I was attacked in my office. You should see the other guy."

"Oh Kelly," she said, shaking her head. "I warned you about the dangers of the job. The dangers your dad wanted you not to face."

"Please Arlene." The pain meds had not kicked in yet, and *I told you so* was the last thing I wanted to hear.

"You need to be more careful if you're going to continue this."

Agreed. "Thanks, but I'm fine."

"I'm just saying…"

"I understand."

"Okay, girls," Jeff said.

"Don't *girl* me," Arlene and I snapped back at the same time. I glanced at her, she at me. Had we ever agreed on anything? No. She cracked first and we both ended up laughing until my ribs ached.

"Well, thank you both for dropping by. Jeff was heading out and sounds like you need a faucet looked at."

"There's no hurry. Tell us more about the investigation," she said.

The doorbell rang. Saved by the bell again before I could answer. I opened the front door and Kyle walked in, dressed in button-fly jeans and a blue plaid flannel shirt over a black T-shirt. He gave me a gentle hug. When he let go, I introduced him to Arlene.

"Nice to meet you, ma'am." Kyle nodded at her and extended his hand to Jeff who shook it. "Nice seeing you again." He turned to me. "I got you in to see Georgette, but it's a short window."

I grabbed my jacket from the closet by the door and slipped it on. "If you wouldn't mind, could you give Floyd a break before seeing yourselves out?"

Jeff nodded and Arlene didn't say a word. For the first time in my life, I'd left her speechless.

WE TOOK KYLE'S SUV. My body had protested during the climb in, but the view was spectacular. In my Spitfire, I sat below most other cars' window-lines. I zipped here, zipped there, and flinched when driving past semis praying they wouldn't mistake me for a speedbump. Here, I could see it all and look down on the Spitfires of the world. When Kyle wanted to change lanes, people fell back and let him in. The Portland P.D. sticker on his bumper could've had something to do with that.

"You socialize with your exes often?" Kyle asked.

I sensed that was coming. "Arlene lives next door to me and she takes care of Mitz if I'm running late. Do they show up unannounced? More often since Georgette hired me. Truth is, Arlene and Jeff have been a part of my life since I was a child." I thought of the concern Arlene had shown when she saw my face. My heart squeezed. "Whether I've embraced it or not, Arlene tried to be a mother to me after my mom died. And Jeff and I had been off and on since I was a teenager. Because we have a daughter, they'll always be a part of me. Like you said, it's more complicated when kids are involved." The other part I hadn't admitted was that I'm not sure I'd want it any other way. Next to my sweet Mitz, they were the only family I had in this world. Argumentative. Judgmental. Over-bearing. Often complicated. And mine. Although Jeff was on my list for pulling the custody crap, one way or another we would find a way to work together for Mitz's sake. We had to. And I may not have helped my own cause over this past year. Perhaps instead of always pushing, I should be pulling them closer. Despite my hurt with Jeff. Something else to contemplate after this case.

Kyle nodded.

"Tell me more about Georgette. They seriously found a fingerprint? I can't envision her being strong enough to kill Nightingale."

"On the doorknob. You'd be surprised. Revenge and rage can make a person do things you'd never expect."

"I suppose." My dad wouldn't knowingly ask me

to help someone he thought would cross that line. But anyone could be driven over the edge. If someone hurt Mitz, every ounce of my logic and self-control would dissipate. I kneaded my hands. "There has to be an explanation for that print."

"For her sake, I hope so. And about that glove they found in Nightingale's bedroom. It's a man's small and has Nightingale's blood on the outside; trace amounts of someone else's were on the inside."

That information sank in. "The killer cut himself?"

"That's the theory. It's not uncommon for a killer using a household knife to get cut during the act."

"But no weapon has been found?"

"Correct, but the wounds are consistent with that kind of weapon. Detective Richmond has run the results through the database and hasn't come up with a match."

"Georgette's hands don't have any cuts, that I've seen. I'm sure the detective has too. Why arrest her?" Had I seen a cut on Anderson's hand? With my focus on him twisting his pinky ring that day in the conference room, I couldn't remember.

"She refused to give a DNA sample. With her in custody, they can get it from her. If it is hers, they'll arraign her in 48 hours. If not, there's still the issue of the print."

Georgette hadn't mentioned the request when she'd gone for fingerprinting. "Then I'll find the evidence you'll need to arrest Dave Anderson long before any of that. It feels like the key to solving what happened to Brooke lies in solving Nightingale's murder. And I can't believe it was Georgette." I went on to update him that Amanda could I.D. Anderson fighting with Brooke outside the bar and that he followed her, and ended with

Mr. Foley's observation of someone standing next to Nightingale, skipping his drinking admission.

Kyle shook his head. "Would've been great to know about a second person that night."

"Agreed. But it supports my theory that if Anderson was involved, he'd have had the clout to ask Nightingale to stay behind. The decision to kill him to keep him quiet could have come later. Any chance you can get Anderson's DNA?"

"Unless there's probable cause, no." He gave me a sideways glance. "You grabbing it isn't admissible by the way."

He was already good at reading my mind—not sure if that was a good or bad thing. "I'll just feel better once I find something physical that ties Anderson to the scene, that's all. Or I'll take an admission."

He chuckled. "Right. That's not likely."

I nodded. "By the way, Rachel who works at the firm gave Anderson an alibi I haven't checked out yet. She says they were having dinner at the Chop House across town that night. Not sure how to confirm that information, but I need to."

"I might be able to help. The restaurant is in my patrol area. I can drop by and call in a favor."

I relaxed into the seat. "Thank you."

We made the rest of our drive with Kyle's Justin Timberlake CD playing in the background. Kyle kept time tapping his fingers on the steering wheel. My thoughts went to Georgette and her fingerprint found in Nightingale's apartment. Had she been there? If so, when? Despite not wanting it to be true, I prepared myself for the worst.

THIRTY

ALREADY THROUGH PROCESSING, Georgette was in a cell when we arrived. Kyle and I waited in an interrogation room until a guard brought her in. She wore an orange jumpsuit and her usually perfect auburn hair fell limp around her face. Tearstains streaked her makeup.

Deep set lines etched around her eyes and face had aged her. She looked tired—and desperate. Her face crumpled when she saw me. "Kelly, I didn't do it."

Without a second thought, I went over and gave her a hug, which she returned as if I was a lifeline that would keep her from drowning. Questions milled around in my head. I waited until I was settled again across from her at the worn gray metal table. "Were you really in his apartment?"

She sniffed back tears, her eyes darting between Kyle and me.

Her lack of a quick answer could have to do with the audience. "Kyle, do you mind giving us a minute?"

He brushed his hand on my shoulder as he stood. "Sure. You'll have eyes on you though." He pointed to the video camera in the ceiling corner.

"Thank you," I mouthed to him on his way out. After the door shut, I rested my elbows on the tabletop. "I need that answer."

She started to cry again. "I only went to talk to him." Of course she did. "When?"

"The day I came to your office." She wiped her face with the sleeve of her jumpsuit. "The police had released him from jail, letting him walk away, and I wanted my own answers."

"The fingerprint on the door is from when you saw him then?"

"Yes."

I leaned back in my chair. "Tell me what happened. The truth this time."

She had a distant look in her eyes. "He was pleasant at first when I arrived. I told him who I was and he invited me in and we chatted. He started his lies immediately."

"Lies?"

"How sorry he was about what had happened to Brooke. That he saw her drunk and stumbling around. I told him to stop lying. He knew more. Why wasn't he telling me? That's when it slipped that she'd been upset. How did he know that if he hadn't talked to her? I didn't let up until he snapped."

That didn't sound good. "Snapped?"

Her body stiffened. "He got this vicious look on his face. Said he could see why Brooke didn't talk much about her family. If they were all crazy like me, he'd stay away too. That Brooke's dominating ways obviously came from me. Which wasn't true. Brooke was strong-headed, but a good girl and she loved us. Then he told me I knew nothing about my daughter and that her life would shock the hell out of me."

He'd dropped the word dominating to elude to Brooke's activities. Brooke's life certainly had shocked. All of us. "Did he say anything else?"

"Not at that point."

"Why have you always thought he knew more? Did Brooke do something that made you believe she'd been lying?"

She lowered her head. "The day before she died, we had coffee. I hadn't seen her in a while and she looked terrible. Sad. Exhausted. She wouldn't say why. She got up to use the bathroom and left her phone behind and a text came in. There was no name on it, but it was unpleasant."

"How so?"

"It was threatening her. Saying she'd better not be serious, or she'd pay."

Did Anderson send that text because she wanted away from him? Finding Brooke's phone could answer so many questions. "Do you remember the number?"

"No, and there was no time to jot it down."

"Did you confront her when she came back to the table?"

"Not in so many words. I did ask her what was wrong."

"You didn't tell the police any of this?"

"I asked them to look into Nightingale. Like I told you from the beginning, the fact he happened to be there didn't make sense to me."

I nodded, feeling weary. Everyone had been hiding something. Is this what being a P.I. was—going from place to place and trying to figure out who was lying about what? Process serving was far more straightforward. "It would have been nice if you'd told me about that text and the meeting."

She looked away.

Georgette may have been wrong about Nightingale, but she'd been right to follow her instincts that something wasn't right with Brooke. While I could give her that, she'd been holding out on me this whole time, and despite her predicament, I was pissed. "Let me understand. When you came to hire me, you'd seen that text and you'd already talked with Nightingale. Yet you acted like your entire theory of him killing Brooke was a mother's intuition."

"Yes."

"Did you know what we'd find in the penthouse?"

"No. He only said she was no saint. I didn't believe that. I still can't believe I was such a horrible mother that my oldest daughter would do such things, but I guess...." Fresh tears streamed down her face.

My sympathy for her remained a no-show. "Why didn't you tell me everything up front?"

"He said if I spoke of our conversation or bothered him again, he'd make sure the world knew what a depraved and perverted piece of trash my daughter had been. That's when I came to see your father, and hired you. If you could prove Nightingale did it, then he wouldn't be able to intimidate his way out. No one would believe him if he was guilty."

Depraved and perverted were interesting word choices coming from him. He clearly wanted her to back down. That only explained our first meeting, however. "After he was murdered, you could have come clean."

"And risk you dropping the case because I'd lied to you? I couldn't."

I raised an eyebrow. "You're at risk of that now."

Georgette buried her head in her hands. "Please Kelly. You haven't uncovered the truth yet. Nightingale also said Brooke had a nasty habit of upsetting

people, and that's what had gotten her into trouble.
You need to find out who she'd upset."

"He didn't give names, I suppose?"

"No."

That would be too easy. "Did Brooke or Nightingale
mention Dave Anderson, Brooke's boss?"

She wiped her face with her hand. "No. Why?"

"I believe they were having an affair and she might
have been blackmailing him." I proceeded to give her
the Cliff Notes version of events, ending with my theory of Nightingale and Anderson knowing each other.

"I see." She closed her eyes. "You have to believe
me, that fingerprint in Nightingale's apartment was
from my visit before I hired you. I never went back to
see him. My not telling you of our meeting was out
of fear."

"I believe that, but you're going to need a lawyer if
they end up indicting you on that print."

"I know."

"If there's anything else you've been holding back,
you need to tell me now."

She stared at me, without blinking. Thinking.

"If I find out anything else..."

She started to cry before I could finish. Her shoulders shook.

Her response had anxiety marching across my skin.
"What is it?"

"Your father."

My stomach dropped. "What about him?"

Her mouth opened. She covered it with the palm of
her hand. She couldn't get the words out.

Did I want to know? "That day you came looking to
hire him. You never did answer how you knew him."

She straightened and clasped her hands together, finding her composure. Not looking at me. "He was an old and very good friend."

The letter that he'd left had told me that much and at the same time had told me nothing. Maybe it was the way she refused to make eye contact. Or the way she said very. Whatever *it* was, I fought the urge to sprint out of the room and keep myself in the dark. "Damn it, Georgette. Tell me."

She didn't.

"I quit. I won't be lied to anymore." I started to raise my hand to the guard.

"Don't." She looked at me wide-eyed, and pale. "He was the affair I told you about."

The information kicked me in the gut and sucked the air out of me. The room closed in on me and spun. It wasn't only an affair she'd told me about. It was an affair and a child. "When?" I managed while I did the math. I was thirty-two. Hannah was twenty-three. I would have been 9. My mom would have been alive. "More importantly, why?"

"Years ago, I hired Roger to find Brooke's birth parents. We were having problems with her at the time. She's always been rebellious. Chester was hard on her. They butted heads constantly. The agency had lost touch with the parents, so I asked for his help. I thought if she knew who she was, she'd feel better about herself."

"Did he find them?"

She shook her head. "But one thing led to another, and we…"

I raised my hand. I got the picture. "Were you in love?" I whispered.

"No," she said. "We were both going through a rough patch. We found comfort in each other, but I got pregnant."

My mom and dad always fought. Yet I couldn't think of any moments that would have caused him to run into someone else's arms. What did I know? Up until that moment I thought my dad was perfect. A person whose character had been worthy of being lived up to. So much that I'd taken this case to help Georgette without question. Everything I'd done since Georgette walked through that office door, from the moment he died, was to make him proud. I had been naïve. Had I lived with a stranger?

I straightened in my chair. "Did he know about Hannah?"

She wouldn't look at me. "He met her once when she was a baby and that was it. I wasn't going to leave Chester, and Roger wasn't going to leave your mother. After your mom died, we were in touch briefly. We agreed it was best to live separate lives and not introduce you girls."

"You said Hannah knows who her real father was though."

Georgette nodded.

I felt like an idiot being the last one to know. "What's her number?"

She gave it to me without protest. She must have known the day she hired me it was inevitable I'd find out. Had my father?

With a sudden need for fresh air, I signaled the officer on the other side of the glass to let me out.

"Will you be able to get me released?" Georgette asked, her eyes sunken.

I was numb. "Doubtful. From what I understand, they want your DNA to see if it matches the glove they found in Nightingale's place."

"It won't. You believe I'm innocent, don't you?"

"Of what? Murder or adultery?"

She winced. "I deserve that. You should have known the truth. I'm done with the lies."

I didn't know what to say or what to believe. "If the DNA isn't yours, that will go a long way in clearing you."

She searched my face. "Will you stay on the case?"

I wasn't sure why I would, or should. Even if the sample came back as no match, the fingerprint tied Georgette to the scene. She could be facing jail time. I might not get paid for the hours I'd already put into this case. But something had happened to Brooke. I'd been hired to find out what and my father had asked me to help Georgette, despite how I felt about the situation—which I couldn't get a read on. Perhaps more than anything, I wanted to know how this sordid story ended. "Yes."

I waved for the officer again, who let me out. An urgency to get this wrapped up pushed me and I was desperate to get out of there. I found Kyle talking to another cop near the elevator.

Back at his truck he said, "How'd it go in there?"

I placed my hand on the seat and he covered it with his. I let the warmth ground me. I wasn't ready to talk about the revelations of my father and Georgette with anyone. Even Kyle. "I'll be glad when the tests come back."

He nodded. "Where to now?"

"Home, please. I need to meet someone."

We rode in silence and I shot Hannah a text. "We need to talk. Pambiche's on Glisan at seven." From the time I told her I was a P.I., she had to know our connection. She'd fed me information piece by piece. I was done with her games. Time for a sisterly chat.

A few minutes later I got, "Sure."

I had a lot to think about with regards to my life, my half-sister, my father. I was beginning to grasp that I knew only the parts of his life that he wanted me to. Like the cases he kept to himself, there was much more to him than I realized. His love for me and his grand-daughter were not in question. And he'd left me his house and his business. But his legacy was not what I thought it was.

THIRTY-ONE

My new half-sister, Hannah, arrived at Pambiche before me. The dinner crowd filled the place and it buzzed with voices and laughter. She'd found a corner table and was nursing a margarita when I joined her.

Hannah and I sat eye to eye. I couldn't stop staring at her. The knowledge of who she was and the betrayal of my father had every nerve including those affected by my attack pinching my spine. How had I missed the resemblance between us? Had I not wanted to see?

"What happened to you?" Hannah stared at my puffy lip. Given the way she'd exited the last time I saw her, I expected more snark instead of her concerned tone.

I patted my lip with my fingertips. The swelling had come down. "The downside of being a P.I. Thanks for meeting. I didn't think you'd show."

She shrugged. "My mom's in jail for something she didn't do. Quickest way to get her out is to get the right person in." If she'd guessed that I knew about our connection, she didn't let on. That might be best.

I cocked my head. "I didn't get the impression you cared about your mom one way or another."

She didn't meet my gaze. "We have our issues and it's complicated. Doesn't mean I want her rotting in a cell."

Issues hardly described what I'd seen between them.

"Am I to believe you've had a change of heart and you're willing to help figure out what happened to Brooke?"

She rolled her eyes. "Not sure I care what you believe. My mom's innocent."

Hardly. "How do you know that?"

She swirled her index finger through the sweat on the margarita glass. "She gets mad at me for every little thing since I'm a walking disappointment. But it takes a lot to rile her up and even then, I've never seen her violent. Not like Brooke, who thrived on it."

"The BDSM stuff."

"Yeah. I always felt bad for the men in her life."

"Like the one you mentioned that she tormented?"

She nodded while taking a long drink of the margarita. "Him especially."

"You really don't have any idea who that guy was?"

"Never saw him. Remember, I wasn't invited to the penthouse." She drew in a breath.

Hannah may never get over that slight. "She never hinted at anyone?"

"I guess she mentioned a couple of times that she liked having her own personal errand boy. And he apparently was *naughty* quite a bit and needed punishing." She shook her head. "Just bizarre."

The waitress approached and took my drink order. I opted for a mojito and Hannah took another margarita.

"And the married guy?" I said once the waitress left. "Dave Anderson. Was he naughty too?"

"They all were in her book. At least he was rich and funded most everything through the firm. More recently, she'd started talking about getting out and dumping him. At least at one point. Like I'd mentioned, he wasn't too keen on that."

"You never said she wanted out of the lifestyle altogether."

"Thought that was implied. Wanting away from him, the lifestyle, sort of the same thing."

Not in my mind. I thought about the text Georgette saw. "You think he could have been angry enough to make her pay if she tried?"

"Who knows. Men are weird."

Some for sure. In this instance, Brooke stopping her activities could have presented a new issue for Anderson. The firm might lose clients if she refused to provide the services they'd grown accustomed too.

Hannah licked the salt off her drink.

Dad had loved the salt on a margarita. For the first time, I noticed the indent in her upper lip that was like his. She had his strong chin, too. I stared past her out the window, forcing myself not to compare. "Did Brooke ever say she was blackmailing Anderson?"

"No. Wouldn't put that past her though. When she was angry, watch out." Her tone suggested a little sister that had felt Brooke's wrath a time or two.

"I need proof. Any suggestions?"

"You checked her place?"

"Only once and her things looked gone through. Nothing jumped out at me as missing. I didn't know what I was looking for either."

"Pictures?" Hannah offered.

"I thought of that earlier."

"Or a contract?"

"What kind of contract?"

"I'm not saying there is one, but a dominatrix often has stuff in writing with the people they dominate."

"They do?"

"Yeah. Not with firm clients, but probably with her minions." She air-quoted the last word.

Kyle had suggested there would be an agreement; I didn't contemplate that being in writing. "If she wanted to quit, and Anderson wouldn't let her, she might use that contract to get out." I was thinking out loud. Would a lawyer be dumb enough to sign a document? If he had, that might be what he'd been looking for in Brooke's place.

Hannah drained her margarita as her next round arrived.

I stirred my drink. "I think he killed her." I scanned her face for any reaction.

She didn't give me one; only nodded. "It sure the hell wasn't me. I wasn't anywhere near those tracks."

"Given your earlier comments, you can't blame me. You never did answer why you hate her. Was she that bad?"

She took a long drink. "If I spent years in therapy, I'd say we both made the best of a shitty situation. We just handled it different because we were treated different. Being adopted, or chosen, she didn't have the whole *my mom had an affair* strike against her. I hated her for that." She held my gaze a little longer. Waiting for a reaction?

Once we went down that road, I might not get the information I needed or keep my emotions together. "How'd you end up in her apartment?"

"She felt sorry for me. When I left home, I had no place to go."

"Is that what setting you up with firm clients was all about? Feeling sorry?"

She tilted her head. "Probably. I got work at Casa Diablo. In the beginning, it was part-time and didn't pay much."

I spooned out a chunk of ice and crunched it, curious to know more about the firm entertainment. "How'd it work? The clients?"

"Rachel gave me the information of where to go and who to meet, and I did."

The margaritas had caught up to her. "You mean Brooke."

"No, some chick named Rachel. She's the one that coordinated and paid me."

My skin tingled. "That's not what you said before. You said Brooke did."

"At first before Rachel took over. Brooke didn't have time for such tasks. My sis liked to tell people what to do, in case you've missed that part."

Rachel had offered to show me receipts of dinners out with clients. She'd played dumb as to being involved. "Did Rachel entertain clients?"

"Think so. I've seen her around town with guys who look like they're from Japan or thereabouts. She's been to my bar a couple of times."

Rachel had also failed to mention that detail. It didn't surprise me that Anderson would have her doing things for him. He was a real piece of work. After our last meeting, I'd already figured she'd do most anything to keep her job. Saying no wouldn't be easy in her position. I'd seen for myself the control he had over her when he'd called her into his office. "What did you do with those clients?"

"Nothing shady. I'd take them to karaoke. Or dinner and the club or a comedy show. Sometimes out to listen to a band. It was all on the up and up."

That sounded hard to believe. "No sex with any of them?"

She shook her head. "Nope."

"Brooke did though?"

"In the beginning. Not towards the end. She'd wanted to get back to a simpler life. Buy a place in the country. She loved horses."

"I saw a picture of her on a horse at your mom's place."

"Yeah. Cowgirl Brooke. She even spent some time with a real cowboy to get her horse fix."

Cowboy? Had I missed someone in Brooke's mix of men? "Who was that?"

"Her landlord at the apartment complex."

The hairs on my arms stood up. The landlord that said he'd rarely talked to Brooke? The landlord who had Floyd a hundred yards from my car? "That's Luke. Did you ever meet him while you've been staying there?"

She shuddered. "God no. I kept out of sight. Brooke said he might hound me about her if he thought we were related. He had a thing for her and it wasn't mutual. He was supposedly nice enough, but odd."

"Didn't you just say she liked the cowboy?"

"No. I said she liked horses."

"At the penthouse you said she liked someone who was more normal. Is that the cowboy, or I mean landlord?"

"Yes. What I actually said was there was one man she tried to be normal with. In Brooke's world, that's not the same as liking—or at least in the way most people think about it. If you didn't have money, she wasn't interested. That didn't stop him. According to Brooke, he held out hope."

My heart felt like I'd finished a marathon and I had to go. Luke *had* spent quality time with Brooke. Why did he lie to me?

I had one last item to discuss. "I know, by the way." It's all I could manage to get out.

She tilted her head. "About?"

I didn't answer.

She swished the margarita around. "How?"

"Your mom told me."

She bobbed her head. "If it makes you feel better, I didn't know about you either, until recently. I mean, I've known since I was 12 about Roger Pruett being my dad. Found it in my mom's diary and looked up what he did for a living. When you came back the second time and came clean about being a P.I., that's when I put it together."

When Hannah was 12, I was 21, and it was long after my mom had died. Why didn't my dad tell me then?

"What do we do with the information now?" she asked.

I hadn't liked Hannah from the start. After tonight, I'd softened that opinion a bit. But I had no idea how to go about this. The betrayal of my father stung. No—it more than stung. It gutted me. If I thought about it for any length of time, I'd end up curled in a corner. "We can start by talking when this case is over."

She agreed. I threw a twenty on the table and walked out.

I ducked into my Spitfire forcing my thoughts back to the case. What had happened to the guy who appeared to be Brooke's slave, or errand boy? He was still a mystery. He might not matter in the scheme of things. Brooke might have removed him from the equation when she scaled back on clients or slaves, or whatever she called them.

The burning question was how did Luke fit in? I was building quite the collection of liars. If Brooke felt the need to warn her sister about staying low-key around him, he might have been the obsessive type. That's why he'd downplayed their relationship—to throw off suspicion from himself. I'd felt the creep vibe after I saw him with Floyd. Exactly how big of a creep was he?

THIRTY-TWO

I'D HOPPED INTO my car gung ho to confront Luke, but my body had different ideas. My ribs ached. My bruises throbbed. My head and heart hurt from hearing about Hannah, Georgette, and my father. Whatever I told myself when I popped the two pain meds in my mouth after leaving Pambiche's, it all equaled stupid. I'd nearly fallen asleep half-way there. I managed to get home, send off a text to Jeff asking him to tell Mitz I loved her, and crawl into bed. Eight hours of sleep later, I was headed out to Meadow Verde.

I left Floyd home this time. I didn't want to have to worry about him alone in the car while I confronted Luke. But morning traffic crawled at the pace of a jogger. Sitting behind a semi that crept along, I had time to play catch up with Kyle and to hear his voice.

"You up?" I asked after he finally answered.

"I'm on duty. Pulling a double to cover for the guy who took my shift when you were hurt."

"Sorry about that. I'll make it up to you." I found myself thinking of a few ways to accomplish that.

"I like the sound of that and I'm glad you called. I was able to get that information from the Chop House. Anderson had been there that night. His credit card receipt shows him cashing out around ten o'clock."

"Which means he would have had plenty of time to get over to the Limbo." Rachel was telling the truth about their dinner. She'd also put Dave Anderson in downtown Portland around the time of Brooke's death. "Appreciate your checking. I wanted to update you too." I gave him the rundown of where I was headed. After being mugged in my office, having someone know my whereabouts made me feel better. My ribs couldn't take another blow. His tracking me via police scanner after the fact didn't offer much comfort.

"You think Luke was involved?" Kyle asked.

Traffic picked up and I took the exit. "I'm not sure how he fits. Yet."

With a promise to fill him in later, I parked in front of Luke's apartment and rang the bell. When no one answered, I banged on the door until I got better results.

The door flew open and Luke peered out at me, his hair on end and sleepy crust in his eyes. "Whoa, lady. What's with all the racket. There a fire out here?" He leaned out of his door and looked both directions.

"Funny." I didn't smile. "We need to talk."

He eyed me and I glared back. He looked like crap with at least a day's growth of beard. "What about?"

"Brooke Hanson. Seems you forgot to mention how much you liked her."

"I told you I like all the residents here."

"Cut the bullshit already."

He ran his hand through his mane a few times, perhaps debating how much I'd found out. "Come in."

He realized enough. I marched past him into his living room and made myself at home on his couch.

He dropped into a chair and grabbed for his pack of Camels. "It's not what you think."

I'd heard that a lot lately. "What do I think?"

He pulled out a cigarette and lit it. "That I deliberately *lied* to you about being friendlier with Brooke than I originally said." His drawl was thick.

"You're a mind reader. Were you two dating? Friends? What?"

He rubbed the back of his neck. "Something like that."

"You sleep together?"

He grimaced. "We weren't that kind of serious. I mean, I wouldn't have minded, but she was old-fashioned."

I nearly choked on my own spit. "What makes you say that?"

"That's what she told me."

This guy might be more naïve than I had been. "How long were you seeing each other?"

"Last couple years. I wouldn't say seeing really. She moved in upstairs and took notice of my cowboy hat. Truth be told, I think she liked Chance better than me."

"And you were seeing each other even after she moved, sounds like."

"She'd always wanted a horse. She'd come out on weekends to ride. On occasion I'd talk her into dinner before she'd head back to Portland."

Until now, Brooke had been hard to see as a regular person because I couldn't relate to her life or her choices. Loving animals—I understood. "Did you love her?"

He took a drag on his cigarette. "She was a good girl. I thought she could feel the same, until she told me to stop calling a few weeks before she died. I was none too happy about that. I thought we might be able to make a go of it. I may not be fancy, but I'm solid."

"When was the last time you saw her?"

"Don't remember."

Hard to believe given what Brooke had told Hannah. "Please."

"Look, I called her a few times. At first, she'd answer and let me down easy. Then she ignored me." He flicked an ash into the tray and took another long drag and blew it out. Buying time. "I decided to go where she goes on Saturday nights," he blurted.

"The Limbo? The night she died?"

"Yup," he said.

Was anyone *not* there that night?

"I called and told her I was coming down and we were going to talk. I didn't see yammering on the phone working to my advantage."

Had Amanda been mistaken? Was it Luke outside the bar? "What happened?"

"She called me back. She'd been drinking and told me to stay away because she was leaving. That's when I heard someone talking to her."

I shifted. "Who'd you hear?"

"Her voice was muffled, but pretty sure she said, 'no David, it's not true.' Then she hung up on me. Since I was close, I kept coming and pulled up across from the bar a few minutes later. That's when I saw Brooke."

My heart raced. "You got out and talked to her?"

"No."

Of course not. "Could you describe who she was talking to at least?"

He ground out his cigarette and lit another. "He was hidden in the shadow of the building. I couldn't tell."

I was desperate for confirmation. "You really can't describe anything about the guy? Anything at all?"

He stood and started pacing. He frowned. "Okay. I don't want you to think something's wrong with me."

His rigid body language had me sitting taller. "What is it?"

He reached into his pocket and grabbed his cell phone, setting it on the coffee table in front of me. "Here's the thing. This guy leaned into her and kissed her, which kind of messed me up."

"Are you sure he kissed her?" Amanda said Brooke and Anderson were arguing.

"Pretty darn sure. And here's the part where you might get the wrong impression of me."

I inched to the edge of my seat. "I won't."

He picked up the phone and tapped open the Gallery. A few slides of his finger and he landed on a picture and handed me the phone.

Brooke's back was to Luke, and a stockier figure was in front of her, in the shadows of the tall building. I swiped to the next one. The image wasn't much clearer, but the arm of a raincoat was in the photo. My mind raced. I wanted that I.D. The third photo. Again no face, but a hand on Brooke's right wrist and clear as day, a diamond set in black onyx on a man's pinky.

Up to this point, I'd had nothing truly concrete. This picture of the ring was a game changer. If I could get this on a computer and use the photo enhancers, I bet I'd find a shadowed Dave Anderson in the background. I tilted my head back and then swiped the next picture.

"There's only the three," Luke said.

I shifted the phone around lengthwise, trying to make out the fourth picture. Was that a person in it?

"Ms. Pruett, I don't want to give you the impression I stalked her. It's just when I saw him lean in, I got the notion to take the pictures. Not sure what I planned to do with them. Maybe confront her later." His shoulders dropped.

"It's okay," I said. It was more than okay. He'd given me evidence of Anderson physically in front of the Limbo. My focus returned to his phone.

"Anyway, when I looked back at them," he said, "they were done talking and she was running off. I thought she'd seen my car and that's why she ran. I debated whether to follow before deciding I didn't want no damn restraining order slapped on me. My mother raised me better than that. The girl did *not* want to talk to me. I had to face that."

I looked up. "Did the man she'd been talking to chase her?"

"I was too upset to notice."

"Had she ever talked about a Dave Anderson before?"

"No. We didn't talk about her friends, family, or even work. She preferred I not ask questions. Me and Chance, we were like an escape to her."

I bet they were. A different world she could melt into, leaving her other life behind. Luke hadn't asked much of her and that would have been a welcome change.

Their relationship could have sparked more jealousy in Anderson. Especially if Brooke was wanting out. "Do you think she talked about you to anyone?"

"Doubt it. She liked to tell me she was an independent woman who did what she pleased and answered to no one." He hung his head.

Anderson could have found out about Luke other ways. "Is there anything else that stands out about that night?" My eyes went back to his phone and at the image of someone on the sidewalk closest to the driver side. I squinted at the photo, trying to make it out.

"I really only took the three," he said. He reached for his cell and scanned the screen. "I'll be damn. That one there is of a woman I saw. Must have shot it when I was putting the phone away."

I grabbed the phone back. I spread the image with my fingertips, the details fuzzy. "Where did you see her exactly?"

"She came out of the alleyway behind that bar where Brooke was. She ran across the street behind me and headed the same direction as Brooke."

"Could you describe her?"

"It was pretty dark."

I kept staring at the picture. "Think, Luke. Tell me what you saw."

"The light above caught the reflection on her glasses and I think that's what got my attention. That and it didn't seem smart for a woman to be in an alley. She was wearing a raincoat, and her hair was pulled up, you know, like in a bun."

Every hair on my arm stood at attention. I said the next words slowly. "Like a librarian bun or a soft and sexy one?"

He thought about it. "Tight, I guess if you put it that way, a librarian."

"You're sure about the glasses?" I could make out an outline of what looked like eyewear, but it wasn't as clear. What was clear was the angular shape of the woman's jaw.

He closed his eyes, as if recalling the night. "Yeah.
I remember thinking that with the rain, she must've
had a heck of a time seeing."

Rachel Mosley. It had to be. She and Anderson obviously had no problem getting to the Limbo after leaving the Chop House. Why chase Brooke though? Did
she realize Anderson was talking with Brooke right
across the street moments before? "Is there anything
else you can remember?"

"No. I should've been honest right up front. I didn't
because me spending time with Brooke wasn't relevant in the scheme of things. Brooke and I didn't have
much other than horses, and that was over according
to her. When you came waltzing in with questions, I
didn't want to reopen the wounds."

His eyes looked more tired than when I'd come in.
"Thank you for coming clean," I said. "I need you to
text me all of those pictures." I sat with him as he sent
each one. My phone dinged as they were received.

As the last one came through he said, "Brooke always made me a little crazy. Got my head spinning,
you know? And I do want to apologize about your
dog that day."

I had planned to ask him. "What was that all about?"

"I saw your car there when I came out to go to
the Dumpster. Your door was unlocked. I wanted to
know more about Brooke, but didn't want to appear to
be skulking around. Thought that would look weird."

Weirder than taking someone's dog out of their
car? Brooke did have him messed up because driving
to Portland to confront Brooke was a bit loony. Not
to mention the photos were creepy. But right then,
based on those pictures, I could have kissed that crazy,

creepy man on the forehead. And he did sound sincere. "I appreciate that, Luke. Some women have the power to screw with men's minds, for sure. Here's a tip for the future. Messing with someone's dog is never going to endear you to anyone."

"Suppose you're right." He thought things over. "The picture of that woman seems to have you excited. She have something to do with Brooke dying?"

That was an interesting question. Rachel had lied since the beginning about her involvement in the firm entertaining. She'd also failed to mention she and Anderson had finished their dinner in plenty of time to have him in front of the Limbo. Or that she'd been on the same sidewalk and followed Brooke. What else was she lying about and to whom? I thought about Chris Foley's testimony that he'd seen someone in a raincoat and heard Nightingale ramble "goddamn her" at the accident scene. Maybe he was never referring to Brooke.

"There's a chance," I said.

I left him and hit the road back to downtown Portland and to Brooke's place to find evidence she was blackmailing Anderson. I had pictures which, once cleaned up, should prove that both Rachel and Dave Anderson were near the Limbo, and headed in Brooke's direction shortly before she was killed. Rachel's presence had thrown me off. She could be protecting Anderson. Would she do anything that man asked?

THIRTY-THREE

IT WAS TURNING out to be a cool, clear autumn day by the time I got back to downtown. Getting past KOIN's security was a breeze. I'd ridden up the elevator, dug out the extra key Georgette had given me for Brooke's place, and fully expected to let myself in. Instead, I found myself at David Anderson's door.

According to Kyle, Anderson shared the penthouse with his wife, Cindy. A part of me wanted to know what kind of woman put up with a scourge like him. But there was more to it than that. If she had seen the comings and goings at Brooke's place, she could provide me a better picture of Brooke's world. With any luck, she might have insight on her husband and Brooke's relationship. Wives were smarter than their husbands gave them credit for. While I hadn't known outright that Jeff was cheating on me, I'd felt the distance between us long before. Mrs. Anderson could have picked up on something that I could use against her husband. Something like a motive.

I pressed the doorbell, and a low pitched three-toned gong sounded. A minute later, my stylish gray-haired elevator buddy from the other day answered. "Yes?"

With a genuine smile I said, "I think we've met before."

She checked her hair and pulled the collar of her

stark white blouse together at her neck. "You asked about our neighbor recently."

I extended my card. "I'm Kelly Pruett and I'm investigating Brooke Hanson's untimely death."

"Barbara," she said.

"Dave Anderson's mother-in-law, correct?"

Her lips tightened, turning down at the ends. "I don't remember telling you his name."

Not wanting to come across, in Luke's words, stalkerish, I shrugged. "I'm sure you did."

"Well, he's not here right now. We don't generally see him until late."

Fine by me. "I'm actually hoping to visit with Mrs. Anderson if she's available?"

Concern bunched the space between her eyes. "For what purpose?"

"Just covering all the bases in my investigation, and that includes Brooke's neighbors." I didn't add that her son-in-law was my prime suspect or my curiosity about his home life.

"She's not up for conversation. I'll let her know you came by." She started to close the door when a small voice came from behind her.

"Who's here, Mom?"

Barbara's jaw tensed. "A solicitor, darling."

Whether Barbara wanted to introduce me or not, I couldn't lose this opportunity. "I'm here on behalf of Brooke Hanson's family," I said to the woman who I'd yet to see.

A mechanical inhaling sound came from behind Barbara. "Let her in, Mom," Mrs. Anderson said.

Barbara shot me an icy glance and I smiled innocently. "Follow me."

She led me to an expansive living room with a full river view before disappearing into the kitchen. Like Brooke's place, expensive leather furniture filled the space. Unlike Brooke's, family pictures and personal mementos were in the mix. Tribal relics and art covered a wall. An entire shelf boasted blown glass from Italy. The décor was classier than Barbara, if that was possible.

A motorized whirring sound came from the hallway before Mrs. Anderson came into view. I tried not to stare. The small, frail woman, mid-forties, sat stiffly in a wheelchair. A strap across her chest held her upright, and an air apparatus tube rested near her mouth.

Her brown bobbed hair had soft blond streaks, and her blue eyes sparkled. Her natural makeup complimented her soft cheekbones. Barbara took good care of her daughter.

Mrs. Anderson drew air from the tube and spoke, "I'm Cindy. You were asking about our neighbor?"

It took me a second to gather my thoughts. "Thank you for seeing me," I said and introduced myself properly. "She died a few weeks ago and her mother hired me. She doesn't believe her daughter accidentally fell under the MAX train. Did you know Brooke?"

She took another breath. "She headed David's accounting department. Such a tragedy. She seemed like a nice girl."

He'd told his wife the same lie. "Did you think it was odd that she lived on the same floor?"

She paused. I couldn't tell if she stopped to catch her breath or think about my question. "No. David told me she'd chosen this building because she loved the view. It is spectacular."

He'd probably told Cindy lots of things to make it seem normal that Brooke happened to choose the same building to live in. "Did you and David socialize with her?"

"I didn't. David had business meetings with her quite often."

"Business meetings?" I tried to not sound sarcastic.

Barbara reappeared next to her daughter. "Darling, maybe now isn't the best time."

"I'm fine, Mom. Thank you," Cindy said. "That's what David called them. I'm not stupid." Another breath. "I realized I couldn't satisfy my husband anymore."

She did know about the affair. "Weren't you devastated?"

Her forehead furrowed. "At first, but David and I've been married twenty years, and half of those have been with me in this chair."

"Can I ask—"

"How it happened?"

I nodded, morbid curiosity getting the better of me.

"Hang gliding. Downdraft smashed me into the ground, headfirst." She sounded detached, like reading a newspaper article on the incident.

I winced at the description, an electric shock traveling down to my toes. "I'm so sorry."

"Me too. Up until then, we were an adventurous couple. He took me to many wonderful places. My accident was hard on our marriage, but David has been a good husband. He'd been faithful up until a couple of years ago. Things changed when they hired Brooke at the office."

More than she could imagine. "You didn't confront him?"

"No. He stayed and cared for me. I've never wanted
for anything. If he needed an outlet, I couldn't deny
him that."

She let him off way too easy. "Does he know you're
aware of his relationship with Brooke?"

"Probably suspects. It's nothing we've discussed."

Barbara let out a disgusted sigh.

Cindy rested her eyes. "You don't have to approve,
Mother."

"And I don't."

Dave's affair had been the topic of many a mother-
and-daughter chat. "Did he love her?" I asked.

"How could you not? She was smart, beautiful, and
able to do everything I couldn't. Hard to resist."

Cindy had made peace with the situation. I thought
of Jeff's infidelity and my father's. She made it sound
like her husband, or any man, couldn't help himself.
What happened to self-control and commitment? Was
no man capable of those attributes? I was becoming
jaded and disliked Dave Anderson more every second.
"Did you see other men or women come and go from
her apartment?"

"There were quite a few of both when she first
moved in, wasn't there, Mom?"

"I didn't live here then, sweetheart."

"That's right. My caretaker mentioned Brooke was
quite popular. In the last year, there have been less."

"Can you describe any of them?"

"I've only seen one man in particular myself,"
Cindy said and Barbara nodded.

"Did either of you talk to him?"

"No," Cindy said.

Barbara shook her head. "I keep to myself."

Recalling my initial conversation with Barbara in the elevator, she'd played the *I don't know a thing* card. Not that I blamed her. At the time, she didn't know me and would have wanted to protect her daughter.

"But you'd said you saw him with things in his hands," Cindy said to Barbara. "You even mentioned we needed someone like that to run around for us."

"Yes, dear." Barbara didn't meet my gaze. "He was always bringing dry cleaning in and out. Or groceries."

That had to be the errand boy Hannah had talked about. She'd also said he was the one Brooke tormented. Was it torment if he'd signed up for the punishment? To make sure I wasn't jumping off in the wrong direction I said, "Did he wear a uniform or anything that led you to believe he was working for a company?"

Cindy made a noise that sounded like a chuckle. "No. I got the impression he was a suitor."

"He often had a bottle of wine in hand. I'd also say he was interested in her," Barbara added.

How had Dave Anderson liked that? "Could you give me a description of him?"

"Handsome. Brown hair. Longer on the top. Nice arms. Looked like he could have lifted weights."

I ticked off a list of who I'd met that fit that description. Only one came to mind. "Were the sides shaved close?"

"I believe so."

My shoulders pinched. I grabbed my phone as my heart raced. I didn't have a picture of Derek Stromenger from the Limbo, so I searched Facebook. While Cindy and Barbara watched me tap the screen,

I narrowed down the possibilities until I pulled up his profile. I flipped my phone around. "Is this him?"

They both said, "Yes."

If he'd been Brooke's gopher, then he knew about Dave Anderson. Why would Derek have protected him? It didn't make sense. "You saw this man go into Brooke's apartment regularly?"

Barbara nodded.

I thought of my prank caller. "Did he have a key or was Brooke always home when he came by?"

"I didn't pay that close attention," Barbara said.

"I didn't see him but once or twice," Cindy added.

"And no other men, or women, came or went from her place in the last year?" I asked. After talking with Luke, I couldn't rule out anyone. Every way I turned new information came at me.

"Not that I saw," Cindy said.

"Me either, but as I'd said before, Ms. Pruett, we don't hang out in the elevator lobby. Cindy, you really should rest."

Cindy didn't respond.

"I only have a couple of more questions if you're up to them?" I asked Cindy, already knowing Barbara's answer.

"That's fine" Cindy said.

Barbara pursed her lips.

"Do you think if David saw Brooke and another man coming around, or if he thought she might end things with him, would he react to that by let's say, physically retaliating?"

Her eyebrows drew close. "He might not be happy, but I've only known him to be very kind and gentle. He must have figured he couldn't hold her back though. And Ms.

Hanson at some point would have realized there was no future with my husband. David would never leave me."

The Dave Anderson I'd seen in the office that day and who'd attacked me was anything but kind and gentle. "That's wonderful he loves you so much." Or that she thought he did anyway. Lying and cheating was one heck of a way to show it.

Her eyes lost some sparkle. "I wish I could say it's all love. In reality, I'm as rich as they come, and I'm sure that holds some appeal for David."

The revelation of her wealth surprised me. Anderson was a taker on every level. The look in Cindy's eyes said she wasn't at peace as she'd first let on. "His law firm does okay, doesn't it?" I asked.

"Not so well to own a cabin in Aspen and million-dollar ocean-front condos in Maui and Italy. My David has expensive tastes."

He had kinky tastes too, but sharing that information felt wrong.

Cindy's face drooped and she slumped in her chair. Despite her willingness to talk, it had taken a toll. I'd overstayed. I thanked them for their time. Barbara tended to her daughter as I left. In the hall, I let out a long-held breath. Cindy Anderson didn't want or need my pity, but I ached for her situation.

Dave may not be the best husband, but he was companionship and he cared for her. Twisted, but it worked for them. Here I was looking to turn Cindy's world upside down. I'd have felt worse if a young vibrant woman hadn't ended up dead because of Anderson's games. I needed to find the proof to nail him for the murders of Brooke and Nightingale. I thought it all over as I inserted the key into Brooke's apartment.

THIRTY-FOUR

AN ARCTIC BLAST of air hit my face when I opened Brooke's door. The thermostat in the condo hadn't been above fifty-five for the last few weeks. The chill added to the eerie quiet. I shivered, pulled my coat closed, and walked in.

During my last visit, I had the distinct impression Brooke's drawers had been rifled through. I believed the person rifling was Anderson. But what if I was wrong? After my conversation with Cindy and her mother, Derek Stromenger could have been the one in here. Except despite the new information, I had a hard time picturing how he fit with Brooke. If one needed money to get her BDSM services, a bartender position wouldn't have much to offer. Unless he was free labor. Someone to *torment*. Either way, it didn't seem likely Brooke would have anything to blackmail him with.

Based on my original assumption of Dave Anderson, which made more sense, physical proof of Brooke blackmailing him had to be here. Even if Cindy Anderson knew about the affair, Brooke might not have realized that. Or it could be as Rachel had suggested that she threatened to take down the firm. I just needed to find out what Brooke had been using that Dave wanted to find.

Starting in Brooke's kitchen, I opened each drawer thinking about where I would hide blackmail-worthy items. I inspected under the silverware tray, finding crumbs. Same in the knife and utensil drawer. I removed envelopes and notepads—reading each piece for juicy info. The few utility bills and junk mail I found had none. An address book had settled at the bottom. I lifted it out excited to find names of friends or associates I could question. Blank pages stared back at me.

In the living room, the fanned books I'd seen that first day were stacked in a neat pile. The hairs on the back of my neck stood up. Whoever had been through here before had come back.

Afraid they'd already found what they were looking for, I strode into Brooke's bedroom. Even with the lamps on, the dark fabrics and walls absorbed the light and life from the surroundings. Opening the dresser, I went through Brooke's things again, hoping that touching them would trigger a thought or a feeling. I'd criticized Amanda for her *feelings,* and here I was reaching for the same thing. At this point, I'd do anything to find proof that Dave Anderson had killed Brooke and Nightingale. I found nothing there.

I slapped off the light and went back into the living room, desperate for inspiration where to look next. My focus rested on the bookshelf where I'd skimmed her selection of crime novels before. I liked a mix of mystery and romance. Brooke didn't share my eclectic taste. Then I spotted something that didn't fit with the others, high on the top shelf. Mixed in with the Stephen King novels sat *The Hobbit.*

It meshed in style and color with the other books; I nearly missed it. The only reason it caught my eye was I couldn't see Brooke being a reader of fantasy. At least not the elf and middle earth kind.

Dragging an ottoman over to the bookshelf, I used it to climb onto the hutch. Being vertically challenged had its frustrating moments, and more so being injured. Standing on the shelf, I had to get onto my tiptoes to reach the book. The stretch caused my ribs to throb, and my eyes watered.

With my fingertips, I wiggled it out of its spot. It didn't have the texture of a book. I pressed it to my chest and stepped down onto the ottoman.

A quick inspection answered why it felt different. It was a box, masterfully crafted to look like a novel. A thin rubber band was wrapped around the hardplastic. The case was locked.

A couple of jiggles to the latch later, it didn't open. I turned it over. Tucked under the rubber band was an *I Love Texas* bumper sticker. Behind the sticker, a picture of Brooke on top of a bay-colored horse. She leaned in the saddle away from Luke, who rested against the horse's side, his hand clutching Chance's bridle. Brooke's distancing body language said she'd used the cowboy for his horse. Poor sap thought they might be able to make a go of it. The picture indicated no likelihood of that.

I removed the picture and bumper sticker and placed it on the shelf before sitting on the cushion to try the lock again with no luck. If pictures of Luke were on the outside, it could be a sample of what was on the inside. But why leave those out and lock something else in? No, whatever was inside had to be more interesting than a picture of Luke, Brooke and Chance.

Another scouring of the hutch for a key yielded

nothing. I hadn't seen one when I'd gone through the other rooms or drawers either. Brooke could have kept the key with her. It may have been with the personal effects that Georgette had, but it would be easy enough to pop the latch with a screwdriver—or something flat.

In the kitchen, I grabbed a butter knife from a drawer. I had it poised on the lock when the front door flew open.

My breath caught in my throat. I tucked the locked box under my jacket and set the knife on the counter. The thump of my heart filled my ears. The nightmare of being trapped and beaten in my office rushed back like a flood. My legs wobbled.

For a moment, I felt rooted. I couldn't stay in the kitchen. And what if it was only the landlord, Ms. Matson? I forced myself to calm down and ordered my legs to walk into the living room to find out. If it wasn't her, better to be the confronter this time, rather than the confronted.

At least in theory. A lump in my throat cut off my air when I saw Dave Anderson securing the front door. Panic at remembering what he'd done to me zapped my resolve. I should have stayed hidden and snuck out when he wasn't looking. What was I thinking?

He turned and saw me, anger flashing in his eyes. "What are you doing in here?"

Wrapping my jacket tight around me like I was cold, I prayed the "book" wouldn't fall. I squared my shoulders. "I could ask you the same question."

"Brooke was my employee."

"I've been hired by the family."

"To do what? Run around and harass my wife. Who do you think you are?"

Had Cindy or Barb called and told him where I was? Or had he come back to resume his search and was updated then? "I'm trying to find Brooke's killer." I met his glare as I felt for my pepper spray in my purse. I found it, just past my gun. Heavy artillery would only come out if it had to. I slipped the spray into my pocket.

He was oblivious to my movements and kept his distance. "What's that have to do with my family?"

"It's pretty obvious you had a thing with Brooke. For God sakes, everyone knows about it." I didn't want to out his wife, but he could take my comment however he wanted.

The vein in his temple pulsated.

"You must have funded this lifestyle, right? You don't do that unless you're head over heels for someone."

"My personal affairs are none of your business."

"They became my business when you murdered Brooke."

He jerked his head back and his body stiffened. "Are you insane?"

"I'm not the crazy one. Did you really think that attacking me in my office would intimidate me into stopping my investigation?" He took a step closer to me and I pulled out my pepper spray, aiming it at him. "Stop."

He did and worked his pinky ring. I expected more reaction when he saw the spray that had nailed him in the eyes the other night. He didn't even blink.

"I didn't attack you," he said. "Or kill Brooke. I'll sue you and take every penny to your name if you try to defame me."

"Did Brooke threaten to *defame* you, too? Is that why you killed her?"

His face grew pensive. "I didn't kill her. I loved her."

"Right. I've seen what's in that bedroom." I pushed, hoping to hit enough buttons to get a confession and not become a casualty. I thought of the gun in my purse.

"What two people do in private isn't for you to judge."

"She wanted out of this arrangement though, didn't she?"

"Not sure where you're getting that information from."

"A source, who also says you wouldn't let Brooke go."

"They're wrong."

I hugged the box closer. "I have witnesses who put you near the Limbo that night, arguing with Brooke outside, and a picture to corroborate it. Save your lies for someone else."

He didn't answer. His narrowed eyes indicated he was thinking about what to say. His hands were in fists. "I wanted to talk some goddamn sense into her."

A small crack in his armor. "Did you follow her to the tracks?"

No response.

"Was she blackmailing you to get out?"

He turned red. I'm sure the lawyer in him endorsed silence. The silence sounded like a *yes ma'am* to me.

"How about Nightingale?" I said. "Did he see you kill Brooke and you had to kill him too?"

"Wow, you think I killed everyone?"

"Is that a confession?"

He waved his hand as if dismissing me. "He was Brooke's friend. I never even met the man. Give me a break. I'm a respected lawyer in this town."

"I'm sure you are. That's why I'm confused why you had Brooke arranging escort services for clients. You should have stuck to law. You honestly thought entertaining foreign clients with sex was a great idea?"

The veins in his neck were corded. "I don't know what you think you know, but you've got it wrong."

"Do I? That you were having Brooke perform sex acts on clients? That you told her who was in town? You can deny it all you want. I have someone who helped entertain those clients, and she'll make a great witness. With the picture I have, I'll just keep putting it out there until you won't be able to defend someone for a parking ticket around here."

Spittle foamed at the edges of his mouth. "Get out of here," he said. "Take your foolish ideas with you."

"I'll be taking them straight to the police," I said.

He barked a laugh. "Go ahead. I'm innocent. Just like Brooke's involvement with the clients. We're talking dinners and dancing. Nothing else."

"You mean, Brooke, the dominatrix?"

He wiped the corners of his mouth with his thumb. "What's that got to do with the firm's clients?"

"Come on. You know as well as me that she and Nightingale were taking care of other needs besides food."

He rubbed his hand over his face. "Maybe Nightingale. Brooke didn't do that."

He sounded convincing. "You're telling me nothing in that bedroom was for the sake of clients?"

"I'm telling you none of this is your business. Get out." His face turned the color of blood.

I could have left then. I wanted to. The memory of his saliva on my face and his hands around my throat sent pings of anxiety through me. But I hadn't finished. I willed myself not to move. I wanted confirmation I had it right. "Did you know about her relationship with Luke?"

He huffed. "What are you talking about now?"

"The apartment manager at her old place. She never talked about him?"

"Brooke and I had an open relationship."

"How about Derek Stromenger? Were you two so open that you didn't mind that another man visited her?"

"Please. We agreed long ago I didn't want to know about what she did. When we were together, she focused on me. Whatever assumptions you've made about me are off base."

"We'll see about that."

He threw his head back and stared at the ceiling.

I ran past him and out the front door with the book hidden from his view. He didn't follow.

THIRTY-FIVE

I KEPT MYSELF together until the elevator closed, and nearly lost it, trying not to hyperventilate on the way down. When the metal doors reopened, I sprinted out of the building and to my car with the book clutched to my chest.

I wanted out of the city and far away from Anderson. Fear had gripped me as I faced the man who'd murdered Brooke. It continued its hold as I crossed into the northeast section of the city via the Hawthorne Bridge. I'd always thought of this part of town as the armpit. I'd take its known vagrants and dope pushers over the high and mighty sex peddlers and killer I'd found in high-rises downtown. The rundown part of this area might be nothing compared to the modern art and glitter across the river, but it was my territory.

As I accelerated out of downtown, my mind swirled with questions. But after I crossed the river my heartbeat started to return to normal as the adrenaline slowed its coursing through me. And the further I was away from Anderson, confusion crept in.

Despite my theory of his guilt, something in his denial rang true. He was almost believable when he said he didn't do it. It was the look on his face; the way he held himself. The surprise in his voice when I'd accused him of killing Brooke. And something else. I hadn't seen a cut on his hand. Of course that only meant he didn't kill Nightingale, not that he hadn't pushed Brooke.

The cut also might have been small and already healed and he was just a damn good lawyer who had his acting skills for the courtroom down pat. My head hurt with my ping-ponging thoughts. What I did know as I pulled into my drive was I had a locked box that needed to be jimmied open.

Ignoring my ribs, I took the stairs two at a time into my house and slammed the door, securing it behind me. Floyd greeted me and I nuzzled him, trying to calm down. In the kitchen, I dug around until I found a screwdriver in the junk drawer, and a meat mallet in another. Since the likelihood of my pounding out a chicken breast for chicken cordon bleu was as likely as going on a spa weekend with my ex-friend Linda, it was nice to finally have a real use for it.

On the counter, I shoved the flathead into the lock. A few pounds later, the lid popped. I'd half-expected to find more pictures of Luke and Brooke. I'd wanted more than anything for there to be proof tying Anderson to Brooke's murder. And Nightingale's. Brooke's diary spelling it all out for me would be even nicer. What I found was a two-page, stapled and folded document. Not sure what it was, I lifted the first fold. *Consensual Slavery Contract* was centered.

This must be the BDSM contract that Hannah had suggested was commonplace. My face flushed and I almost cried. Not from the find, but from the adrenaline releasing out of my body. Okay, maybe both. Finally, something tangible tying Anderson to Brooke. I let out a whoop that made Floyd's ears perk. "Sorry, boy." I got up with the box under my arm and would have skipped to the living room if I hadn't been in pain. I curled up on the couch. With anticipation like it was Christmas morning, I opened the paper and read the first paragraph:

THE SLAVE AGREES *to submit completely to the Master in all ways. There are no boundaries of place, time, or situation in which the Slave may willfully refuse to obey the Master's directive without risking punishment, except in situations where the Slave's veto applies at said working place during working hours.*

THAT EXPLAINED HOW they worked it while at the law firm. I settled deeper into the couch.

THE SLAVE AGREES *their body belongs to the Master. All of the Slave's possessions likewise belong to the Master, including all assets, finances, and material goods, to do with as she so desires. The Slave agrees to please the Master to the best of his ability, in that he now exists solely for the pleasure of said Master.*

I SHOOK MY HEAD. I hadn't realized what signing one of these agreements could mean. All the slave's possessions belonged to the Master. The slave existed solely for the pleasure of the Master.

It was hard to believe anyone would sign this. Especially a lawyer who had a lot to lose. Even harder was to imagine he'd enjoy having no control. How would his wife feel about that since it was her money? Did she also have to share his time when Brooke demanded he be with her? That couldn't have gone over well in the Anderson household when both Brooke and Cindy required his attention. There must have been exclusions or it wouldn't make sense.

No matter what had put him over the edge in the end, I had proof of their relationship and he wouldn't be able to deny their connection. It wasn't a leap to believe the threat of losing everything was strong motivation. I flipped to the second page and scanned the rest of the document, eager to see his signature on the master and slave contract. My eyes locked onto the signature line. I finally blinked. It wasn't Dave Anderson who had signed the contract—it was Derek Stromenger.

With the document on my lap, I slouched back into the couch. If Derek was a slave, this wasn't that shocking. In fact, it made sense. Hannah said slaves signed contracts and Derek had been Brooke's minion. I'd simply missed Anderson's contract. Right? I inspected the box again before flinging the box on the couch next to me. It wasn't there.

I stared at the contract again, willing the information to be different, and spotted the handwritten scribble at the bottom. "Cancelled—October 2, by Master."

October 2 was the day before Brooke was killed. The day Brooke had received the text Georgette saw. "You better not be serious or you'll pay."

It had been Derek all along. My mouth felt dry. Blinded by my certainty that it was Anderson, I'd ignored the other signs. The way Derek downplayed his feelings towards her from the beginning. Changed his story. Left early, right after kicking Brooke out. He'd known Amanda had talked to me. That's why he'd harassed her. I'd been stupid. He had the motive, and the opportunity. I jumped off the couch with the paper in my hand.

The night Brooke was murdered, she'd been belligerent with Derek. They must have been arguing about her canceling the contract. Or maybe he was furious and didn't want her in the Limbo anymore to flaunt her relationship with Anderson. Or whoever she chose. That's why he'd kicked her out of the bar that night.

While it was Anderson, not him, that stopped Brooke outside the bar, Derek would have had time to chase Brooke down to those tracks. Derek had lied about everything. Like everyone I'd encountered. Floyd whined, feeling my frustration. I trotted him out the front door and waited for him with arms wrapped around myself. I was shaking, but not from the cold.

Derek didn't admit that he and Brooke had a relationship because I would have asked more questions. The only reason to lie was because he killed her.

My theory of Anderson crumbled, replaced by one for Derek. As her errand boy, he would have had an extra key to her place. He would have wanted to retrieve this contract so that no evidence led back to him. I thought through the last few days. He could have certainly made the prank calls to me and been my attacker. He was a similar build. He was strong. Always chewing gum. If I'd been close enough, I bet I would have smelled the mint on his breath.

What I didn't quite understand was why he killed her. If I'd been released from a contract like the one he signed, I'd have taken that as a blessing.

Waiting for Floyd, I kept reading, wanting to learn more about this relationship where Derek had signed away his life to Brooke.

THIS CONTRACT MAY be terminated at any time by the Master, but never by the Slave, except under special conditions to be agreed upon by signers. Upon termination, all materials and belongings shall belong to the Master, to be shared or kept as they see fit. The Slave, owning nothing and having agreed to give up all worldly possessions and body to the Master, shall once again own their body, but nothing else, unless the Master decides to give back their possessions.

IF BROOKE HAD canceled the contract and then wanted to enforce the possessions part of it, Derek could have been angry enough to kill her. While not knowing what Derek would be giving up, even if it wasn't much, the idea of it could have enraged him. I thought of my Triumph, and the earrings my mother gave me. Someone trying to take those away would make me livid.

Floyd and I came back inside, and I paced the living room. Derek had motive to kill Brooke. I wasn't sure how Anderson stopping Brooke out front and Rachel on the other side of the street fit. Or why Nightingale would have covered for Derek. I was missing something; something right in front of me.

My phone rang. Jeff. I almost let it go to voicemail, but it could be about Mitz and I wouldn't make that mistake again.

"Hey, we're eating up at my mom's house. Come join us. It's meatloaf."

Mitz was okay, and I was on a roll, about to bring this case home. "I'm kind of busy at the moment."

"Mitz is here."

A few more paces and I stopped, pulling myself back. I had to refocus. I couldn't miss an opportunity to make things right with my daughter no matter how amped I might be. And with Jeff wanting full custody, I wouldn't let him think for a second she wasn't my priority. "I'll be there."

Stuffing the contract back in the box, I went into the kitchen and put it in a white paper bag and set it on the top shelf in the refrigerator behind a gallon of milk. If someone came looking, they'd think it was Chinese takeout. I gathered my strength for dinner at Arlene's.

"I SAW YOU drive up," Jeff said when I reached the top of the stairs to Arlene's place. "How's your day been?"

"Good. Where's Mitz?" I said as we approached the front door.

"Inside." He inspected my face. "I told her you fell. How are you doing?"

Before I could respond Mitz bounded out of the house straight for me. The sullen girl of before had disappeared and my arms prickled with relief.

"Are you okay?" She let go of me and signed the question at the same time with her already healing hand.

"I'm perfect, now that I'm with you."

She touched my lip and frowned.

"I got clumsy."

"Be careful," she scolded.

Tears moistened my eyes and I blinked them back. "Always. I have to take care of my girl."

She nodded, satisfied I was okay.

Jeff took lead, and Mitz and I followed him into the house. Arlene was unusually quiet after our back and forth yesterday about my being attacked. I'd take this version of my ex-mother-in-law any day.

For the next half hour, we sat and ate together as a family. While I tried not to rush, my thoughts were on the contract and why Derek killed Brooke—and how I'd fell for his lies from the beginning. Mitz signed about her day, and I nodded catching the main points.

Arlene brought a pineapple upside down cake to the table and set a slice in front of me.

"By the way," she said as I took a bite. "I saw someone around."

"Around?" I said, chewing.

"Yes." She took a seat. "You'd said kids were in your backyard a couple of nights ago."

"Kids?" Jeff asked.

Someone had been at my house again. "Right." I looked at Jeff. "Thought I told you about that."

His forehead wrinkled. We both knew I hadn't, and I wasn't going to fill him in now—or ever.

"I just wanted to make your mom aware in case she saw anything unusual. Was that someone in my backyard, Arlene?"

"No. In the front. Wandering."

"Man or woman?"

"Man."

My stomach tightened. "What did he look like?"

"He was," she waved her hand about six inches from her head, "about that tall. He was wearing a white shirt with a black vest and had brown hair with that weird thing going on that you young people do these days. Shaving the sides, I guess. It looks horrible."

Derek. "And he wandered around my property?"

"Yes. He knocked and tried to look in the front door. When I saw him from my bedroom, I went outside and stood on top by the stairs and hollered over to him. Told him you weren't home."

I could barely swallow my food. "When was that?"

"Today."

Derek must know I was onto him, otherwise why would he come by? "What happened when you called out?"

"I startled him. He didn't say a word and took off in a fast walk down the road. I didn't see a car anywhere."

The contract. I had to get home. Taking the last couple of bites of cake, I eased out of my chair and signed. "Hate to cut out, but I'm exhausted, you know, from my fall. Bed is calling my name."

Jeff gave me a small nod. "I'll walk you out."

"I'm good." He might want to talk about my safety, or despite our agreement to chat later, custody. I just wanted to make sure my doors were locked and the box was still in my fridge.

He stared at me.

"I really am okay. I'll have this case wrapped up in the morning. Thank you, Arlene. For everything."

She smiled. "You are welcome—anytime."

I wasn't used to this behavior. We might have more hope than I'd ever thought.

After a kiss and hug from Mitz, I walked toward the door before turning one last time. The three were back to giggling and signing. One happy family. I used to be an integral part. Now I lived on the outside, but as I'd told Kyle, we would always be connected. They were mine regardless of our issues and despite the possibility of my family changing with the revelation of Hannah. I hadn't let myself contemplate what that meant. Not yet.

Not reconciling with Jeff had been my choice, like keeping my dad's business going and honoring his request to handle this case for Georgette. That didn't mean I was willing to give Jeff full custody of our daughter. I wasn't the kind of wife or mother to Mitz that Jeff wanted, someone who would be home and not working. I liked working and being a mother in a way that worked for me. Maybe that was exactly why Mitz needed me in her life. To know she could light her own way.

At home, with Floyd on my heels, we made the rounds to confirm we were secure. After the fourth round, Floyd tired and fell asleep on his bed. I couldn't sit. Not until I figured out the missing piece. I texted Kyle to call. I wanted to update him about the book. I paced some more.

After a couple of hours, pain and exhaustion won out. I hadn't heard from him by the time I relented and crawled into bed.

Not that it did me any good. My body was tired; my brain refused to shut down. Opening the box had given me some answers. Did those answers add up to murder? In my original conversations with Kyle, he'd been good at punching holes in my theories and getting after me for leaping to conclusions. With missing Derek as the killer, I'd lost some confidence that I could solve this. I had to try. The contract provided proof that Derek had been enslaved by Brooke, and that she'd cancelled their arrangement. Had he come here looking for me because he suspected I'd found that contract? He could be afraid I'd make the connection if I had.

Derek and I needed to talk but it couldn't be here.

He'd violated me twice by hanging out in my tree and attacking me in my office. I didn't like the idea of him on my turf a third time. This time I'd go to him.

First thing in the morning, I'd pay Derek a visit. Once I told him he could dispense with the lies because I had the contract in my possession, I might catch him in some more that would seal his fate.

Only problem was I'd promised Mitz I'd be careful. That meant Kyle had to go with me. No more going rogue when I could have help. Especially if I was about to confront a killer. Another check of my phone confirmed no response from Kyle. He must be on duty.

I glanced at the clock every ten minutes until 2 a.m. when I gave up trying to sleep. Downstairs, I started a fresh pot of coffee and paced around the kitchen until it finished brewing, nervous about confronting Derek.

With a cup of coffee and a full carafe, I sat in front of Mitz's computer upstairs. My first quest was to educate myself on slave and master agreements. A Google search offered plenty of reading until my eyes burned. Everything I saw supported the contract from the box.

Next, a bit of research on Derek was in order before our meeting. I'd already discovered his Facebook profile when visiting Mrs. Anderson, but wanted to check him out more thoroughly.

On his page, he hadn't posted many status updates. However, he loved pictures of himself. Derek at the bar. Derek at a recent Oktoberfest celebration. Derek striking some muscle poses. The pictures showed a confident and attractive man. What had been the appeal of being a slave? I hit the photo tab to see if I could find any indicators. He hadn't set up his privacy settings, giving me full access to his albums. I expected to find a few with him and Brooke. At least then I'd have additional ammunition if he tried to deny their connection.

Instead, as I went through the pictures, nothing linked them. Only a couple showed Derek wearing leather pants and a harness, and one with a studded dog collar. Most were of him partying and having fun. Derek shirtless at the beach, holding up a Hefeweizen. Derek water skiing. Derek hamming it up with women at the Limbo.

No Brooke anywhere. That's the way the *master* must have wanted it. I refilled my coffee cup to the brim and kept searching.

An album labeled "Family" caught my attention. Curious if those family photos would shed any light on what kind of kid Derek Stromenger had been, I clicked it open.

The first ones showed Derek at his graduation party and coming down the aisle, wearing cap and gown, at the ceremony. A picture of him with a white-haired woman sitting in a chair; could be his grandmother. Another showed him as a little boy around five, and an older girl around nine next to him. Her brown-hair surrounded her boyish face. Their body language suggested they were family and were close.

The next was Derek in a more recent photo since he was sporting the same haircut I'd seen him with at the bar. His arm was wrapped around a grown woman with the same boyish look of the little girl in the previous photos. The caption read: "Me and my only sis. Thank you for helping me get through life. You do more for me than anyone ever should."

The woman looked familiar, but hard to tell in the

quarter screen shot. I enlarged it to full screen, recognition kicking me. Her light brown wavy hair cascaded onto her shoulders. The librarian glasses were identical. She was far more fit and muscular now than even in that picture, but I had no doubt—Rachel Mosley was Derek Stromenger's sister.

I hopped up from the desk, nearly toppling the chair. Floyd, startled by my excitement, barked. My heart pounded as I bent down to reassure him. If my lip didn't hurt, I'd be chewing it off. She was the missing piece.

Both times I'd spoken with Rachel, she hadn't thought much of Brooke. Rachel must have known about her little brother's involvement with her coworker. Did she know about the contract? I had to assume so. If Derek had felt wronged and stood to lose everything, he might ask his big sister for help.

Derek's photo caption spoke volumes about their relationship. Could *doing more than she should* have included covering for her brother who committed murder?

I texted Kyle again and paced until my legs shook. I dropped onto the sofa at five to rest—and to think.

THIRTY-SIX

MY FATHER BOUNCED me on his knee. I was five, and I touched the soft folds in his face, a smile spreading across mine. His warm strong arms were wrapped around me. My safe place. I wiggled, and he shifted at the same time, his arms opening. With nothing to stop me, I tumbled backwards. Frantic, he reached for me. My hand slipped from his grasp.

I sprung off the couch as fast as my stiff body would allow, trying to shake the dream. Anxiety raced through me as I shoved down the dread in my chest and looked to see if Kyle had texted me back. He hadn't. It was seven thirty. He should be off duty by now. I punched in his number and hit SEND.

To get the blood moving, I stretched and walked into the kitchen waiting for him to answer. He came on the line as I poured cold coffee into a cup and put it in the microwave.

"Morning, sunshine," his deep voice sounded over the phone.

Any other time, my heart would have skipped a beat. With so much to tell him, it only pounded. "Did you get my message?"

"Just saw it. I've been handling a call all night and I'm just finishing the report. What's going on?"

I launched into the list of what I'd learned in the last twelve hours and landed on who had killed Brooke.

"It's Derek. He's lied about everything, including taking a break. He clocked out and left after removing Brooke. He was her slave, except she'd cancelled the contract the night before. A contract that allowed her to keep everything of his, even if cancelled. Everything." Excited to lay out the facts end to end, I raced ahead. "Rachel Mosley is his sister. She's been covering for him. Luke gave me a grainy picture he accidentally took of her running towards the tracks after Brooke."

Kyle drew in an audible breath, no doubt trying to keep up.

I'd at least had a night to absorb the information. "Are the DNA results back yet on that glove?" I asked.

"No," he said. "I've put a rush on it. We should have it by the end of the day."

"I'll bet it's Derek's. We just need to get a sample to compare." I was thinking out loud.

"Impossible without an arrest or him volunteering. Both unlikely."

"Right. Which is even more reason for me to see him this morning to press for the truth. With some luck, I'll get an admission, or at the least, get him tripping up on his answers. In my search last night, I found his address. Will you meet me there? I'd like backup for this conversation."

"Okay, slow down," Kyle said. "You've got a lot of theories. Solid or not, you don't bust in on people unannounced and expect them to cooperate."

"I've gone in as a friend and as a P.I. and he didn't cooperate either way. With the information on the contract, I think I can rile him up enough."

"Rile up someone you think is a killer?"

"That's why I want you close. If nothing else, our

presence will let him know we're on his trail and he may start screwing up. Making mistakes."

"If the DNA is his, the detectives on the Nightingale case will do that."

"Not if there isn't anything in the system to compare it to, they won't. I can't take that chance."

Kyle didn't say anything.

"Please Kyle. I'm doing this, with or without you."

We were in a standoff. I didn't want to battle him, but I'd come too far to stop now.

After a tense few seconds, he said, "Fine. Where am I going?"

I relayed the information and we agreed to meet in forty minutes outside Derek's house.

After a quick change from P.J.s into my jeans and Nike jacket, I was in my car. A few false starts later, the engine hummed. Thank God. I punched Derek's address into my GPS and hit Interstate 84.

Derek's southeast neighborhood was a mix of new and old construction and he lived in an older brown duplex. I parked a block away between a Ford truck and a Toyota Camry, which hid me well enough I'd be able to see when Kyle arrived. Keeping the engine running for warmth, I went through my questions for Derek about the contract and about whether killing Brooke had been premeditated. Had he been upset that she blew him off? And why Nightingale?

My other question was how Rachel fit. In our conversation, she'd confirmed Nightingale handled the clients who preferred men. According to Hannah, Rachel arranged client visits. She must have sent work his way. Derek could have killed Brooke, but Rachel was the one who would have been able to convince

Nightingale to stay and take the rap. If he hadn't done what she ordered, she could have cut off his very lucrative income.

Before I had time to contemplate further, Derek's front door opened and he walked out, dressed in long black nylon shorts and a dark hoody. My eyes went to his hands, remembering what Kyle had said about Nightingale's killer cutting himself. The fingerless gloves he had on made it impossible to tell. He ducked into his sedan and backed out, heading the opposite direction. When he was far enough away, I did a U-turn and followed from a distance. Kyle would be at Derek's in ten minutes. I'd wait to see where we were going before updating Kyle on the change of plans.

A few miles later, Derek pulled into the driveway of an all-white, one-level rambler on Oak Avenue and got out. I swung in behind a parked car about a block away from there and killed the engine. Hunkered low, he didn't notice me and entered the house using a key. A stream of exhaust came from Derek's car. He hadn't turned his motor off. He must not expect to be there long.

I texted Kyle. "Derek left. I'm following. Will update you soon."

Next, I punched in the house's address into my browser. It only took a minute for the internet to tell me it belonged to Rachel Mosley. What better place to confront Derek than right in front of his sister's home? There'd be no denying the connection. But what if he tried to attack me again in broad daylight? I did have my gun. Before I could debate further, Derek jogged out, slunk into his car, and took off.

The decision made for me, I popped my gear into

drive and pulled out. It might have been a bad idea to have a throw down in front of Rachel's anyway. I'd have had to explain to Kyle why I didn't wait for him. But as I neared Rachel's house, I slowed. Why had he gone in there? It was his sister's place. Why not go in there? But what if it wasn't a leisurely check to see if she was home? He'd come to my house, perhaps thinking I was onto him. What if he had come here to hide evidence? If she was willing to cover for him, it wasn't outside the scope of possibility. Like a magnet, the house dragged me in and I swerved the Spitfire next to the curb.

Derek was getting further away and the plan was to confront him. Except the words on his Facebook picture bothered me. The way he thanked Rachel for doing more than she should. What had that included, other than convincing Nightingale to create a cover story for her little brother? I had to know.

It was a weekday and Derek's brief stay suggested Rachel had left for work. I'd make it quick and get back to Kyle who'd be getting close to Derek's duplex. He should have also seen my text by now, and I'd wait to give him the next update. Making a police officer an accomplice to breaking and entering wasn't a good idea.

I grabbed my wallet and selected an old library card. Its flexibility should do the trick on the door lock if this untested skill my father had taught me years ago even worked. The movies made it look easy. I'd know soon enough.

With my purse over my shoulder, I approached the house in long strides like I lived there. There were no signs of movement in or around the house. A work-

ing neighborhood, it appeared everyone had already
left for the day.

At the door, I rang the bell once to make sure Rachel wasn't home. Then I shoved the card in the ver-
tical crack between the door and the jamb. My heart
pounded. Once I stepped in, I'd be breaking the law.
Finding the truth for Brooke was more important.

With my shoulder, I pushed the door as far as it
would go. It only gave me 1/8 of an inch. No deadbolt
had been engaged. Lucky for me. With a tilt, the card
forced the lock down. Another bend the opposite way,
a bump with my body weight behind it, and pop. The
door swung open. I slipped in and closed it behind
me. My mouth was dry, making it hard to swallow.
I gripped and released my hands, trying to calm the
shake and steady my nerves.

When my internal racket quieted, the only sound
in the house was the tick of a clock and the hum of the
furnace. "Rachel?" I said in a loud whisper. If I got a
response, I'd have to come up with a convincing reason
for having busted in. The silence suggested I wouldn't
have to get creative. I checked the house anyway and
found it all clear.

In the living room, I began a thorough search. A
cream-colored fur area rug anchored the room, which
also had sage green velour couches, a glass coffee
table, and a bowl filled with potpourri. Her home
smelled like cloves and spice, and fall. Personal pictures in ivory frames lined a bookshelf. Her brick fireplace had never been used. Not one Asian architecture
or Japanese garden book was found anywhere. Whatever firm entertaining Rachel did, the clients didn't
appear to come to her house.

Ribbons and awards for bodybuilding hung on the wall. At some point in her life, Rachel had done well in the bodybuilding circuit. A search through her drawers and cabinets didn't produce anything that connected Derek to Brooke. The junk mail, the pictures, they were all Rachel's.

The first bedroom I walked into had been converted into an office. I skimmed Rachel's desk. More bills. Student loans. Nothing suspicious. Until the phone—a Samsung Galaxy lying near the printer. The case was Kate Spade with flower sparkles. Not very Rachel like. My heartbeat quickened again.

I pressed the power button with no success. The battery was dead. Slipping the phone out of the case, I turned the phone over in my hands. No SD card. The SIM looked intact. My stomach flipped. If this was Rachel's phone, it wouldn't be dead on her desk. This could be Brooke's missing phone. Which meant I'd been right to believe that Rachel was helping Derek.

My mind raced on what to do. Was it better to have the police find it here, or for me to take it, hoping it linked back to Derek? My guess was the text that Georgette had seen with the threat to Brooke would tie back to his phone. One more piece that would put him in jail. I was convinced it held the key to what happened to Brooke that night, which was why Rachel had taken it for her brother. If I left the phone behind, Rachel would destroy it the minute Derek told her we were onto him. If I took it, the prosecutor wouldn't be able to use it as evidence. To get this far only to have Derek walk free for something I screwed up, would haunt me. It had to stay.

Forcing myself to keep searching, I went to the

guest room, where no evidence of the child Rachel said she had was found. The lies were endless with these people. Using the mother card may have been a play for sympathy so I wouldn't ask too many questions.

In the master bedroom, I checked the closet. Mostly work clothes and shoes. No whips, chains, or gags. I didn't know what I expected to find. Nothing would have surprised me.

Up to this point, I hadn't seen anything else damning and I needed to catch up with Kyle and get back on Derek's trail. I was on my way out when I saw a coat tree and bench in the entryway. Shoes were tucked under the bench and coats and hats hung on antiqued brass hooks—including a long raincoat and a black jacket. A barely visible glove had been stuffed into the pocket. A black glove.

I couldn't be sure if I recognized that glove as matching the one in Nightingale's bedroom. I moved a little closer to inspect what was visible. It had the same stitching. Made of the same material. Black gloves weren't rare, by any stretch, but I couldn't leave without knowing.

In the kitchen, I rummaged through the drawers for a utensil that could help me pull the glove out of the pocket without contaminating any possible evidence. I returned to the entry with silicone tipped tongs and retrieved it from the pocket, rotating it side to side to find anything that could prove it was the match to the one found in Nightingale's apartment. As the light hit the leather, dark dots became apparent. I shuddered at the realization that the spots could be blood, and that this could be that glove. Rachel was hiding evidence for her brother in plain sight.

I shoved it back into the raincoat pocket, having the same issue with it as I did the phone—removing it would make it inadmissible. But if I left now, Rachel might have time to hide it before the police could do anything about it.

The only way around that was if I was arrested inside this house. Kyle could come across the glove while taking me into custody. If Nightingale's blood was on there, and the DNA inside the glove matched Derek's, it would be irrefutable proof that he'd committed Nightingale's murder. Just as important to me now, that Rachel was an accomplice. My P.I. license would be on the line for breaking in here. But I was in this far, I had to take the risk.

Kyle must be wondering where I'd gone at this point. I sent him a text telling him I'd found the matching glove and Brooke's phone. I emphasized he needed to get over here ASAP and arrest me for breaking and entering.

While I waited, I saw no harm in seeing if Rachel had hidden anything else incriminating. I headed to the garage. When I stepped out of the door, my gaze landed on the black Cadillac in the farthest stall. Fear gripped my throat at the memory of the near miss. My eyes locked onto a pair of women's blue shoes caked in mud. The mud from my backyard when the intruder made their escape. Crap.

I swung open the door into the kitchen, glancing at my phone to see if Kyle had texted. The message hadn't gone through. Panicked, I hit resend.

I stepped back inside and saw the flash of copper of a frying pan coming straight at my face.

THIRTY-SEVEN

TERROR JOLTED MY body like an electric shock and my neck vein pulsed in rhythm to my pounding heartbeat. Stabbing pain pierced my skull. A scream sliced through the air before I realized it was me. I lurched back and crashed onto my bruised side in the middle of the kitchen. My head landed on the cold tile floor with blood trickling from my nose and tears blurring my eyes. Rachel was a few feet away—a pan in one hand. A revolver in the other.

"What the hell are you doing in my house?" Rachel demanded. I blinked up at her dressed in spandex running tights and a sports tank that framed her muscular veined arms. A headset hung around her neck.

My brain froze. When I opened my mouth, nothing came out.

She marched out of the room toward the front door, probably thinking I was incapacitated or near death. The click of a deadbolt made every muscle in me clench. She'd locked us in. Frantic, my eyes searched for cover. The pantry was a few feet away. My purse, with my gun, had landed a couple of feet to the left of the pantry door. My fogged brain couldn't decide what to do first. Survival kicked in. If I didn't get to safety, I'd have zero options.

Arms shaking, I lifted myself onto my hands and knees and crawled into the pantry. In the cramped space, I turned my body toward the door. I was about to grab for my purse when footsteps echoed. Rachel was coming. I had to try anyway. I reached for the strap. A bullet whizzed past my arm.

Breath caught in my throat as I snapped my arm back, purse-less, like a cable breaking from a heavy load. "I've got my gun." I lied, trying not to sound desperate. "I don't want to start a shootout with you, but I will." I scanned the confined space. Canned food, energy bars, and cereals stocked the shelves. Nothing substantial enough to do real damage as a weapon. A can of pork and beans would have to do. I grabbed a couple of cans from the shelf and clutched them in my hands. "Let's end this now, okay?"

"We'll end it with you dead. You're the intruder here. You broke into my house. I'm only defending myself."

She'd have a point if she wasn't guilty of murder. I had to believe that trumped anything I did. "That'll never fly." Shifting onto my feet and crouching low, I positioned myself for a peekaboo view of Rachel. My head throbbed.

"You'll never know."

There was no use trying to reason with crazy. If Kyle had received my text, he should be on his way. Until I had confirmation of that, I had to buy time. "It was you that killed Brooke, wasn't it?" The error of my previous theories came to light the moment I'd seen the blue shoes.

"Since you're in my house, you must have figured it all out by now."

"Only that it has to do with your little brother, Derek."

"Ahhh—you discovered that connection. You are smarter than I thought."

"Which means you knew about Brooke and his contract," I said.

She grunted.

"That contract had to be upsetting."

She let out a guttural laugh. "She actually owned my brother. Owned. Who does that? She didn't even love him. She used him like he was a barnyard animal."

Telling her that some found pleasure in those arrangements didn't seem like a good plan. "Yeah, that's pretty screwed up. Can't blame you for being mad. I'd be upset about it, but you didn't have to kill her."

"If I wanted her out of my life completely and to stand a chance with David, who she only used for his money, I did. He was as stupid as my brother."

Rachel paced like a caged cougar. She could be contemplating her dilemma of my knowing the truth. I needed my gun. "You love David?"

Her face contorted and she pointed her gun my direction. "More than she ever did. I'd been at that law firm for fifteen years, always by his side. I'd helped him through the trauma of his wife's accident. He cared about me until Brooke was hired."

"Looks like he still cared. You have a good job there. It's not like he replaced you with her," I said.

"He didn't have to. She got the perks. The office, the money, the man. The only thing that bitch had to do for it was wear some leather and spread her legs. She got everything that should've been mine."

Rachel's nostrils flared and she limbered her shoulders and neck, as if readying for a fight. Talking about

Anderson had upset her, making her more unstable. My purse was too far. I had to figure out a way to get it to me. "I still don't understand the firm entertainment thing. It sounds like she wasn't even doing that this past year. And you lied completely about your involvement."

"Oh please." She paced again. "The whole thing was her idea in the first place. Like everything Brooke did, she got it started and then wanted out. She had her affair going with David, and my brother licking her kitchen floors. When it became more complicated and the clients wanted more, David asked me to handle them and to keep it quiet." She had a far off look in her eyes. "And I did. I did what I always do. I took care of things."

I was drawing her out. Good for buying time; bad in the long run. People only overshared when they weren't worried about anyone being alive to tell about it. "Killing Brooke took care of things for Derek and got you that corner office, how convenient. How'd it really go down?"

A smile covered her gaunt face. "I texted her that David wanted to see her, that it was urgent, and she left the bar to find him."

That had to be Brooke's phone in Rachel's office. I'd thought the phone would lead to Derek—but it led to her. She wouldn't have wanted anything that could link her to that night. Even though phone records might have proven the same thing, police wouldn't have checked those records unless there was cause. "Okay, so Brooke was easy enough to get to. How did you get David in front of that bar?"

"Over dinner I'd told him that Brooke was blackmailing the firm. I mentioned she kept a dossier of the firm's clients and intended to release their names that night if she didn't get a huge payout, despite their relationship—which meant nothing to her. If he wanted to talk sense into her, he had to go to her immediately. He and Brooke were both gullible. It would have been perfect, except when Brooke got outside she saw someone she knew and took off after her."

Hannah.

"I thought at that point my plan would fail, until David caught her and they argued. Then she broke free."

Rachel was lost in her recounting of Brooke's demise. The next time she walked away from me, I'd go for my purse. "You just happened to be waiting and watching in the alley?"

"Exactly. She ran and I followed. The train was passing between her and whoever she'd been chasing. I'm not sure I'd planned to kill her until that moment at the tracks. I had dreamt about it, but to actually do it…" She chuckled, amused at herself. "My plan had been to destroy her with David—having her ass thrown out of that penthouse and out of the firm. But there she was. She made it easy; I couldn't resist. Shoving that drunk bitch right into the train felt good."

Her callousness shocked me. "What about Nightingale? Did he cover for you because he did work for the firm?"

"He and Brooke often met to discuss business. It was a fluke that he'd been there that night and down at those tracks. I took full advantage. If he hadn't lied for me, I would've cut him off. He was paid handsomely for his services." She laughed again. "He didn't like it, but he stayed behind."

That explained his bitterness. She turned her back to me. I was about to reach for my purse, but she whipped back around. *Shit*.

She continued. "When Georgette went to confront him and then hire you right after, I was concerned he'd talk. After he'd arranged to meet with you, he had the balls to tell me I needed to line his pockets with some cash if I wanted to keep him quiet. He had to die."

I shook my head. "Brooke's murder was almost the perfect crime."

She cackled. "If Brooke's nosy mother had stayed out of it, it might have been. She couldn't leave it alone, but Brooke deserved it. I don't feel a bit sorry about how it worked out."

"You've screwed Derek at this point though. Doesn't that bother you?"

Every muscle in her body went rigid. "He didn't do anything wrong. Other than being stupid, which no one will ever know about. I've been protecting my brother for a very long time. The idiot was devastated when Brooke canceled that contract. She'd apparently decided she wanted a different life. To start over. Like it would be that easy. At some point he'll get over it and her."

Rachel was so entranced that when she glanced away, I reached for my purse again. Another bullet whizzed at me. Wood cracked close to my ear. I recoiled, desperate to become one with the drywall. I didn't see the blood at first. The gray of my jacket turned red around my bicep. A sharp hot pain reached my fingertips. They were on fire.

"Bullseye," she said.

"You wish," I yelled. I'd seen too many episodes on Shark Week. If she sensed blood in the water, she'd be in a frenzy.

I couldn't wait any longer if I wanted to survive. I took the can of beans and flung it straight at her head, followed immediately by the other. At the same time, I stretched for the purse strap, grabbed it, and flung it back into the pantry with me. Fighting through the searing pain in my arm, I gripped my gun and yanked my phone out with the other hand.

Blood drips trailed on the floor outside the door. A wave of dizziness and nausea hit me.

Rachel laughed. "I did get you."

"Even if you did, we're both armed and I'm not surrendering."

"I can wait until you bleed out and lose consciousness."

Warm blood trickled down under my sleeve and into my palm. My legs were noodles. Panic was setting in. I didn't want to die. "Except I just dialed 911." And I did.

She didn't respond. Fast footsteps echoed on the linoleum followed by sounds from the other room. I peeked my head out from around the pantry to an empty kitchen and ordered myself up. I'd just stepped out from my hiding spot as the front door slammed. The house shuddered in response. I tucked my Glock into the waistband of my pants.

My arm exploded in an ache that made childbirth feel like a yoga class. I swayed at the sight of my own blood but refused to pass out or die. Rachel wouldn't get off that easy.

I stumbled out the front door and spotted her sprinting down the street. I wasn't Wonder Woman, but I had to keep eyes on her so the police could find her. She took a left through one of her neighbor's side yards about a block up. Trailing, I followed and cut through the wet grass.

On the side of a garage was a locked cedar gate. Rachel must have gone over it. There'd be no getting my ass over that fence with one good arm. As I calculated another route, I spotted Rachel behind a recycling can leveling her gun at me. I grabbed the lid of a garbage can and flung it at her. She jumped out and clutched my bleeding arm, her thumb digging into the bullet hole. The high pitch scream that exploded from my mouth pierced my own ears.

She whacked me in the nose again with the butt of her gun. My whole face shattered. Blood flowed into my mouth. Primal instinct took over and I flailed at her with both arms. My mind raced to Mitz. I wouldn't go down like this and leave my only child. I broke free and punched, kicked, hit, and scratched. Rachel was stunned with the force I'd summoned. We both were. What happened in my office would not happen again.

Another hard right with my fist and her gun flew into the air. We tumbled to the ground. She tried to crawl away. I yanked her flat like she'd done to me and pulled her arms behind her. For once, my pudge played to my advantage.

Rachel bucked and thrashed, launching me forward onto my injured arm. Pain bolted through every nerve. She stood and stumbled toward her gun. I reached for mine. In one motion, I had my Glock aimed and fired. The bullet caught her in the back of her thigh. She crumpled, writhing in pain.

Distant sirens filled the neighborhood. A Toyota 4-Runner screeched to the curb and Kyle raced to us, reaching Rachel's gun to secure it before calling for an ambulance. By then, the police cars had pulled up and were getting Rachel into custody.

I leaned against the gate and Kyle walked over. "You couldn't wait for me?" He bent down, put an arm around me, and gathered me to my feet.

"It's a long story."

He stared at my beaten face and blood drenched arm, his face creased with worry. "You can tell me on the way to the hospital."

"I'll be fine. You should see the other guy."

"You have a thing about doctors?"

"I have a thing about needles."

THIRTY-EIGHT

LATER THAT AFTERNOON, I waited in front of the Justice Department, sagging against my car. It had been one long day. Kyle had taken me to the hospital and after an excruciating wound clean and a detailed report to the police, I'd learned Georgette was being released. I wanted to be the one to meet her so I could wrap up the case, and a few other loose ends. It took convincing Chester this was best done privately since that's how I'd been hired. He finally agreed it would be okay. He'd wait for her at home.

Georgette appeared through the revolving door and I waved her over with my good arm.

"Thank you," she said as she dropped into the Triumph.

"No worries. I have some selfish motivation for getting some alone time with you."

She nodded. "How's your arm?" Her face furrowed in concern.

"Nothing that codeine and time won't heal. It was just a graze."

"I understand Brooke's co-worker was at the root of everything."

I pulled out into traffic. "Yes. Rachel Mosley. An indictment should be handed down for two counts of Murder in the First Degree, and my attempted murder, in the next couple of days."

Georgette leaned her shoulder against the door, gazing out the window. "What had Brooke gotten herself into." It wasn't a question; more a sad statement.

I'd tried to come up with reasons for why Brooke had gone down the road she did. I didn't have any words of wisdom or great epiphanies. Her lifestyle wasn't one to evoke sympathy from those who learned of her death. Some might think she'd deserved it. I didn't agree. She'd been a loving daughter. Even a loving sister. While Hannah didn't see it, Brooke had cared for her in her own way. And like it or not, BDSM was a choice shared by consenting adults. Who was I to judge? Finally, I said, "I think Brooke felt strong and in control as a dominatrix. In the end, however, that wasn't why she was killed. Rachel was a jealous, angry woman, and overprotective of her brother. I'm sure Brooke never counted on that."

Tears filled Georgette's eyes.

"The DNA tests came back a bit ago."

"Your friend, Kyle, gave me the run-down before they released me."

I nodded. "Then you know the glove I'd found in Rachel's house matched the one in Nightingale's house and confirmed her as the killer. And the phone in Rachel's office did belong to Brooke. It still had the text Rachel had sent to lure her out of the bar, as well as the threat you saw the day before from Derek."

"How did he fit in exactly?" Georgette asked.

Defining his and Brooke's relationship for Georgette wasn't necessary. She'd dealt with enough. "Let's just say, his being so upset at Brooke ending things is what triggered Rachel in the first place. If there's any good news, it's there won't be any problems with a conviction. Rachel's admitting to everything to keep her brother out of trouble."

"Thank God for that."

I pulled onto her street and in front of her house. We sat silent, the car running. I had a million questions.

"I'm sure you want to know more about me and your father," she said.

She read my mind. The answer was yes and no. "I knew he and my mother had problems; I just always saw him as perfect. I would never have believed he was fallible in that way. Or of wanting other things besides our little family."

Georgette stared at me. "Is that what you think? That he didn't want you and your mother?"

I directed my focus out the window as my eyes filled with tears.

She put her hand on my arm. "That wasn't it. We had a moment of weakness. That's all. We weren't proud of it, and he never pursued anything with me, or I him. He never told you because he wanted to protect you. Even after your mother was gone, he couldn't burden you with the knowledge."

"I guess I'm surprised you didn't have an abortion, given that."

Her face wrinkled. "For me, keeping Hannah was the only option. I'd been told earlier in life I'd never have children of my own and regardless the cost, I would've never given her up."

I thought of the anger Hannah had shown towards her mother. "Do you ever regret that choice?"

She hung her head. "Not for a second. I understand why she's been bitter all these years. Chester and I will make amends. She should have never paid for my mistake."

A little late. Or when it came to love and family, was there no such thing?

Georgette climbed out of my car and walked to her front door, where Chester stood. He opened his arms when she approached and wrapped them around her. He'd forgiven her for so much. I didn't feel capable of such forgiveness toward her, or my father. Not now. I was numb.

I headed home ready for another pain med. Truth was, Rachel's bullet had done more than graze my arm. It had taken a chunk. The bullet only hit fat—thank you extra pudge—but it would leave a mark.

When I got home, the codeine put me out for nearly 15 hours. I woke the next day not feeling much better. Healing would be a process. Though the bullet had hit my left arm, it would make chores and cooking difficult, for a few weeks, anyway. Which is why I'd asked Arlene to help me and why she stood in my kitchen that night cooking up mac and cheese. Jeff had let Mitz come over and she was upstairs doing homework, and I sat on the couch thinking about recent events.

My phone rang. It was Kyle.

"How's my favorite patient?" he said.

I closed my eyes, listening to his deep voice. This time, my heart did skip a few beats. "I'll live. Did you hear whether Vice was going to do anything with the law firm?" I settled deeper into the sofa cushions.

"They're opening a full investigation. Anderson's not saying much. He might be innocent of murder, but it sounds like he had a hand in the entertaining of the clients and he's not going to incriminate himself. We'll see what happens."

Not surprising. "With Rachel in jail, and Vice on their butts, whatever entertaining they were doing has at least come to a screeching halt."

"For sure."

"Did you ever find out why Derek came to my place?" I asked, the fact that he'd shown up here still bothering me.

"He said when you'd dropped in, asking about Amanda, he felt concerned. He said something about a co-worker that went missing to Rachel, and she commented that she'd take care of whoever or whatever to keep him safe. A bit into their conversation, he realized Rachel may have done something to Brooke. He said he was coming to talk to you about it."

"You believe that?"

"Nothing ties him to what happened to Brooke or Nightingale."

The evidence supported Rachel having acted on her own that night. She'd made those calls to me and been in my backyard. At the point she'd begun harassing me, I hadn't even met her yet. Officially. She was the woman at the end of the bar with the Asian man when I'd first visited the Limbo and started nosing around on Georgette's behalf. She knew I had begun to ask questions. To my surprise, she'd also admitted to attacking me that night in my office. Not Derek.

The doorbell rang. "Are you coming by later?"

"I'm working a double, but I'll swing by tomorrow."

"Cool. I'd like you to meet my daughter, properly this time."

"I'd like that."

I smiled. This might work out just fine. I let him go and shouted to Arlene. "I'll get the door."

It took a few tries to get off the couch. When I did, I opened the door to Hannah. "Came by to see how you were," she said.

"On the mend. Come in?"

She sat at the end of the couch, with her leg tucked under her and I eased onto the other side with my leg tucked under me.

"You been by to see your mom yet?" I asked when we were settled.

"Earlier today. She and my dad want to make it right."

The fact she'd referred to Chester as her father was a good sign. "I hope you can work it out. Family's important."

She nodded. "We'll be okay."

Arlene poked her head out. "Another for dinner?"

I turned to Hannah. "It's mac and cheese and hot dogs."

"My favorite," Hannah said.

It was mine too. Mitz came bounding down the stairs and I introduced her to Hannah. "She's mama's half-sister," I signed and said, my voice hoarse with emotion. In all that I had lost this year between my dad, my husband, my friend, I had gained a sister. Family. Something that I thought I had truly lost. And something I hadn't realized until the word sister had come out of my mouth.

It was in that moment I understood why my dad had left me that letter. He knew he wouldn't always be around. While he couldn't know for sure when or if Georgette would come looking for help, perhaps he hoped if she did, it would lead me to Hannah.

"I have an aunty?" Mitz signed, her mouth opened with excitement.

"Indeed."

Hannah smiled at me and I could see in her face that neither of us were sure what to think of this new situation.

Mitz started telling her about her school. Hannah would need to learn to sign if she planned to spend time with us. In the meantime, with my good arm I helped when needed.

I hadn't even begun to process the revelations about my dad. He'd always been my hero. I felt like I'd just been told Santa wasn't real. Despite my confusion, Hannah shouldn't pay for the sins of our father—or her mother. Or me for that matter. Being an only child had been lonely. Although no guarantees on how it would turn out, it was worth a try.

We gathered at the table. A misfit group of Arlene, Mitz, Hannah, and me. Jeff was at his home and while his betrayal might always sting, I wasn't sad about it. We were two very different people with one thing in common—Mitz. We needed to be united for her. He'd backed off his threat to go after full custody—temporarily at least. My getting shot didn't bolster my position, but since it was related to the case that was now over, we were at a truce. I was afraid the issue would come back around as soon as I took on another investigation. I'd deal with it then.

Truthfully, I'd learned a lot about being a P.I. during the case. I'd made some mistakes. In not looking at everyone as a suspect, I almost got killed. Next

time I'd do better. And there would be a next time.
I'd known the moment Rachel had hit me in the face
with the frying pan. A weird time to find certainty,
but the fact I'd picked myself up and fought, meant I
had what it took to do this job. Ultimately, I had solved
the case. Even if what Arlene had said was true about
Dad wanting me to sell the business, that's not what I
wanted. I loved being a P.I. And given that I had hon-
ored my father's wishes to help Georgette, I believed
I had done my dad proud. After dinner, I planned to
update the company website. Putting *In Memoriam*
next to my dad's name might be hard, but it was time.
I might even let Arlene help me bring those boxes up
from the garage and start unpacking them. Baby steps.

   We ate and I waited for Arlene to lay into me about
my arm, my profession, and my inadequacies as a
mother. Instead, she and Hannah were lost in conversation about street life and being a free spirit, something
Hannah knew plenty about. Mitz paid close attention
to them, following their every word. I'd once believed
my family had the San Andreas Fault running through
it. Tonight the fault line had closed some.

   Then Arlene turned to me and said, "Are you planning to take on more cases?"

   Maybe not. "Yes."

   "Then you're going to need some help. What do you
think of hiring me?"

* * * * *

ABOUT THE AUTHOR

MARY KELIIKOA spent the first 18 years of her adult life working around lawyers. Combining her love of all things legal and books, she dove into mystery and suspense writing at the age of 27. Life happened, and after a fifteen-year hiatus, she picked up the pen again at 50, returning to her passion of creating a twisting mystery where justice prevails.

At home in Washington, she enjoys spending time with her family including ten grandchildren and her writing companions/fur-kids, Bella, a bossy golden retriever and August, her mischievous kitty. When she's not at home, you can find Mary on a beach on the Big Island where she and her husband of 30 years recharge. But even under the palm trees and blazing sun she's plotting her next murder—novel that is.

For more information, please go to marykeliikoa.com.

Get 4 **FREE REWARDS!**

We'll send you 2 FREE Books plus 2 FREE Mystery Gifts.

Harlequin Romantic Suspense books are heart-racing page-turners with unexpected plot twists and irresistible chemistry that will keep you guessing to the very end.

FREE Value Over **$20**